To Hannah,

Thank you for your support!

MALKONAR

ALEX JACKSON

Copyright © Alex Jackson, 2015
Cover Art Copyright © Francisco Ruiz (feintbellt), 2015
All rights reserved.
ISBN: 1508493413
ISBN-13: 978-1508493419

For Graham Elsdon.

ONE

On the 29th of October Peter Vaughan made the biggest mistake of his short and fruitless life. He answered the phone.

He grunted as the familiar trill tore through his ears. He had never been fond of telephones; they were such needy machines, as needy as the people who used them. The very people who made Peter the man he was. He rolled his eyes, what was it this time? Insurance? A Nigerian lottery win? His expatriate parents trying once again to re-establish contact? But as much as they frustrated him they still had to be dealt with, and he gently rolled his dog Pepper from his lap and walked into the jaws of his worst nightmare.

He grabbed the receiver with a careless grasp and pressed it to his ear, and with a barely-disguised contempt spoke,

"Hello?"

"Hello, is that Peter Vaughan?" a voice replied. A voice without provenance, speaking an English so stark and perfect it seemed inhuman. A voice that kept him from slamming the phone down for the first time in three years.

"Yeah," he said, shifting slightly, "Can I help you?"

"You can indeed. I am in need of your assistance, and I would be very grateful if you could help me out."

"If you're from a charity you can sod off," he snapped, then recoiled at his lack of grace. To his relief, the voice laughed.

"No, no, I'm not from a charity," it sneered, "I merely need you to do something for me."

"What could you possibly need from me?"

"Do you know of a stone..."

"Not personally, mate. It's hard to strike up an interesting conversation with one."

"If you would let me finish," the voice snapped, "Things would become clearer. A lot clearer."

"Sorry."

"Thank you. Now, are you familiar with a stone that is shaped like a pentagon, is roughly the size of a dinner plate and has a small, red spiral at its centre?"

He gulped. That stone. The one his ten-year old self had found tucked away in the corner of the attic, the forbidden room of his childhood home. The one of only five things he had taken with him upon moving out on the grounds that it was 'a part of his childhood'. The one that was now gathering dust deep inside his bedside drawer, forgotten about for six years before now. How the hell did this person know about it? He felt his throat tighten.

"Erm, no?"

Silence. The receiver was clamped to his ear expectantly but no response arrived. A small voice inside his head told him to slam the receiver down while he had the opportunity, but the rest of him was too intrigued to let him do it. Moments later the return of the voice signalled the end of his last chance.

"Are you lying to me, Peter Vaughan?" the voice asked.

Peter's lip trembled. What should he say? What should he do? He gazed out of the window, onto the grimy streets of Averton and beyond to the greenery of the Northumberland countryside, hoping for inspiration, but saw only the setting sun and the encroaching darkness that accompanied it.

"Well?" the voice demanded, and Peter saw no other option than to speak. Holding the receiver tighter against his face, he let his brain improvise.

"How do you know I'm lying about just that?" he said desperately, "Why haven't you accused me of lying about my identity? Anyone can lie about their name. Sometimes I'm called Adam Jorvill and live in Cambridgeshire, so how did you know I wasn't lying about that? How much do you really know about me?" his grip on the phone tightened, "Have you been spying on me? I'm warning you now, I will call the Police if I have to."

More silence. A wash of relief sponged his sweating brow as he sensed victory, but then the voice let out a snigger and he tensed up again.

"An excellent deduction," the voice said, "And I will admit that I knew that you possessed the stone prior to our conversation, but I have not been spying on you."

"I'll still call the Police, I'll hang up right now and call them!"

"Wait!" the voice panicked. Peter froze, the receiver held slightly away from his ear, ready to slam down.

"What?"

"Alright," the voice said calmly, "Let's say that you do call the Police. They'll want names, locations and reasons. Do you know my name?"

Peter whined as he sensed what was coming.

"No."

"Do you know where I live?"

"No."

"Can you trace me?"

"I'll get your phone number. I'll dial 1471," he said triumphantly, but the voice wasn't deterred.

"Try it and see," it teased, "And finally, what crimes can you hold against me?"

"Suspected..." He stopped, not knowing what words to fill the gap with. "I don't know."

"Will the Police go hunting for me?"

"No."

"Exactly, so that is why it is imperative that you stay on the phone, Peter."

Peter felt his blood run cold. Whoever this was had no intention of hanging up empty-handed.

"What I want you to do," the voice continued, "Is take the stone to the old grain silo in Edgeley Park. Around the back of the building there is a hole in the wall shaped like the stone in question. The stone used to occupy that spot in the wall, and all I ask of you is that you return it to its former home."

He frowned. The grain silo in Edgeley Park, of all places? The stone cone that had been on the verge of collapse since long before he was born?

"Why?"

"I'm afraid I cannot tell you all of the details, but doing as I say will help both yourself and I greatly."

"Why?" he demanded.

"Like I said, I can't tell you everything."

"Then no deal."

"Will a financial incentive turn your head?"

Peter snarled. Taking the stone to the silo seemed innocent enough, but being bribed, the universal symbol for deceit and betrayal, to do it? It was enough to bring him to a final decision.

"I don't take bribes," he said.

"Does your heart change its beat to the tune of five hundred pounds?"

"No."

"One thousand?"

"No."

"Two thousand?"

Peter clenched his eyes shut. The money was getting better and better, but morals were more precious to him than money.

"No, and that's final."

"I see," the voice said, rather annoyed this time, "Well, if I cannot change your mind I see no reason why we should continue this discussion. Good day to you."

"Wait!" Peter blurted, his sense of curiosity hijacking his voice just in time.

"Yes?" the voice said, intrigue ringing in the word.

"What's your name?"

"Why do you wish to know my name?"

"You know mine; it's only fair that I learn yours."

There was a hostile pause, as if the voice was contemplating handing over the secrets to the Universe.

"Alright," it said eventually, "My name is Malkonar."

"Malkonar?" Peter frowned.

"An unusual name, I know, but it is mine and I treasure it. So, is there absolutely nothing I can do to change your mind?"

"Nothing."

"Very well then, good day to you," and with that, the line went dead.

Peter didn't drop the phone, nor did he sigh or even breathe his relief. He stayed still, the receiver still clamped to his ear. Why had Malkonar been so smug when he had threatened to call 1471? Even if he was calling from a payphone, there must be some sort of number that the service could trace. Surely there was no way he could hide, but he had to know for certain.

With a frantic finger he dialled 1471 and pressed the receiver to his ear until it went numb.

"Caller number," the automated voice said, then silence.

Peter felt anxiety weight his stomach again. How could there be nothing? A line in the vein of 'Number withheld' would have made more sense, but silence?

Then the voice returned. "If you wish to return..." but instead of returning the call he slammed the phone down in anger.

He stayed still even as silence began to settle again, eyeing the phone with curious caution. He glanced over his shoulder to the window, checking Averton's dreary skyline for an intruder that he knew wasn't there yet somehow was, one he didn't like. What it was he couldn't tell, but it made him reach for the wall and disconnect the phone.

The lights embedded in the plastic died, and it satisfied him enough to turn his back and retreat to the sofa. Only then did the lights flash, unnoticed. Then again, and again, and then one final, prolonged time to the sound of someone far away laughing.

TWO

Peter had been looking forward to Friday evening. Once more the working week was over, and he no longer had to go outside and suffer the inhumanity of Averton's stained concrete. No more cramped commutes or having to interact with people he had little time for, or typing code he knew was faulty into an overpriced piece of software. Just him and his apartment for two more glorious days.

He thought of it with relish as he pushed his way into his apartment, but it was gone in an instant the second he locked eyes on the phone. Its disconnected cable trailing from the floor, but the beady yellow light of the answerphone flickering at him.

He dropped his keys, ringing like church bells as they hit the floor. Impossible. No one could call a disconnected phone. No one with a phone number, at least, and he knew someone who had no such thing.

Suppressing the shudders in his stomach, he licked his lips and edged towards the phone, and with a trembling finger pressed the answerphone button.

"You have one new message," the smooth voice announced, "Received today at four twenty-eight PM."

"Cron asken nin jakov! Cron asken nin jakov! Cron asken nin jakov!"

"If you would like to..."

He slammed the phone down, the plastic cracking under the force, and felt his heart pound against his ribcage.

"Bloody hell," he wheezed, gasping for air. What the hell was that? Had some angry Russian got the wrong number? Instead of screaming at an enemy, he'd made a costly long distance phone call to the UK? Yes, it had to be that. Or maybe it was just scrambled. He covered his mouth to stop his hyperventilating. Yes, that was it. He slumped down to the floor to rest his quivering legs. It was just scrambled. Not Malkonar, just an ordinary phone call twisted and skewed horribly by a mistake somewhere. Yes, a scrambled message. It wasn't anything dangerous. Not at all.

He pressed the delete button on the answering machine with a vicious stab, then stumbled to the sofa, massaging his temples as he went, and landed heavily among the cushions. The noise drew Pepper's attention, and the husky lay down next to him, burying his head in his stomach and whining softly.

"It's alright, mate," Peter sighed, stroking his furry mane, "It was just a scrambled phone call, it won't do me any harm."

His words were sincere, but as he looked into Pepper's multicoloured eyes he could see the heavy doubt reflected in them, and though he tried he found himself unable to dispute it.

* * *

The next day he took Pepper for a walk. Most days the duty fell to Don, his former schoolmate and now full-time dog walker, who he endeavoured to avoid beyond the daily handover of Pepper before he went to work, but he was keen to get out of the house and away from the phone.

A week, that was all it had taken. Two questionable phone calls was the only excuse he needed to torment himself with absurd possibility after another. What was Malkonar really after? Did he want to hurt him? Had he done something accidentally that had put his life in danger? Was his life actually in danger at all? The questions were constant and alarming and he couldn't stop them no matter how hard he tried. He hated himself for it, and he hated himself even more for doing nothing about it. He hadn't researched who Malkonar was; he hadn't looked to find how he had called without a phone number, and, worst of all, he hadn't even bothered to look at the stone. He had done everything a detective shouldn't do, but he had never wanted to be a detective. He was an utterly confused IT technician praying that he could find his way back to normality, but even with the winter sun in his eyes he could sense he was a long way off-course. The only consolation he had was that his dog-walking route meant taking a reluctant trip to Edgeley Park.

He strolled through the rusted gates, their hinges begging to be put out of their misery, and along the tarmac path slithering towards the lake. The murky waters came into sight at the crest of a hill, but his eyes fell on the grain silo that stood next to it.

It was a conical building, crafted from weather-worn stone, that towered over everything else in the park. Its peak slouched with age, watching over the grass like a chronically-depressed overlord.

Peter ambled up to its base, his grip on Pepper's lead growing limp and eventually non-existent. With one hand on the silo wall he began to walk, caressing the stone and mortar with hardened fingers. With each step he felt more and more uneasy, the influence of the silo pressing down on his chest, and when his hand suddenly descended further into the rock he whimpered in fright.

Trembling, he examined the wall. Staring back at him with invisible but frowning eyes was a pentagonal hole in the rock, roughly the size of a dinner plate.

Bile was the first thing to rise in his throat. He swallowed it before it could fill his mouth and sat down before the accompanying nausea knocked him off his feet. That was his fears confirmed. The stone definitely belonged to the silo, which meant this was no prank. Malkonar really did want the stone to go into the silo wall.

The first question that hit him was simple: why? Every action had a consequence, but what consequence did Malkonar want him to create? And more importantly, what effect would it have on him? He bit his lip, and bit harder when he noticed the set of feet at his side.

"Enjoying a bit of lone time, Peter?" the Park Keeper said.

Peter leapt to his feet and brushed himself down, shoving aside his anxiety in the presence of another human being. The Park Keeper was an aged man who had cared for Edgeley Park for as long as Peter could remember, but despite his many years of loving service he appeared to be ignorant of the shadow cast by the silo just inches away from him.

"Oh, aye," he replied as calmly as he could muster, "Just thinking."

"What about, if you're okay with me asking?"

"Erm...the hole in the silo wall," he said, patting the indentation in the rock, "I've always wondered how it got there, it just seems weird that it looks like a pentagon. Was it deliberately cut like that? Or did it just erode away in that shape?"

He shook his head. "I'm not sure," but then he added, "Though my Father told me a story that he was told by my Granddad which supposedly explains why the hole got there."

"Really?" Peter said, surprise elating him, "Care to tell me it?"

"Oh, I don't know," the Park Keeper said, stroking his white moustache, "I'm not convinced it's true."

"It's just a story, there's no harm in telling me. Will you?"

There was a short pause, then the Park Keeper sighed.

"Aye, alright then. But let me warn you, it's a weird story."

"I've never been bothered by that sort of thing."

"Okay."

He rested his rake against the silo and stood up straighter.

"The story goes that the silo was closed for absolutely no reason. It was an extremely useful building. It stored most of the town's grain originally, and when it fell out of use clubs hired it out to hold meetings in private. Then," the Park Keeper paused, as if reminiscing about something, "Then they say something happened. Someone did something to the silo and ruined it."

"What exactly?"

"I don't know. About a hundred years ago the council suddenly decided to seal it and cut some of the rock out of the wall, as you've noticed. The official reason given was that the silo was structurally unstable and needed to be sealed to protect the public, but my Granddad, who sealed the door, reckoned it was something more complex than that."

"In what way?"

"Well," the Park Keeper dimmed his voice, trying to conceal something from no one in particular, "He reckoned there was something witch doctor-ish going on."

"Like magic?"

"Nah, not that, but definitely something not natural. He tried to find out what exactly, but when he went to study the silo before he sealed it they wouldn't let him in."

"Why not?"

"Don't know," the Park Keeper shrugged, "But it's clear whatever was in there was meant to be hidden from public view."

"So what happened next?"

"He persevered. He went into politics and got a job at the Mayor's office, which gave him access to confidential files. There he found that there were some weird experiments going on at the time by a man called Armstrong. He paid the Mayor handsomely to let him carry out some experiments in the region, and he was certain the silo was one of his ingredients."

"So his theory was this," Peter thought aloud, "This Armstrong guy used the silo in experiments; the experiments went horribly wrong, and because of this they sealed the door to keep people away and cut a hole in the side?"

"That's basically it," the Park Keeper said with a shake of his head, "But I wouldn't dwell on it for too long. Getting involved in things you have no business with will lead you to no good."

"But I'm not..." Peter protested, but his plea was ignored as the Park Keeper picked up his rake and walked away to greener pastures.

He sat down again, leaning against the stone, and thought. Malkonar wanted him to put the stone back in the silo, but why? He didn't know, but it had been removed around the time the silo was sealed, so could it mean he was trying to undo whatever removing the stone had done? Possibly, but he raised a sceptical eyebrow to his thought. What could removing a slab of stone do that he so badly wanted to reverse?

He tried to think, but his train of thought rolled no further and he was forced to try again from a different angle. Maybe it was something to do with that Armstrong fellow, but again, what could he have done to create Malkonar's desire to return the stone? He tried in vain to think of a feasible explanation, but again he hit a dead end. He groaned and rubbed his pale face. Another mystery, and that meant another problem to violently oppress him.

He heard a whine and a nudge against his leg. Pepper was getting sick of sitting out in the cold.

"Oh, sorry mate."

He took Pepper's lead and joined a procession of dog owners traversing the winding path, skulking their way back home with coats pulled up to their noses. He reached for his collar to blend in, but not before he took a cautionary glance around. The shadows were gone, melted into the light chocolate of mid-evening. On the horizon loomed the dying strands of daylight, but as Averton dictated there was no orange flare of beauty. Just a watery grey, like everything else in the city.

An icy breath slithered down his neck and he hastily tugged his collar up, teeth chattering.

"Bloody hell," he breathed, voice muffled by layers of fabric, "Another parky night, eh, mate?"

Pepper didn't listen, but that didn't deter Peter.

"Another cold, crappy night," he continued, spitting his words at the sky. "Another Avertonian night."

He stole one last look back at the gates as its hinges creaked in the wind, and though he intended that to be his last look at that sorry wreck of a park, it wasn't. He would be back in a matter of hours.

THREE

The journey home was not a comfortable one. The hands of the approaching winter wrapped themselves around his exposed hands and cheeks and burrowed under his clothes to numb the rest of his skin, but inside his head was an unbearable furnace of heat.

The questions were inescapable. One after another they came, banging against his skull, demanding his will be broken and the mystery challenged, and with them came the emotional baggage he needlessly attached to them. By the time he reached Averton City Centre he was barely aware of his own mortality, the city lights blurring, the people slender shadows he stared warily at as they dived out of his path. The only feeling he could sense was the desire to unleash his paranoia before it turned on himself.

He ran at full pelt up the stairs to his apartment, praying none of the neighbours were there to slow him down. He rammed open the door, fracturing the lock, and grabbed a piece of paper. His hand did the rest on its own, channelling every thought and replicating it without him having to think. Writing fast but eligibly, drifting across the page like it was an ouija board, casting out the questions as smudges of ink that drained the pressure from his mind.

Once it was done he lay back like an exorcised victim, arms spread limply across the sofa, and proudly inspected his work:

1. How did I end up in possession of the stone?

2. What did Armstrong do that caused the silo to be sealed?

3. Who is Malkonar?

4. Why was a hole cut in the side of the silo when it was sealed?

5. Why does Malkonar want me to return the stone to the silo wall?

6. How significant was the scrambled phone call in relation to the call made by Malkonar?

7. Why can't I trace Malkonar's phone number?

8. Who made the scrambled phone call?

9. Why is the scrambled phone call scrambled?

His silent ritual drew the attention of Pepper. He sat himself in front of Peter and sniffed the sheet of paper, and his master hastily withdrew it from under his nose.
"No," he said firmly, "This isn't for you."
Pepper gave a demanding whine.
"It's mine, not yours."
Another whine, pitched just perfectly to grate Peter's vulnerable nerves.
"You can't play with it, Pepper. This is for me, it has important human things on it."

Pepper's lips parted to whine again, but Peter's frustration meant he beat him to it.

"No, you can't have it!" he yelled, standing up and glaring down at his pet, "This is not a toy, it is full of serious things that I really need to deal with at some point." He paused, his white face somehow growing gaunter. "Well, not immediately," he said quickly, "I'm sure this is just me getting worked up over nothing again, and all of this will blow over pretty soon. I'm not doing anything unless I absolutely have to, but if I do, I have this to help me. Not that I think anything too problematic will come of this, it's just in case."

Pepper didn't whine. He tilted his head like he did when Peter had pretended to throw his ball and he'd seen through the ruse. It unsettled his master greatly.

He squirmed on the spot, one of his eyes twitching like he didn't want to look at him but couldn't tear his gaze away. He didn't look as sincere as his words at all, not until he shook his head and sharply announced,

"I'm going to bed."

He folded up the question sheet until he could no longer see the letters and shoved it deep into his bedside drawer, then fell under the covers. He lay with his eyes open for a long time, the look Pepper had given him burned into his mind, trying in vain to unravel its meaning.

In the other room, Pepper tilted his head at an orange on the kitchen counter that didn't look familiar.

* * *

02:36 was the time his projection clock displayed in relentless infra-red light on his ceiling when he woke up screaming.

He felt a boulder slam against his forehead, and his eyes were barely open when a second one hit. He cried out in panic, writhing until he was able to force himself upright and grab his head.

"*What the hell...*"

A third vicious sting robbed him of the thought. Dizziness made the darkness spin, and he frantically massaged his temples to slow it down, gulping air until his chest strained. This wasn't right. Headaches didn't feel like this, and he'd never had a migraine in his life. Another unusual happening; it made the pain in his head feel worse.

He stood up, still rubbing his head, doing his best to control his breathing against the demands of a reflex. The agony began to subside near instantly, but as it seeped away the sound of a voice took its place.

He froze, still enough to hear his surging heartbeat, and listened. He could definitely hear something emanating from the base of his skull. Tiny rustles of breath, ever so faint, but definitely a voice aching to break through.

A nightmarish scream burst from his chest. He clutched his head tighter and tried to shove the voice out, but he could still hear the murmurs no matter how hard he tried. He began to walk in circles, stomping his feet and panting like a wolf to drown out the sounds, but they refused to go unheard. The world began to spin, spurred on by the babble that was growing louder with every pace. He screamed and sunk to his knees.

"What's happening?" he bawled, "What's happening to my life?"

He rolled onto his back and curled into a foetal position, desperate whines escaping with every breath. He squeezed his eyes shut and threw all his strength into forcing the voice out, but his effort was in vain and succeeded only in draining him of what little energy he had.

"What have I done to deserve this?" he sobbed, tears spilling from his tired eyes. The world didn't answer, but the voice in his head did by screaming words at him.

Hafte yar! it shrieked, words blended with teary gasps, *Lest ignor vokter acher! Hafte yar! Lest horket! Lest horket!*

Peter's eyes tore open. Fright shot stings of intense pain through his chest, but it broke his hyperventilation. He lay there silently and wiped the tears from his eyes. His fear had gone. That voice was not a voice he could fear. Something sounding so desperate couldn't possibly endanger anyone, even if he recognised it instantly as the same screech from the answerphone message.

He chewed his lip until he felt it tear. It was no technical error. Whoever had phoned was a real, breathing person, and a hysterical one. Not seeking to torment him, but reaching out to him with a desperate plea. Begging him for his help, and that made him beat down his cowardice and listen to the voice.

Suddenly, the words changed.

Heede Edgeley! the voice screamed, more frantically than before, *Heede Edgeley; trose shovel! Lest ignor sider silo! Hafte yar!*

The words repeated themselves over and over again in his head, a broken record on his brain that made his nerves shudder. He could make sense of a few words: Edgeley had to mean Edgeley Park; shovel was self-explanatory, and the word silo cropped up in that sentence too, so that meant the voice wanted him to take a shovel to Edgeley Park and start digging near the silo. Why would anyone want him to do that? He collapsed back onto his bed in deep and desperate thought, and shot back up again as he worked it out.

"Oh my God!" he screamed, unable to silence himself as the reality dawned. Someone who was scared out of their wits wanting him to dig a hole for them? Whoever was pleading for his help had been buried alive.

He pulled on the first set of clothes he saw; grabbed a torch and ran out of the door, almost falling down the concrete steps in his distraction. He needed a shovel, but where could he get one? The blast of ice as he stepped out into the winter night knocked his thoughts off balance, but he recovered them enough to find a solution. He was going to a park, and all parks had gardening equipment, didn't they? He didn't let himself answer that question.

He weaved his way through the concrete maze of Averton, guided only by instinct in the rows of broken streetlights, and to his relief the turret of the Edgeley Park grain silo burst out of the gloom.

He launched himself at the gates and clambered over, serenading the night with the squeaks of hinges and chains. He rolled across the tarmac and straight back to his feet, flicked on his torch and stumbled into the darkness.

The path was alien in the dark and he feared he had lost his way when the ground turned to grass, but was elated when he brushed up against the Park Keeper's wooden hut. Surely that would have a shovel inside it. He felt his way along the timber wall of the building until he found the door and shone his torch at it. The hut was locked by a small padlock, definitely breakable with force. For a moment he hesitated, but the unwavering roars in his head reminded him of what he had to do.

He slammed his shoulder into the door with all of his might. It caved slightly, but the lock stayed strong. He rammed the door again and it flew open, an array of cobwebs greeting the torchlight. With twitching eyes he gazed into the battered building and found a rusted shovel close to the door. He lunged at it then sprinted off to the silo.

The voice in his head was getting louder and louder, so much so that he didn't need to concentrate to hear it anymore, and its manic pleas drained his concentration until he stumbled into the silo wall. Holding his bleeding nose, he stepped back. The voice grew stronger, and as he walked around the base of the silo it grew stronger still. Each step boosted the volume, guiding him closer to its location, and two steps later the voice screamed with everything it had.

Haer! Haer! Haer! Haer! it roared, and he needed no encouragement.

He thrust the shovel into the earth and began to dig with all of his strength. Grass gave way to soft mud, a steady mound of earth quickly growing behind him. All the while the voice bawled, screaming at him to hurry and straining as air drained away, but he was going as fast as he could.

His muscles began to seize up but he pressed on, begging to hear the sound of metal on wood. Sweat dripped off his forehead and into his eyes, but he didn't dare stop to wipe it away. His conscience wouldn't allow failure, there wasn't a second to waste. His heart and shoulders roared their frustration at being ignored, but he dared not let himself rest, and he was rewarded moments later with a resounding *Clunk!*

He dropped the shovel and shone his torch into the hole. Inside he saw a small stone coffin, a red spiral of three anti-clockwise turns engraved into its lid. With trembling fingers he lifted it out of the grave and onto the grass. The voice had stopped talking, but a hiss of pained breathing from inside the stone told Peter whatever was inside was alive.

He eyed it warily. What was inside? The box was small – only an infant could fit inside it, and as far as he knew infants didn't possess the ability to invade peoples minds. He felt his body simmer in angst again. Whatever was inside the coffin wasn't human, and if it was then it wasn't a human as he knew it. For a moment he considered running away, but another painful breath from inside the box reminded him of his compassion.

Nervously, he lifted the lid of the coffin off and shone his torch inside, and nearly died of shock. Pressed against the stone walls was a small, blue dragon. The creature was curled up tightly in its tomb, its arms and legs drawn into its body and its wings wrapped around its skeletal frame. Mud and dirt formed a blanket over its faded scales, but the silver tears that were creeping out of its eyes had washed its face clean.

Peter tried to speak, but the look of terror the dragon was giving him yanked his voice away. He tried again, but the most he could manage was a burbling sound. He couldn't do anything other than stare into the eternal, weary gaze of the dragon's eyes. He knelt there in silence as the dragon watched him, shivering against the cold. Then it opened its mouth, screamed a nightmarish scream, and blacked out.

Peter's breaths became whines as the horrific roar coursed its way through his body, carving itself permanently into his mind. Only once its horror had slackened its grip on his chest did he remember what was lying at his feet.

He sat down and crossed his legs. What the hell did he do now? He had gone to so much effort to save it and he couldn't leave it alone in the winter, but it was a dragon. Dragons breathed fire and ate humans, would it really be wise to let one of them into his home? His head told him no, but another part of him spoke otherwise. The dragon was clearly a young one, and the look of innocence and fright he had seen was not the face of a ruthless beast.

He laid a hand on its slight frame, feeling its freezing scales. Cold, alone and scared half to death, but carrying three wickedly pointed claws on each limb, claws that looked more than capable of tearing flesh. He didn't know what to do, but that scream had stretched him to the end of his tether. He had to make a decision, and as he crouched there in the mud, staring at the calm yet restless body of the dragon, fingers stiffened and skin reddened, he made up his mind.

Ten minutes later, a sore and tired Peter clambered over the gates of Edgeley Park, an unconscious dragon slumbering across his shoulder.

FOUR

Peter had long suspected that everything he knew was wrong, but having it confirmed by the creature lying next to him was still a harrowing experience for his shattered nerves. Weird phone calls, dodgy experiments and now dragons. If there was ever a moment where he wanted to throw himself off the top of his apartment block, this was it. Not even the overly-strong espresso he was wincing his way through could lull him back to calm, but there was still a curious part of him keeping his feet on the ground. He had written a list of questions just a few hours ago, and even though they were separated by a room he could still feel it in his hand.

He took another sip and stared at the dragon to counter the vile taste. The new arrival was napping peacefully, shrouded by an old blanket he'd found in the utility cupboard. Nervously, he reached out and stroked the creature's scaly head, and as he did thoughts of the dragon's primal scream seared through his body. He winced again. Those sort of screams didn't happen in real life, but dragons didn't belong in real life, and he didn't belong in a fantasy. At least not in a fantasy where people were buried alive.

He lay back and released another painful breath. He had entered a new plane of reality, no longer a part of his dimension but rather a pseudo-real state where the fictitious were all too real, and he was a tourist without a map. He took another sip, but the vile taste that lingered wasn't espresso.

He looked at the clock; 04:26 was what it read. It was practically morning, and staring out of the window told him that a few Sunday workers and insomniacs were on the move already. Groaning, he crawled back to his room and slithered under the covers. He didn't feel like sleeping, but having spent half the night running through the streets he had to get some rest.

As he lay there he looked across his apartment, eyes fixed on the peaceful figure of the lodger, and he panicked. He was about to sleep, and he was trusting it not to harm him. Could he though? He took deep breaths to reassure himself. He would be okay. He was fairly certain that all animals could recognise a random act of kindness, but at the same time he could see himself scrawling 'What the hell have I done?' onto the kitchen tiles with his own blood.

He shut his eyes and did his best to settle down. He was tired, scared and nauseous, but he wasn't defeated. Today had been a nightmare, but tomorrow was another day. As far as he was concerned things would be better in the morning, but the small reptilian eye covertly watching him from the sofa knew otherwise.

* * *

Peter woke to the feeling of warm breath on his face. He winced at its smell. It wasn't a scent he recognised, but he could tie it to one animal.

"Pepper," he said, rubbing his eyes, "I've told you before not to climb on my bed."

The world came into focus, but it wasn't Pepper he saw. Where the heterochromatic dog should have been standing was a blue dragon.

"Ah!" he screamed, flailing in despair and making the dragon roll across the bedsheets. He sat up and wheezed the morning air, eyes locked on the intruder. Small and blue, with flecks of burgundy and yellow on its wings and spines; a light brown painting its horns and tail stump. Three claws on each limb sent signals to Peter's mind, but its face of soft jaw and glistening eyes betrayed no menace, and this absence of aggression brought his pulse down.

"H-hello," Peter panted.

"Gruto," the dragon yapped back, and he almost collapsed back onto his bed. That word wasn't English, which meant he had another problem to wallow in.

"Oh, for God's sake," he whined, but a flicker of intellect ignited in his mind at the sound of the strange tongue, and it gave him the answers to two of his questions.

Elated, he leapt out of bed and claimed the list from his nightstand. The dragon followed suit, its sharp paws carrying it to the living room where Peter now sat, writing eagerly on his question sheet.

8. Who made the scrambled phone call?

A dragon of some description, who later contacted me through his own mind to save him from being buried alive.

9. Why is the scrambled phone call scrambled?

It wasn't scrambled, just spoken in a different language.

With his questions filled in, he watched as the dragon clambered onto the sofa and sat alongside him, perching itself like an obedient dog.

"Tidden sine," the dragon said cheerfully, nuzzling his arm.

"You're welcome?" Peter replied.

The dragon beamed at him, then began to chew the stump at the end of its tail, making approving noises as it gnawed. Peter watched the ritual with a degree of uncertainty, and glared at his feet because of it. He was scared of this chirpy creature that was chewing on itself rather than him. Who cared it if was a dragon? It was his idea to bring it home, so he would have to learn to be comfortable around it. If he couldn't at least accomplish that then he didn't deserve to have any of his problems solved, and the thought of having to deal with Malkonar for the rest of his life encouraged him to take the first step.

He coughed to get the dragon's attention and spoke as slowly as he could.

"Do. You. Speak. English?"

"Eng...Lish?" the dragon asked, staring at him with narrowed eyes.

"No to that then," he mumbled, running through his head the various languages that he knew. "Sprechen Sie Deutsch?" he asked hopefully.

"Deutsch?"

"Parlez-vous Français?"

"Français?"

"Vi parolas Esperanto?" he said desperately, trying the last language he knew a word of, but his hopes were crushed as the dragon shook its small head. What now? Well, if the dragon couldn't understand him then he could try to understand the dragon. Languages weren't hard to pick up, but to learn the words he had to get the dragon to speak, and to do that he would have to ask it to in a language it clearly didn't understand. It seemed futile, but with Malkonar's seductive tone crawling across his head he found himself speaking again.

"What is your name?"

"Name?"

"Name," Peter nodded, pointing at its bony chest, "What is your name?"

The dragon rolled its eyes for a moment, then replied. "Vornt?"

Peter didn't know how to react. He had a word, but what did it mean? Probably something along the lines of 'what are you on about?' Still, it was a breakthrough, and where there was one there would certainly be more.

"Yes! Oui! Ja!" he said, feigning excitement. The dragon cocked its brow at him.

"Damn," he muttered, feeling his hope drain away yet again. He looked to the window for inspiration, but only saw the sun slip behind a cloud and turn his living room a shade darker.

"Vornt?" the dragon said again, "Yar vornt? Sine vornt?"

His ears pricked up at the sound. More words but still no meaning, but at the back of his mind inspiration struck again. Could 'Vornt' mean name? Name had been the only English word the dragon had reacted to, so it seemed plausible, but how could he develop that knowledge? The only idea he had was to try and give the dragon his name, and with nothing else working he went for it.

Clearing his throat, he spoke in the slowest and clearest voice he could muster.

"Vornt Peter," he said, gesturing towards himself.

"Feela."

"No, no, Peter."

"Feela."

"Peter."

"Feela."

"Pet...Oh, never mind," he grunted, balling his hands into fists, but the dragon seemed to sense what he was trying to convey and helped him out.

"Yar," it said, pointing to itself, before turning its claw to point towards him. "Sine."

Peter frowned, nodded dumbly and repeated the dragon's moves.

"Yar," he repeated, pointing at the dragon. The creature shook its head.

"Denor, denor," it exclaimed. "Yar," it said, slower this time and jabbing at itself in an exaggerated manner, "Sine," it added, poking Peter's knee. This time he understood.

"Yar," he tried, pointing at himself. "Sine." He pointed at the dragon. The reptile smiled and clapped its claws together.

"Wess!" it grinned, and Peter gifted himself a rare smile. Sine and Yar, You and Me, and that meant he had words to construct a sentence with. Plucking up confidence, he stuck two of the new words together and asked another question.

"Sine vornt?"

"Yar vornt sit Septimus," the dragon replied, and sunlight returned to the room. Septimus, he had his name. Well, he assumed the dragon was a He. Septimus sounded like a masculine name, but he couldn't be sure.

"Boy?" he asked hopefully, "Or Girl?"

"Boy? Girl?" Septimus asked, but this time Peter was prepared. He picked a magazine up off the coffee table and thumbed through it until he found a picture of a couple standing side by side. He turned the magazine so that the image faced Septimus and pointed at the picture.

"Boy?" he said, pointing at the man. "Girl?" he added, pointing at the woman. Without hesitation he received a reply.

"Boy," Septimus smiled, and he returned the favour. What did he have so far? A dragon called Septimus who was male. Not major progress, but good enough for a Sunday morning, and certainly further than he'd got with Malkonar, Armstrong, the silo and the stone.

He instantly regretted remembering the stone. It dredged up all the negative emotions it had been blessed with in the last few days, but this time he shoved them aside. No more excuses. He had left it alone for far too long, thriving on the idea that everything would blow over in a few days, but with a dragon chewing its tail on his sofa he knew he was well and truly stuck in this conundrum. He had to start tackling the problems pressing down on him, and he could begin by shedding some light on the most mysterious problem of all.

He stood up and wandered into the curtained gloom of his bedroom, pulled open the bottom drawer of his bedside table and rummaged through the contents until he saw the stone, biting his lip a little too hard at the sight of it. He eased it out of the drawer and held it in his hands, peering through the half-light at its blood red spiral. Three clockwise coils of crimson red were daubed into its surface, glowing slightly. He ran his finger over them a few times and felt smooth stone, no grooves or indentations to be touched. The jaws of unease clamped round his throat again. They weren't painted or engraved, but a part of the rock. That wasn't possible, was it? He turned back to the light of the living room, staring at the impossibility grooming itself on the sofa, and realised that nothing was impossible anymore. He grunted his frustration, but another idea hatched in his mind. The mysteries of the stone evaded him, but this time he wasn't alone in the dark.

He made his way back into the living room, the stone concealed behind his back, and discreetly sat himself opposite the reptile.

"Septimus?"

"Wess?" he said in his quaint voice.

Peter held the stone up for him to see, and Septimus' tail fell from his mouth. He crawled frantically to the other end of the sofa, attempting to get as far away from the stone as possible.

"Splowe gant!" Septimus shouted, "Splowe gant!"

"What?"

"Splowe gant!"

"What does 'splowe gant' mean?"

"Splowe gant!"

Peter sighed and shut out Septimus' babble in order to think. What did he want him to do with the stone? 'Splowe gant' it, whatever that was. As he pondered what that could mean he didn't notice Septimus creep forward, and he only became aware of the dragon's movements when the stone was ripped from his hands.

The shock paralysed him for a moment, only able to watch as

Septimus unleashed another cry of "Splowe gant!" before throwing the stone to the floor.

He stopped breathing as the precious slab flew to the ground, and oxygen only returned to his lungs when it bounced harmlessly off the carpet, settling down without a scratch. His eyes darted back to Septimus, the dragon's face filled with panic at his failure, and he raised a claw to slam down on the rock. Alarm finally brought life back into Peter's body.

"No!" he shouted, swiftly swiping the stone from the floor before Septimus could move. "No splowe gant! No splowe gant on the stone! The stone is precious! The stone is not to be touched!"

Septimus watched Peter clutch the slab tightly to his chest, and his wings slumped in defeat.

"Feela," he whined, but Peter's mind was elsewhere. Septimus had not only recognised the stone, but had tried to destroy it. He clearly feared it, but what exactly was he afraid of? He bit his tongue as the pieces slotted together: Malkonar wanted the stone; Septimus was afraid of the stone, so were Septimus and Malkonar connected? He turned to Septimus again and breathed a single word.

"Malkonar."

Septimus whimpered. Not the downhearted sound of an unhappy child, but the heavy, tearful squeak of a victim. Peter watched as he curled himself into a defensive ball, shielding himself from the horrors associated with that word. There was his answer, but as quickly as one question was answered another, much more crucial question presented itself to him. One that took him full circle and brought everything, from the phone call to now, onto the same plane: why was Septimus so afraid of Malkonar?

FIVE

Most days Peter spent as little time out in Averton as possible. It was a way of living recommended by just about everyone around him, judging by their hunched-up forms nestling in the protective layers of their coats, eyes directed to the pavement as they pushed past. The thought of stepping out his door after work was at one time unthinkable, but that was exactly what he was doing. He had Septimus now, the bridge between him and Malkonar, and he had to exploit it. He had to change his attitude entirely, stop ignoring the insanity around him and use whatever time and resources he had to find answers. He had to find out more about Malkonar and the stone and their significance, but there were only two places he could think to look. There was Septimus, but that was impossible given their inability to communicate, so that left him with only one option: Averton City Library.

He stepped through the revolving doors and was instantly hit by the smell of disinfectant that all libraries used to disguise the stench of decaying paper and humans. Closing his nostrils, he wandered over to the Librarian's desk and looked at the solitary figure sat tapping into a keyboard.

She was a very generic-looking woman, with hair pinned back

so tight it looked like it was about to rip out of her scalp, complete with ringed spectacles that seemed older than her middle-aged self. Without looking up from her computer screen, she spoke,

"How may I help you?"

"Erm, right," he stammered, not sure how to phrase his query, "I'm looking for a book."

Her eyes rolled upwards, staring at him as if he'd scored 17 on an IQ test.

"Most people who come in here are looking for those."

"Yeah," Peter said, blushing slightly, "But I need a book about someone called Malkonar."

She stopped typing and raised her head.

"Malkonar?" she said, intrigued.

"M-A-L-K-O-N-A-R. I'm not sure what it is, I just need a book on it," he explained curtly. She glanced at him for a little while longer, then tapped the word into her keyboard.

"Ah, there is one book that can help you. *The Complete Guide to Mythical Creatures* by Nelson Jakes, you'll find it on row 208 on the second floor."

"Thank you," he said, charging off towards the stairs.

"No running in the library!" she shouted after him, but his mind was elsewhere. The Complete Guide to Mythical Creatures. Mythical Creatures. The onslaught of fear against his stomach was brutal.

He traced the signs with his stiff finger until it slid over row 208. The vast majority of the books on the shelf were leather-bound relics, but the book he was after was fairly new, with a plastic cover and neat illustrations of dragons and gnomes and pixies down the spine. He prised it out of the shelf and sat down in one of the obligatory beanbag chairs, flicking the book open and sucking in as much air as he could before delving into the unknown.

The Complete Guide to Mythical Creatures

By N. Jakes

Contents:

Introduction – 1
Orcs – 7
Griffins – 12
Fairies – 18
Elves – 26
Centaurs – 33
Unicorns – 39
Dragons – 45
Gnomes – 57
Pixies – 69
Giants – 75
Fauns – 85
Epilogue – 91

Peter cocked an eyebrow. There was nothing about Malkonar in this list, just a scattering of other fictional beings. Well, he thought they were fictional, but if a dragon had turned up God only knew what else was out there. On a hope, he turned to the chapter on dragons and began to read.

<u>*Origins*</u>

Dragons are one of the older mythical species, appearing in various forms across numerous different works. However the word itself didn't appear in the English language until the 13th century, courtesy of the French, and came to light as a creature in the King James Bible, where Dragons are mentioned as a creature of evil (though the word Dragons is used interchangeably with Serpents and Jackals).

This was of no use to him, so he read on.

There are many different 'species' of Dragons, ranging from the Slavic Dragon, a creature that is regarded in Slovenia as the 'Protector of Ljubljana', to the Chinese Dragon, a popular 'species' that is recognised to this day.

Unimpressed, he slid his hand under the plastic to slam the book shut, but a small text box caught his eye in the nick of time. It was easy enough to miss, tucked away in the top corner of the page, but his eye latched onto the title of the box: the word 'Malkonar', scored under and adorned with sharp serifs. Excited, he read it.

A Malkonar is allegedly a 'species' related to the Dragon. Appearance-wise they are said to be largely identical, but there are a handful of differences that separate the two species.

Unlike dragons, Malkonars are alleged to be able to breathe more than just fire, with ice, electricity and an ability known only as 'turquoise' being recorded. Malkonars are also said to be capable of numerous mental powers such as telepathy, telekinesis and the ability to possess individuals by the power of the mind.

Not much is known of them in folklore, the few references to the species coming from scraps of parchment found in an undisclosed location in Dorset, England. Due to the text being in an early form of the English language and lacking in significant detail, not much information has been lifted from its pages, though it is known that within the writing the creature is considered to be the 'father' of Dragonkind.

The knot in his stomach tightened. He slammed the book shut and shoved it back on the shelf without so much as looking at it, trying hard not to think about what he had just read, but he did, and doing so sent him hurtling back towards the Edge. He was taking phone calls off a psychic dragon that breathed rainbow fire; just thinking of that sentence melted his sanity. He would have laughed if he didn't think it could kill him. Was that what Malkonar had in store for him?

He quickly distracted himself with a question before he could ponder it too long. A good, relevant question: why did the book refer to Malkonar as a species rather than an individual? That was worth knowing, and the sheet of questions pressing against his thigh agreed. He unfolded it and wrote along the bottom:

10. Why is Malkonar referred to as a species instead of a person?

In the process he realised he had an answer. It didn't fill him with the joy that he had hoped for, and he wrote it down unable to think of anything other than a scaled hand holding onto his own and making him write; unable to think of anything other than that mischievous voice reading it back to him as he crammed it back into his pocket and ran sweating for the door:

3. Who is Malkonar?

Malkonar is a person or species related to the dragon, only capable of telepathy, telekinesis and possession via the power of the mind.

* * *

Peter returned home to the sound of fighting. The first thing he heard upon stepping through the door was a venomous hiss, swiftly followed by Pepper bolting from the kitchen. It took his mind off Malkonar for the first time in nearly an hour.

"Woah!" he cried, leaping out of Pepper's way. He dropped his bags and scuttled forward, standing between the kitchen door and the sofa that Pepper was now cowering behind. "What's going on?"

He received no response bar the whines of a distressed canine, and while the noise hurt him something pressed harder. "Septimus?" he called. "Where are you?"

The sound of his name brought louder cries from Pepper, and this time Peter gave him his attention. He was curled tightly into a ball, tail shielding his nose, moist eyes looking fearfully at the kitchen before turning to him as if to say *save yourself*.

Peter nervously turned towards the kitchen, but didn't budge. He had to do something but he wanted to do nothing, but as he peered over his shoulder to see Pepper's doting gaze he forced himself to make a sacrifice.

He cocked his head so that he could see inside, but saw nothing out of the ordinary. He forced himself forward, and this time he spotted a blue tail dangling off the top of the fridge. He inched a little closer, just enough to let him see the ceiling in the far corner of the room, and the strand of blue became connected to a pale blue lump that was quite obviously Septimus, but all he could see of the dragon was his horns, his tail and a furious left eye.

"There you are," Peter said, but he wasn't relieved. "What's wrong? You don't look very happy." There was no reply.

Slowly he crept into the kitchen, departing carpet for tile, and with each step he took he was greeted with hisses.

"Come on," Peter said, drawing close to the fridge and swallowing the fear clogging his throat, "Tell me what's wrong." He rubbed his stomach, then made a drinking gesture. "Hungry? Thirsty?"

"Hourt," Septimus mumbled, "Lest croat hourt."

"Hourt? What does that mean?" he asked himself, but Septimus heard, and it displeased him.

With a malicious grunt he leaned into Peter's face and opened his mouth, and his eyes were greeted with the most horrendous set of teeth he had ever seen. Two rows of at least thirty teeth, top and bottom, each one a wicked-looking canine, all slightly discoloured and emitting the foul stench of curdled milk. Peter bit his lip to stifle a scream.

"Wow," he squeaked, taking a small step backwards, "Those are some nasty looking teeth, how about you close your mouth before you hurt anyone?"

His words did nothing, and Septimus roared. The scream burned his face and stung his ears, but he stood still and didn't react. The final fuse in his head had blown. This was what his life had come to, and being roared at by a furious dragon, scalding saliva spraying in his eyes, was not how he wanted to live. No more tolerance, no more passivity. He was going to get things, work things, leisure things, Malkonar things, done.

When he stopped screaming he looked Septimus straight in the eye, utterly fearless. He had to get him off the top of the fridge, but since talking to him wasn't working that meant handling him, and though he was no wildlife expert handling an angry animal didn't sound like a good idea.

He studied him for weaknesses he could exploit, but then he noticed the wisp of smoke trickling out of Septimus' nostril. The colour drained from his face. He slowly raised his hands to grab, but the grip of hesitance on his throat held him back. He fought the feeling with every nerve in his body. This was no time for backing down, there could only be seconds between now and getting a ball of fire in the face. His cowardice told him to jump aside, but that meant his house taking the blow. What were the options? Lose his house or his life, but at least the latter had a chance of positive outcome. Then he saw his jaws snap open and a bolt of searing air hit his face, and he acted.

Septimus shrieked as Peter's hands grabbed at his body, thrashing as they lifted him from his perch. He swung his claws, catching Peter's tie and ripping the fabric away.

"Ah!" he screamed, looking down at the three claw marks mere centimetres from his chest, "Calm down, mate! I don't want to hurt you."

Septimus slashed again, this time only catching thin air, but shock broke Peter's grip. He couldn't stifle his scream of fear when Septimus clattered onto the kitchen bench. He backed away, expecting claws to latch onto him, but what he received instead was an agonising moan. He looked up to see the dragon in a heap, clutching his side and fighting the tears forming at his corneas.

"Septimus?" Peter said slowly, inching forward, "What's wrong?"

He drew up to the kitchen bench and gently eased Septimus' claw away from his side. What was wrong was a cut below his ribs, angry red and staining his side a thick maroon.

"Ouch," Peter winced, and his emotions softened. He placed a hand on Septimus' head and stroked him. "It's alright, mate, I'll get you patched up."

Septimus wriggled as he was laid on a bed of bandages; he squirmed as antiseptic lotion was rubbed into the wound, and he shifted awkwardly as Peter wrapped the bandages around him, but once the job was done he smiled.

"Tidden sine!" the reptile cheerfully announced, running an experimental claw across his dressings. He looked at Peter's face apologetically and held out a claw. "Apoligek."

Peter shook it, and Septimus gratefully nuzzled his wrist. Peter smiled his appreciation, but again his elation was dampened by something lurking at the back of his mind. Who had inflicted the cut? He couldn't have done it to himself, not from that angle, but then who did? His face slumped as an uncomfortable truth began to surface. There was only one other creature in this house, and those scratches had looked suspiciously like teeth marks.

"Please, no," he whined, pressing a hand to his head.

"Tant?" Septimus asked. Peter reopened his eyes and looked at him exasperated.

"Please," he begged whatever Gods were out there, and tested his theory.

He scooped Septimus up and carried him into the living room, and the first thing to greet him was a series of furious barks. Septimus responded with an equally sinister growl, and Peter responded with the hopeless sigh that only the truly frustrated could muster.

"Oh, for God's sake," he shouted, "I've had just about enough of this!"

The two animals fell silent, turning their surprised eyes up to Peter. He towered over them, his face tight with determination. He wasn't going to be bested by two animals, not when he had bigger things to deal with. They may have got off on the wrong foot but he was going to fix that, and he would succeed whether they liked it or not.

Blood pressure soaring, he plonked himself down on the floor and stared down on the beasts with ignited eyes.

"Right," he snapped, placing Septimus down by Pepper, "I know you can't understand a word I'm saying but I'll say it anyway. Pepper, don't hurt Septimus. Septimus, don't get angry at Pepper. I want you two to play nice, I've got enough on my plate at the moment and I don't need you two giving me more problems." He grabbed a handful of Pepper's toys and dropped them between the two creatures. "Play."

The animals regarded one another with contemptuous stares for a moment, then Pepper scooped up a foam ring in his jaws and all pretence was abandoned. Peter watched as his housemates traded toys, the bridges building with each curious flick of a ball or fling of a rope, and he smiled. His world might have been collapsing around him, but at least he was still in control of something.

The air in the room grew warmer and he soon found himself joining in with the games of dog and dragon, shielding himself from the outside through the innocence of play. Then the phone rang again, and the protective bubble shattered beyond repair.

SIX

Ring! Ring! Ring!

Peter stopped, tightening his grip on a chewy duck. He slowly glanced over his shoulder to see if what was happening was an illusion, but there was nothing there to mimic the sound of his phone.

Ring! Ring! Ring!

Peter felt his palms sweat. The phone was disconnected, it had been since the first phone call, but a message had reached him before so complaining was of no use to him. What he was dealing with wasn't restricted by the boundaries of humanity.

Ring! Ring! Ring!

He looked at his housemates. Both had stopped their games and were looking back at him with the same hopeful gaze. He was their leader, and it was up to him to decide what to do. He looked back at the phone and squirmed. Power was something he didn't want, but it had been thrust into his unwilling hands and there was nothing he could do to reverse that, so he swallowed the lump in his throat and rose to his feet.

He heard the scuffle of claw on carpet as he approached the phone and braced himself for a confrontation that arrived seconds later, when Septimus leapt from behind and shielded the phone with his body.

"Denor," he shouted, "Malkonar."

"Let me answer the phone." Peter shouted back. He knew he shouldn't answer the phone to Malkonar, but he also knew of his question sheet, and the only way to get that needed information was to let him say his unwelcome piece.

"Denor," the dragon shouted again.

"Why?"

"Malkonar."

"Let me answer the phone."

"Denor."

"Why?"

"Malkonar."

The argument repeated itself several times, and it was only after ten minutes of solid bickering that Peter realised that the phone was still ringing. He stopped speaking. How could a phone ring non-stop for ten whole minutes? Because the person on the other end was going to speak whether he liked it or not.

He looked at Septimus, who seemed to realise, and without protest he climbed off the phone and leapt onto his shoulder, his flimsy body trembling. Peter gave his back a soothing stroke with an equally shaky finger, then picked up the phone.

"Hello?"

"Hello, Peter," Malkonar said, "A little bird tells me you've been hard at work."

"I always work hard."

"I didn't dispute that."

"I never said you did."

"Quite. Now, there's a small matter I wish to pursue with you."

"I know what you want," Peter blurted, fear assuming control of his vocal cords.

"Very blunt, aren't you?"

"I might as well be since you aren't. If you want to get a point across, spit it out here and now. Don't bore me with all of your puzzles."

"Well if that's the case allow me to be blunt as well: give me the stone."

"You can't have it."

"And why not?"

"I might not know what you're up to, but I know it can lead to no good."

"How can you prove that?"

"I know what you are, Malkonar, you're a...well, malkonar. You're a dragon-like creature who has psychic powers," he paused as he realised how ridiculous that sentence sounded, "And you want me to help you in whatever madness you've got planned."

"Impressive, Peter Vaughan," Malkonar said, "But there's still much you have to learn. There are many questions you must have at this moment in time, but why put yourself through the gruelling struggle of finding answers when you can give me the stone and discard them all?"

"Is that the best you've got?"

"Many people feel the need to take the easy route out, and I'm giving you that option."

"You're too strange to ignore. You take every opportunity to say nothing, and given how you kept quiet what you really are I'm going to find out what else you're hiding."

"That will take a long time, my friend."

"I'm not your friend."

"If we are not friends then why are we talking?"

"You called me."

"But you had the option to answer the phone."

"I didn't, the phone rang for ten minutes straight, and the only way to shut it up was to answer it."

"You could have hung it up straight away, though. You didn't have to hear a word of mine, yet here you are happily chatting away. That is one of the many things you have to learn, Peter: self-restraint."

Peter let out a small grumble of despair. The reptile was right, and the sudden realisation of how vulnerable he was made his legs tremble.

"You see?" Malkonar crowed, "You don't know the answers to the basic questions. Do you know why I can call you without a telephone?"

"No," he admitted, leaning into the wall to steady himself.

"And do you know why Septimus is residing with you?"

He almost hit the floor again. How the hell did Malkonar know that? He couldn't have seen the episode in Edgeley Park, could he?

"What do you know about Septimus?"

"Oh, far more than you do."

"Define 'far more'."

"Well, to put it cryptically, I know fewer facts about him that aren't true than you do."

Peter rolled it through his mind, and eventually cracked its meaning.

"Something I know about Septimus is wrong?"

"Yes," Malkonar smirked, "Have a guess what it is."

"Erm..." He looked at Septimus, but saw nothing that didn't match what he thought. "I don't know."

"Oh dear, Peter, such naivety," Malkonar tutted, "It's obvious, but sadly you are looking in the wrong places. Think with your mind, not your eyes."

He thought harder. Whatever he had wrong mustn't be physical, but what was it instead? He looked at the blue dragon again, and only then did he realise he had the wrong animal.

He choked on oxygen. It slammed against his chest with unimaginable force, sucking the breath right out of his lungs, and to make the pain throb even harder he heard the devious cackles of Malkonar ringing in his ear.

"I assume you've solved the puzzle."

"I think so," Peter breathed.

"So go on then, what is your guess?"

"Septimus is a malkonar, isn't he?"

"Indeed he is," Malkonar chuckled, "The answerphone message and voice in your head weren't coincidences, my boy. He is inferior to me in every way, but he is of my species. That's one fact I'm donating to you, but I no longer have the desire to be charitable so you're on your own from here on in, I'm afraid."

Peter stood still, mouth ajar, hunting for more words to say, but his vocal cords were squeezed tightly together. He looked at Septimus again, Septimus the malkonar, in the hope that he could help him find a path through the fuzzy maze of his head. He only blinked at him.

"Feela?" he said, but Peter wasn't the only one to hear the question.

"Oh, Septimus is with you right now? Marvellous, I would very much like a word. May I speak to him, Peter?"

Peter once again found himself unable to react, but Septimus helped him along by pointing at the receiver. Peter hesitated, memories of his reaction to his name fresh in his mind, but then he remembered his questions and he obliged.

There was a small murmur as Malkonar spoke, and Septimus whimpered in fear as he heard the sound of Malkonar's voice. He barked something back through the receiver in his language, voice taut.

Their conversation went on for a while in short, sharp sentences, and as it continued Septimus' voice became more frantic. He grew tenser, his claws digging into Peter's shoulder and drawing blood, and his replies became desperate, descending into tearful mumbles before a particularly long-winded comment by Malkonar made him clamp his eyes shut and push the receiver back towards Peter.

Thick silver tears dribbled out of his eyes to soft whimpers, his chest convulsing with sobs. It filled Peter with an uncontrollable rage, and he grabbed the receiver and screamed down it,

"I hope you're proud of yourself."

"He has been told."

"Told what?"

"That is none of your business."

"It is my business!" He spat venom down the phone. "Anything that's his business is also mine, so spit it out, you rat!"

"He has been told," Malkonar repeated, "About his fate."

"What fate?"

"His fate for running away from me. To sum it up in brief terms I will catch him, and there will be blood." Then Malkonar hung up.

Peter felt a scaled head rest against his neck, tears warming his skin, and he reached around to comfort him. He couldn't disguise the repulsion on his face. That voice, that condescending attitude that emanated from every word, and now this. Making somebody cry grated Peter regardless, but the fact that Septimus was so small and fragile sharpened every nerve ending in his brain to a wicked point.

"F-Feela," Septimus burbled between sobs, and Peter shifted his grip so that he held him like a baby.

"It's alright," he soothed, repressing his anger for Septimus' sake, "He isn't going to hurt you. I won't let anyone hurt you."

They stood there for a while, man and malkonar in an embrace. Peter watched the sun dip behind a wall of cloud as he stroked Septimus' hurt away. He was hideously confused in a world which now made even less sense, but right now the ensuing questions didn't matter. Damning things had been said to Septimus, and with no one else to turn to it was up to him to pick up his pieces.

"You'll be okay," he added, and this time Septimus reacted. He looked up at Peter with red-ringed eyes and shook his head mournfully.

"Denor," he whispered, choking back his hurt, "Denor, denor."

"Huh?"

"Yar Mama," Septimus croaked, burying his head back into Peter's neck, and though Peter did not understand what had been said he felt the words puncture another hole in his heart.

SEVEN

Septimus wasn't the same after that. Thursday crawled into Friday, Friday seeped through into the weekend and everything dribbled into Monday morning, but the sprightly creature Peter knew had died and didn't look like returning. He did his best to bring the cheery smirk back to his face: toys, games, food, any form of entertainment he could think of was placed before him, but the glisten didn't return to those giant eyes. It hurt Peter greatly to see him so jaded, but the phone call had at least given him an answer to one of his questions:

10. Why is Malkonar referred to as a species instead of a person?

Because he is a species: Septimus shares the mind reading skills of Malkonar, meaning that they are the same type of creature.

Leaving him alone again was heartbreaking. He watched from the doorway as he crouched over the English dictionary he had given him to study, scraping the words with a sullen claw, and though his heartstrings pulled him back into the comforting warmth of his home he forced himself off to work. It wasn't such a bad thing, as around him any feeling other than sympathy had been shoved away, and now they could be released. Now he had the chance to properly panic over the fact that Septimus was a mind-reader, a panic that sent him stumbling towards Averton City Library at lunchtime.

The Librarian with the tightly-pinned hair was waiting for his arrival, and he didn't bother to disguise his disgust.

"Sorry sir, but the children's books are over that way," she said, gesturing with her thumb and grinning all the while.

"Piss off."

"Language!"

"English," Peter mumbled. "Anyway, do you still have the guide to mythical creatures?" he said as casually as he could. The Librarian looked at him through curious eyes for a moment before tapping something into her computer.

"Yes, we do. It's still on Row 206."

"Thank you," he said, shooting off.

"No running!"

"I'm in a hurry!"

He landed on the second floor and stormed up to Row 206. He traced his finger over every single spine on the shelf until his hand brushed against the plastic backing of *The Complete Guide to Mythical Creatures*. He ripped it out of the shelf and slammed it down on a nearby table, turning swiftly to the page on Dragons, keeping an eye on the clock counting down the final ten minutes of his lunch break.

He found the page with the short paragraph on malkonars and read it over multiple times, hoping it would suddenly expand into an essay on the behaviour and psychology of malkonars, but it was just a paragraph and it wouldn't become anything else.

He turned the page on a hope, and what greeted his eyes was a two-page spread of a size guide for dragons. The silhouette of a 6-foot human stood alongside varying sizes of reptile. Some small as a child's toy, some the size of lorries, but it was the second largest silhouette that made his eyes widen so far his eye sockets threatened to snap. The second largest silhouette, roughly the size of a digger, was marked with the word 'Malkonar'.

He looked away, but he had stared too long and now the image was burnt into his retinas. He threw the book back onto the shelf in disgust and slumped down at the table, cradling his head in his hands. He had picked a fight with a ten-foot reptilian war machine, and all he had to fight him with was a much smaller malkonar who spoke in tongues and a hyperactive dog. The crushing weight of injustice crashed down on him again. It wasn't fair. His life wasn't fair, and as he glanced the time on his watch he realised just how unfair it was.

"Shit!" he cursed, leaping to his feet and swinging his bag over his shoulder. 13:28. He had two minutes to complete a five minute journey.

He ran to the stairs and leapt down them two at a time, landing on the ground floor with a resounding thump that drew the attention of the bespectacled woman a few feet away.

"What's the hurry?" she asked, frowning at his lack of respect for public spaces.

"I have to go, I'm running late."

"Late for what?"

"Nothing."

He took off for the door, but a firm hand grabbed his shoulder and locked his muscles.

"Sir, you have shown a great deal of disrespect to council property over the last few days. The least you can do is answer a simple question."

Peter nodded dumbly, shocked that a librarian had ground him to a halt.

"Good, now why do you run everywhere even though you know it is impolite?"

"I'm in a hurry."

"Why are you in a hurry?"

"I'm late for work."

"Okay, and why the fascination with mythical creatures?"

Peter frowned. "What does that have to do with anything?"

"Please answer the question."

"No, it has no relevance."

"Please answer," she snapped, and Peter's fuse blew. He ripped himself clear of the Librarian's grip and spun around to face her.

"If you must know," he scowled, "My fascination with mythical creatures is none of your business. It's a problem I have and I don't need any help with it."

"What sort of problem?"

"I don't have time to..."

"What?" she demanded, and another fuse fried.

"Look, it's complex and difficult for you to understand. You have no right to know what I'm doing, which is just as well as the less you know about what I'm doing the better. I guarantee that if you were in my shoes you'd want to step out of them as soon as possible, and I think that tells you everything you need to know. Good day."

He turned on his heel and rocketed away. The Librarian followed him onto the street and watched him tear down the cobbles, a look of intrigue etched into her features.

"I wonder," she said, and returned indoors.

*　*　*

Peter didn't do socialising, but tonight he was left with no choice other than to share an evening with Don. He had only gone to his house to pick up Pepper from his afternoon of sniffing at empty vodka bottles, yet he had returned home with his evening fully booked and his mouth full of curses at being lured in.

Though they weren't the closest of friends Don still knew him inside out, so he knew exactly when to hit Peter with the proposal, which was why he was now sat on a barstool in the corner of the seedy dump he called the local, sipping half-heartedly at a warm beer with Don slumped next to him, swigging from a pint of cider and shouting expletives every now and again.

He tuned himself out of Don's tirade and stared at his amber reflection, admiring how the colours emphasised his downturned lips as he fretted over Septimus and Pepper. Was it wise to leave them alone together so soon after their fight? It was a question he had been lost in all night, but he still hadn't found an answer when Don tapped him on the shoulder. He willed himself towards his drunken, maniacally-grinning face.

"What?"

"You going to the Rangers match tomorrow?" he asked.

Peter sighed. Averton Rangers, another relic of his youth he had repressed. From a regular on the terraces to a complete stranger. Just thinking about them made him uncomfortable.

"How're they doing in the league?" he asked, hoping to deflect the question, but forgetting Don was swaying in his seat.

"You don't know how they're doing?" Don slurred, greatly offended.

"No."

"I thought you were a fan," he exclaimed, showering him with drunken foam. Peter's temper began to bubble. Couldn't he see he had other things to worry about?

"I'm not," he snapped.

"What?!"

Peter leapt out of his chair and leaned into Don's face.

"I'm not a fan of Averton-fucking-Rangers, Don! I haven't watched them in four years, I've stopped supporting them!"

The room hushed, and Peter shrivelled back into his seat. What a marvellous thing to say in a pub wrapped in the blue-and-white of the Rangers, and as he glanced over his shoulder he saw the undiluted disgust of his fellow drinkers, all of whom carried far more muscle than his scrawny figure. Panicking, he pulled Don in close.

"Just answer his question," he hissed.

"Fifth," Don shrugged, his alcohol-fuelled rage fading away, "Reckon we'll be in the Championship in no time if we keep it up."

"Who are we playing?"

"Newcastle, so are you coming or not?"

The reply was already in his mouth, but he couldn't bring himself to say it. What had he just said? Him, the eighteen-year old who had risked missing a vital exam to go to the League Cup final, not a fan of Averton Rangers? It was embarrassing, and his regret opened him up to an even more oppressive truth. He was about to do what he always did: isolate himself.

The actions of six years of independent adult life flashed through his memory, and a great red line of shame tinted his cheekbones. All he had done in that time was remove himself from the people he knew until they removed themselves, all gone until only Don was left. That was only because he was too drunk to properly realise who he was calling his best friend, and as he looked at him slumped over the bar he sensed his growing alienation. His last friend was on his way out unless he did something to win him back.

Visibly shaken, he straightened in his seat and forced a more composed look upon his face.

"I'll come," he said, and Don's face brightened. He slapped him hard on the back, causing him to spill his beer.

"Good man!" he said, "I'll meet you at the gates at half two, and bring your dog."

"Why?"

"The steward who keeps telling me to shut up hates dogs, and I think it's time I got my own back."

"Alright then, half two and Pepper comes with us," Peter laughed, slurping down the last of his beer. That was four pints, his usual limit, but he raised his hand for another round.

* * *

The key turned, the lock clicked and Peter stepped inside, flicking on a light as he went. The slamming of the door drew the attention of Pepper, and the husky leapt at his master with glee, his weight almost pulling him to the floor. Peter tried to manoeuvre around him, but Pepper had no intention of letting him go.

"Down, boy," he commanded, but Pepper only growled in response. Peter froze. Pepper always listened to the command of Down, and he certainly never growled at his human as a response.

Pepper shifted his weight, attempting to push Peter over. His arm flailed and grabbed the dog's face. He saw Pepper's eyes and stifled a scream. They were not blue and hazel, but red.

"*What the...*" he thought, but was unable to finish it before Pepper thrust his weight into him and he fell to the floor.

Pepper was on top of him before he could register what was happening, pinning his arms with firm paws and leaning into his face, teeth bared.

"Off!" Peter roared, ripping his arms free and lifting Pepper's teeth away from him as he began to bark, spraying his venom with every blood-curdling roar. "Septimus!" he screamed, "Help me!"

He swung his head from side to side, hunting for the malkonar, but he was nowhere to be seen.

His arms started to throb, he couldn't resist Pepper's weight for much longer. Man and mammal looked one another in the eye, and Peter saw things he had never seen nor expected in his dog: bloodlust; viciousness and insanity, his red eyes twitching as he gnashed at Peter's agonisingly close face. He saw the gleam that relished the moment he got to sink his teeth into human flesh, and the drops of saliva that awaited the chance to infuse themselves with blood.

A small tear trickled from his eye. He hadn't pictured it ending this way. He had imagined something banal, something normal, like going to bed in a nursing home and not waking up. Maybe even something a tad more insane, like a mad battle with Malkonar ending with the death of both good and evil, but not this. Not the canine he had nursed from a fluffy puppy to the hyperactive hound who had loved him until about five minutes ago, but that wasn't how life worked, and life loved to deal him the worst cards in the deck.

"Septimus!" he screamed again, but once more his call went unanswered. He chewed his lip until it turned white. He was dead, wasn't he? A hundred shades of regret flew before Peter's eyes. He had left Septimus alone with someone who could and would harm him. He was an idiot. Malkonar was right, he knew nothing about what he was doing, but he had fooled himself that he did, and now he was about to go the way of all fools.

A sting of pain in his arms dropped them. Paws slammed into his chest. Weeping, Peter closed his eyes and braced himself for the worst.

EIGHT

Then there was silence.

Peter's eyes split open and he sat up, heart slamming against his ribcage. Pepper wasn't tearing chunks of his skin off, but lying on the floor with his eyes half closed, licking his paw clean and eyeing Peter with an apathetic gaze. Panting, he leaned into Pepper's face. His eyes were no longer red, just blue and hazel like they always had been. The eyes of the dog he loved.

"Bad dog," he wheezed.

He stood up on quivering legs and made his way towards the living room. His mind was a muddle, but it suddenly straightened when he walked past the phone and it started to ring.

He stood and listened to it in livid silence as the story straightened itself out in his head. He grabbed the receiver with a snatch, took a few deep breaths to calm the swelling fury in his stomach, then abandoned his restraint and hissed down the line,

"What?"

"Did you enjoy my little show?" Malkonar sniggered. The vein in his temple bulged.

"You..." he seethed, drawing more chuckles from the caller.

"Calm yourself, Peter, or risk amusing me even more than you already have."

Peter reluctantly swallowed the bile he was ready to spit. "So that was you, was it? You playing sadistic games with me?"

"I was merely having some fun."

"Well your fun is pissing me off."

"Calm yourself, I advise against being irrational with me. Do you not remember what the book said I was capable of?"

"Telepathy, telekinesis and the ability to possess individuals by the power of the mind," he recited.

"Exactly, and I believe that you have experienced phenomena three for the second time."

"Second?"

"Remember the time you came in from work to find Septimus on top of the fridge?"

He went silent as the world pressed down on him a little more.

"That was you?"

"Yes. Seizing control of objects is nothing new to me. I've possessed your telephone multiple times already, I've merely upgraded to a larger target."

"So you're calling me by possessing my phone?"

"Yes."

"And now you can take control of Pepper? Pull his strings and make him turn on anyone you like?"

"Do the red eyes lie?"

"The person they belong to does."

Malkonar laughed.

"Indeed, but the intent you saw in Pepper's eyes was as earnest as can be. Red is my colour, and anything I gift my hue to does not use it in vain."

"So that's why you don't like Septimus, is it? You're red and he's blue?"

"I'd have thought you'd have more pressing worries about Septimus. You don't know where he is, and with Pepper now my plaything I sense you're very worried about his well-being."

"Of course I am, I'd just never show it in front of you."

"Well, you may relax, as I decided to leave him alone tonight..." he paused as Peter's gasp of relief echoed down the phone. "As you were ripe for the picking. Why attack the pawns when the king's weaknesses are waiting to be exploited?" He laughed again. "Such fun it was to see the unabashed fear on your face. So many years have gone since I last saw that look, how sweet it was to see it again."

"You're insane, you know that?"

"Insane I may be, but if insanity will get me what I want then so be it. My request is simple: give me the stone, or next time I may not be so lenient."

The line went dead. Peter slammed the phone down and threw his fist into the wall in anger and frustration, but his rage dissipated as one word occupied his mind: Septimus.

He found him in the bedroom, curled up amongst the covers and sleeping peacefully, unharmed and undisturbed. His release of angst was immense, his breath so heavy it sunk to the carpet and spread like smog over an industrial town. Everyone was fine, and with his fears alleviated he sat down and slid a hand into his pocket, withdrawing the question sheet. With a trembling hand he pressed pen to paper and wrote down an answer.

7. Why can't I trace Malkonar's phone number?

Malkonar is communicating with me through his mind. He is not calling from a phone, but is connecting his brain to my phone and talking to me, hence why he doesn't have a phone number.

The gentle scratch of ink on paper soothed him, repairing the frayed nerves in his head, but they snapped again as the padding of paws on carpet bounced across the air. He jerked his head to the door to see Pepper, wagging his tail, tongue hanging from his mouth playfully.

"Sit," he ordered instinctively, and Pepper sat. That was better. He licked his lips and crept towards him, laying a hand on Pepper's head. The dog didn't attack. The hound he knew was back, but for how long?

He sat down on the floor and Pepper slid into his lap, letting himself be stroked.

"You really scared me tonight, mate," he whispered, tickling behind Pepper's ear. "I'd like to say you won't do that again, but you're not in charge, are you?"

Pepper yapped.

"Yeah," he grunted, "But what can I do with you?"

He licked his lips again. What could he do? He had a killer's puppet in the house and there was no way in hell he could keep that around, but he was a dog. He was a domestic pet, not a scavenger. He would starve out on the street, and that was not something he was prepared to let a friend who had doted on him for seven years do.

He leaned forward and kissed Pepper's neck. He couldn't go, not yet. He would just have to tie him up a little more. Yeah, that would do. Just keep him tied up in the house so that he couldn't go charging after Septimus should Malkonar take control. He smiled. Perfect. He kept his dog and Malkonar took one mighty step away from the stone he desired.

He heard Pepper yawn and settle into his lap, and glanced at his watch. Time to sleep. He gently prised Pepper away from him and clambered over to his bed, rolling onto his back and falling asleep before he could feel the night's trauma sneaking into his dreams.

* * *

Peter began the day the same way he had done for most of his life: in pain. He sat up and rubbed the sleep from his eyes, and slowly but surely he felt the sharp sear of spikes impaling his leg. Clenching his teeth, he felt along his leg and touched the rough spines of Septimus' back. His eyes widened.

"Oh, shit."

He rolled over and the spines on Septimus' back slurped free from his thigh. An excruciating pain consumed his leg. He resisted its scream and limped to the bathroom, rooted through the medicine cabinet and bandaged his wound. He didn't fuss or whine, he had no right to. Doing stupid things had been second nature to him recently, and it was high time he started showing a shred of responsibility.

He hobbled back to his room and saw Septimus awakened, curled up on his bed and scowling at him.

"Sine smoodet yar," the malkonar hissed, pointing to his bloodstained spines. Peter raised his hands as if to declare surrender.

"Apoligek," he said, and Septimus nodded his appreciation. Peter smiled. Progress.

"Breakfast?" he asked, rubbing his stomach to signal the word. Septimus nodded and Peter limped back to the kitchen, and returned with the breakfast dishes to the sight of a heavily bloodstained carpet.

He dropped the plates, spilling orange juice over a bloody trail at the end of which sat Septimus, chewing happily on a mutilated rabbit. He gnawed his lip to stop himself from cursing at him. There were no rabbits in the apartment block, so it could only mean one thing. He felt an all too familiar feeling of rage in his veins.

"Septimus!" he shouted, "How did you get outside?"

"Tant?" he replied, sucking out the rabbit's intestines like spaghetti. Peter pointed to his meal.

"How?" he said slowly, and Septimus understood.

He discarded his snack and pointed to an unlocked window, gave his wings a slight flutter and bit down furiously with his teeth. He expected to receive congratulation on his hunting prowess, but instead he got to witness Peter slam the window shut and slide the lock into place.

"Denor!" he snapped, bringing to life one of the few words of Septimus' language he understood, "Denor hunting!"

Septimus whined miserably and collapsed into a heap on the bed. He felt a kick of guilt and pity ride across his organs, but he stood his ground.

"Sorry, mate," he muttered, grabbing his clothes from the dresser, "But I've got to keep you safe."

"Tant?"

"Yeah. I know you can't understand a word I'm saying but I'll say it anyway. You're in danger, mate, and I'm in danger too. We're all in danger, and we need to stay safe. You want to go outside but I'm afraid you can't, it's just too dangerous. Outside isn't even that good, anyway. It's dirty and noisy and full of nasty people who will shun you and ignore you and say hurtful things and even hurt you because you're not like them. I know it must be boring being cooped up in here all day, but hey, watching TV is better than that, right?"

The question was rhetorical, but as he went to exit the room he glanced back. He regretted it. Septimus' posture and position hadn't changed, but his eyes were locked on Peter, and in those eyes he saw something he had last seen in Pepper's possessed state and horrified him to see again. Dissent.

* * *

"Having fun?" Don asked, taking another sip from his bottle of whiskey-spiked cola.

"Yeah," Peter lied, snuggling deeper into his many layers of clothing.

Thistledon Park was only three-quarters full that afternoon, but Peter had still ended up sandwiched between Don and a steward who didn't particularly enjoy the fact that a dog had snuggled up against his shoe. Not that it made a difference, as the bitter temperatures of winter meant no amount of crush would squeeze the feeling back into his fingers. For a fleeting moment he remembered why he had withdrawn from all of this, but he forced his eyes back onto the game. He just had to relax, enjoy himself as twenty-two overpaid men hoofed a ball around for an hour and a half, but that wasn't easy under the grip of panic.

He had made sure to lock every window and door before he had left, but still feared Septimus would be out and about. He tried again to concentrate on the tedium on the pitch, but he still saw that angry look in the reptile's eyes, the look that told him that he was the boss of no one. He didn't need that. Septimus was his way in, lose him and he was back at square one. Lose him and he could be that bloody smear he had feared a month ago. He groaned in anguish and pulled his hat further over his ears just as Rangers blazed yet another shot wide of the mark.

"I know how you feel, mate," Don said, patting his back sympathetically, "This is painful to watch."

"You have no idea," Peter mumbled.

"Hmm?"

"Nothing."

He sat back and watched a goal kick fly into the air, but as he followed the white blot's climb it distorted in front of his eyes, and then came a sharp pang in his head.

He grabbed his skull to steady his vision, biting his lip to silence a cry. Jesus, that hurt. Like someone had pushed a needle into his brain. Like the pain that had racked his head the night Septimus pleaded for his help.

He closed his eyes and a small whimper escaped, but not loud enough for anyone to hear over the songs of Saturday. The world was swirling again, colours flashing about, bouncing off his eyelids, hurtling through his nerves and into his throbbing head, but he didn't let his concentration waver, and through the insanity came a familiar voice.

"Thefte! Thefte!" Septimus screamed in his head, the words

repeating again and again in his brainwaves. Peter's throat went dry. Was Septimus in danger? Not with those claws and teeth, surely, but then he remembered the scratches Pepper had dealt him, and then he remembered the look of defiance on his face. He hadn't gone outside and found trouble, had he? No, he couldn't have, everything was locked and he had the key, but what about the opposite? What if someone had broken in? The colour drained from his face. Thefte. Theft. Someone was in the house with Septimus.

He grabbed Pepper's lead and shoved his way out of the aisle, jogging down the concrete steps of the stand at speed.

"Where're you going?" Don shouted after him. Peter whined. Now wasn't the time for this.

"I have to go."

"Where?"

"Home."

"Why?"

"I just have to."

"But it's not full time yet."

"It's urgent," he pleaded.

"It can't be that urgent, you never do anything," his voice grew frustrated, "I'm the only thing in your life, mate, but all you ever do is try not to be around me. C'mon, just relax and enjoy the game."

"Don, I really have to go."

"I'll not walk Pepper anymore," Don threatened, but with Septimus and his stinging accusation in his mind Peter was in no mood to negotiate.

"Don, it's your job!" he roared, and the heads of seven-thousand people swivelled towards them. "You've been on the dole since being laid off by the shipyards. That was three years ago and you haven't even thought of work since then. The money I give you is the only thing that keeps you alive, and you spend all of it on beer. I might be an ungrateful sociopath but you're a lazy, aimless bastard, so be grateful for what you have and don't bite the hand that feeds you. Now if you'll excuse me, I have to go."

Without waiting for a reply he ran off, averting his eyes from the shrivelled figure of Don, cowering under the glares of an accusing crowd.

He weaved out of the stadium and through the streets of Averton, dodging shoppers and tourists with previously unknown dexterity. Cramp racked his stomach as he charged around, but the voice in his head and the pace-setter that was Pepper kept him going.

He charged across a road, narrowly avoiding traffic to the furious squeals of car horns, and into his apartment block, leaping the stairs three at a time. He drew his keys from his pocket, but found out seconds later that he didn't need them. His house didn't have a lock anymore: the remnants of it were lying in small pieces on the floor. Peter felt his blood pressure surge and he opened the door, and what he saw sucked the breath from his lungs.

The contents of his desk had spewed onto the floor, mingling among the overturned drawers of the coffee table, their rollers snapped by force. His grip on Pepper's lead tightened, knuckles turning white. The damage appeared to have been limited to the living room, but the house and his head were quiet and Peter feared the worst.

"Septimus?" he called, and to his relief the reptile slinked out of the kitchen, his body clenched tight. Peter gratefully picked him up and held his face close to his. "Thank God you're okay," he said, cradling him. "What happened?"

"Thefte," Septimus said timidly. He pointed to the door and ran his claw in a line until it reached the desk. Then he pointed to the coffee table with the drawers pulled out and then to the papers all over the floor. Peter nodded nervously.

"Did they take anything?" he asked, picking up a paper and nodding at the door. Septimus shook his head, but he had another, vastly more important question for the only witness,

"Did they see you?"

Septimus cocked his head in confusion, and with his pulse rocketing he grabbed a piece of paper and sketched a stickman and a stickdragon, drawing an arrow from the stickman's eyes to the stickdragon. He almost looked away as Septimus contemplated the doodle. What if he had been seen? That was bad. That was very, very bad. Unwanted attention, maybe even more thieves, and Malkonar would still be there. The eye of a larger storm. An even bigger nightmare than he was already having. He felt his body begin to quake, but then Septimus shook his head.

"Oh, thank God," he said, pressure releasing with orgasmic intensity, only to fall victim to another panic attack as he remembered the stone.

He sprinted over to the sideboard like a prisoner running from guards and ripped open a drawer. It was still there, its red spiral winking at him, mocking his pale face. He slammed the drawer shut in disgust, but with the last of his immediate fears quelled he finally ground his anxiety to a halt.

"Fucking hell," he said. He slumped against the wall, the only thing strong enough to cope with the weight of his body and his burden. Septimus leapt from his arms and onto the sideboard and studied his solemn face. He didn't do anything, but that suited him fine. He didn't want an interruption from someone without a solution. "When will I catch a fucking break?"

Septimus raised his brow, stretching his eyes so that they bore into his soul. He softened a little under his gaze.

"Sorry," he sighed. He reached out and stroked Septimus' head, "I'm just fed up, and I'm sure you'd understand if you knew what I was saying. But it's okay. You're okay, I'm okay; the house hasn't burned down. We're fine. For now." He turned a mournful gaze onto the mess at his feet. "Do you want to help me clear up?"

He didn't understand the question, but as Peter crouched down to shuffle the papers back into line Septimus leapt from the sideboard and landed at his side.

As they worked Peter began to slot the pieces together. The thief had obviously arrived with a motive if the damage was restricted to drawers full of paper, but what motive? He cycled through the thick collection of papers in his hands. The majority of the sheets were work-related: invoices, business letters, programming notes and the like, but a smaller group of these were Malkonar-related. His anguish disappeared as it became apparent that all the Malkonar pieces were present, and while that relieved him it sent another mystery hurtling towards his problem pile. Why had the thief taken nothing? The neighbours hadn't called and they hadn't seen Septimus so clearly no one had intervened, so what had made them voluntarily leave empty-handed whilst leaving such a great mess behind? He shoved the question away and went back to cleaning. He'd suffered enough for one day and it wasn't even sundown.

He placed the sheets neatly in his desk drawer, and was about to close it when he felt a nudge against his leg. Smiling, he picked up Septimus again and let him add his own stack of sheets to the pile.

"Cheers, mate," he said, pushing the drawer shut.

"Comarden," Septimus said back, an earnest grin stretched across his juvenile face. Peter beamed. The word meant nothing to him, but the smile was all he needed.

NINE

Peter spent the night worrying. It was nothing new to him by any means, but under the weight of Malkonar, Pepper and the thief the subject of his paranoia surprised him: Don.

He squirmed under the sheets as his words at the football match played themselves out in his head again. He was an awful person. No one lashed out at their friends like that, let alone announced their pathetic life story to thousands of people. He dejectedly rolled over. It was the end of the road for them as friends, surely. He would find out for certain in the morning, and knowing Don's fists were hardened by four years of amateur boxing he shrivelled at the thought of what would happen when he arrived to collect Pepper. But he needn't have worried, as Don didn't turn up at all.

He sat fidgeting on his sofa, staring at his watch with heavily bloodshot eyes. Where was he? Well, he knew where he was, and he knew why he wasn't walking off his hangover with a lead in his hand too. Guilt resurging, he looked at his watch again. Only seconds had passed, but those were seconds too many. He was running late, but without Don there was nowhere for Pepper to go other than here, and there was no chance of that happening. Another glance at his watch. Three more precious seconds wasted, and that was too much for him to take. If Don wasn't going to collect Pepper then he'd have to make a delivery.

Don lived in East Thistledon, an industrial wasteland that was near single-handedly responsible for the River Tuskant's pollution, where the idea of policing was smashing intruders over the head with a golf club. He screwed his face up at the rows of Victorian terraces, smeared with the soot of now dismantled industry and smelling faintly of the numerous takeaways spread across each street. His feet crunched over the glass of a broken bus stop, its frame staring apologetically at a shuttered shop across the street, metal rusted and defaced with anti-Government graffiti. He shook his head pitifully. How Don was content to live in a slum like this he would never know.

He reached his house: a piece of rotting brickwork with an overgrown garden to match. He wandered up the cracked path and rang the doorbell, then remembered it had been broken for a year and a half and knocked on the door. A minute or so later Don appeared, in his dressing gown, clutching a mug of what smelled like liqueur coffee and judgementally stroking his five o'clock shadow.

"Hey," Peter squeaked.

"What d'you want?"

"Why didn't you come and pick Pepper up this morning?"

"Why should I?" Don slurred, placing a hand to his head as his hangover reminded him of its presence.

"Look, Don, I'm sorry about what I said," he grovelled, "It was inexcusable and I don't deserve your help, but I really need you to look after Pepper. I'm late for work."

"Oh great. Rub it in, why don't you?"

"What?"

"You're late for work. At least you have a job to be late for."

"You've got a job. You walk Pepper."

"That's not a proper job."

"It is. You work Monday to Friday, twenty past eight 'til five and you get paid for it."

"Oh, don't charm me, Pete." Don snapped, taking a swig from his mug, "You were right, mate, I'm a failure. I've been doing this pathetic shit, collecting dole and being your slave, for two years now, and I've never bothered to try and get out of it."

"You have!"

"When?"

Peter thought, and gave up seconds later.

"See? I'm a nobody, a benefits scrounger. There's a queue of people out the door who'd want to put a bullet in me, and thanks to you I've had my eyes opened to that. So cheers Peter, you've helped me realise that I've fucked up my life."

"You haven't!"

"Yes I have, and you know what? I'm going to prove you wrong. Seeing as you think I'm going nowhere I'm going to get a job. I'm going to work nine 'til five and get a wad of cash for it. I'm going to work hard and get promoted until my job has a fancier name than yours. Then I'll be above you, looking down on your life like you've done on mine, and best of all I'll never have to walk your bloody dog ever again!"

He slammed the door in Peter's face. Peter hammered on it desperately, but as the seconds ticked by it was clear Don wasn't coming back.

"Don, please!" he begged, but his plea drew no mercy from the man behind the door.

He looked at his watch again. Now he was late for work. He had never been late for work before, and with his perfect record history his composure went. He lifted open the letterbox and shouted something he had never dared shout before.

"Gareth Sheldon, listen to me!"

The sound of feet pounding across carpet filled the air, and the letterbox reopened to reveal furious eyes.

"Do you want to get punched?" Don hissed.

"Look, I know you hate your full name, but I had to get your attention."

"Well you've got it, so what do you want?"

"Alright," Peter said, choosing his words carefully, "Could you look after Pepper for me just one more time? You can do whatever you want after, but please, I'm begging you, just for today will you walk Pepper? C'mon mate, I really need your help. I can't leave him alone in my house."

There was a pause as Don rolled his eyes.

"Fine, just for today."

The door opened and Don yanked Pepper's lead out of his hand, slamming shut before he could offer his thanks. Peter could sense his contempt resonate in the air that blew into his face, but it pushed him down the path and into his stride, sending him towards the city smiling.

* * *

Peter left his office to feel the first snowflakes of winter catch in his hair. He greeted them with the same scowl of restlessness he'd worn for most of the day. The buzz of success had died not long after he'd sat down at his desk nine hours ago, and the lesser side of his brain had instantly taken over.

Within the reams of code he pored over he saw names. Septimus, Malkonar, Don, Pepper, disappearing after a double-take but always reappearing further down the line. It spooked him, and though he tried to force them out they refused to leave his mind. The sound of Averton Cathedral's bells tolling the end of the working day didn't come soon enough.

He was the first out of the building but walked the slowest once he stepped into the street. It was nice to escape the claustrophobia of work, but going home wasn't a prospect that thrilled him. Home was where Malkonar could get him.

He sauntered up the steps to his apartment, but froze halfway up as he saw Don sat outside the door, Pepper lying submissively at his side. They locked eyes, and he withered. He was probably going to get another thoroughly-deserved lecture, and by this hour Don usually had a unit or two inside of him so his fists moved more freely.

He stood silent and meek, waiting for Don to say something to break the tension, but he was content to let it float in the air. Peter wasn't.

"Hi," he whispered, raising himself to the top of the steps, "Why are you here? Pepper doesn't need to come home for another hour."

"I can't wait 'til then," Don shrugged. He sounded reserved, not drunk. Peter felt himself relax a little.

"Why d'you say that?"

"I..." he sighed, "Look Pete, I'm sorry about this morning. I was hungover and I didn't mean to act like I did. I'm sorry."

He was caught off-guard by Don's apology, but the stash of guilt he carried meant finding a response was easy.

"You don't have to be sorry," he said, "I shouldn't have done what I did, and I did it in front of about five-thousand people. I'm meant to be your mate," he scuffed his shoe against the floor, "Some mate I've been."

"I know," he nodded, "It hurt, y'know. Those last fifteen minutes were the most uncomfortable of my life, but at the same time I think you gave me an overdue wake-up call. I've spent a lot of today thinking about you and me and..." he rubbed Pepper's furry mane, "I'll walk Pepper for as long as you need. I'm grateful for your support, and I know I haven't really shown it but I am."

"Well, that's good to hear," Peter said, but a flicker of instinct twisted his words in a split-second, "But I think you should work for yourself instead of me for a change."

"What?"

"This morning you said you were going to try and get a job, and I think you should do it."

"Oh, I don't know Pete," Don replied, turning away from him,

"Where would I begin? University dropout and laid off from the bloody docks, of all places. They're hardly gonna jump over walls for that, are they?"

"It doesn't have to be corporate banking or anything. Shops on the high street are always looking for cleaners; shipping companies need drivers."

"Lorry driver," Don sneered, "No chance of that, that's the job of a Pole."

"It's only the job of a Pole because people like us don't want to do it. Just go for it, man. I'll help you in any way I can, I promise."

"Well..."

"And in the meantime you can carry on walking Pepper to keep you going," he added. "Go for it, mate. You won't regret it."

Don considered his options, swapping glances with Peter and Pepper, then smiled.

"Alright then, ten quid says I have a job within the next two months."

"Deal!" Peter said, reaching out to shake on it. Don met his gesture.

"And are we even?"

"We're even."

"That's a relief," Don said, "And if it's okay with you I'll be here to pick up Pepper at the usual time tomorrow."

"Great."

He bid Don farewell and watched him descend the stairs, grinning from ear to ear the whole time. He had actually managed to solve one of his problems! A sense of elation flooded him, making his fingertips tremble. After twenty-four years of existence he had finally grown.

He disappeared back into his apartment and felt something new bubble inside him: confidence. Right now he could deal with Malkonar. Actually, not just Malkonar but everyone. Pepper; Septimus; the thief, right here and right now they weren't problematic.

He collapsed onto the sofa and basked in the good feeling. It was the first time he'd had the chance to do such a thing, and as it transpired it would also be the last.

TEN

Christmas season went into full swing and, in typical Peter Vaughan style, he carried on as if everything was exactly the same. He woke up, lived his worthless life, tried and failed to teach Septimus English, and went to bed to repeat the cycle the next day. The only thing that varied was the success rate of his tutoring, but it only ever fluctuated between ineffective and poor. Everything taught was forgotten in a matter of days. It did nothing to aid his shortening fuse, but he didn't have any more time to spare. In the background life was continuing as normal, and it wouldn't allow him to remove his restrictive veil.

    He collapsed into his office chair and, rubbing some life the bitter December wind had stolen back into his hands, reluctantly set to work. As he tapped in the various commands he began to tune out of the world, the office fading to a blur as he fell into his mind. His crooked mind, polluted with Septimus. What was he doing? Had he got out? Had he broken something? Set it on fire? Had Malkonar got him? Constant, erratic fears that accelerated his heartbeat, but once his bubble had closed there was no escape. Just him, his paranoia and the reams of code on the screen in front of him.

Septimus
Septimus
Septimus
Malkonar
Help me
Help me
HELP ME

The sound of clicking his fingers in front of his face finally broke his trance. He jerked back in his seat, and blushed as his boss eyed him coldly.

"Welcome back, Peter," he murmured, running a hand through his thinning hair.

"Sorry, sir."

"It's alright. If only the others were as enthusiastic about this bloody job as you are."

Peter grinned uneasily. "Yeah..."

"Anyway, Peter, question: do you know the Librarian down at Averton City Library?"

Peter frowned. "Yeah, I do."

"Well, on Friday night she came in here, saying she needed to talk to you."

The fingers resting on his keyboard went taut.

"What?"

"Don't know why she wants you, maybe you have a book overdue or something."

"How does she know I work here?"

"Don't know that, either," he shrugged, "Anyway, I suggest you get yourself down to the Library at lunchtime to see what all the fuss is about."

With a sigh he sauntered back to his office like a man walking to the gallows and slammed the door. Peter licked his lips as a cold feeling squeezed on his guts. What on earth could she possibly want from him? Did she know something? He stared warily around the office. No one paid him any heed, no one would notice if he sneaked out...

No, he couldn't. He turned back to his screen, hoping for a distraction, but saw properly for the first time what he had typed in his trance. He licked his lips again. Slip out to the library and solve another mystery, risking his job in the process, or two more hours of that?

He squeezed through the automatic doors at an impossible angle and slammed his hands down on the Librarian's desk. She carried on typing for a few moments longer before looking up.

"Can I help you?"

"What were you doing asking around my office for me?" Peter spat, suspense overcoming his sense of decency.

"You have a book overdue."

"I don't have a library card."

Her thin-lipped grin drooped slightly. Peter spotted something in the gesture, but he wasn't sure what.

"And furthermore," he said, "If I did have a book overdue, it would have my name and address on that computer you type into so often. Give me the real picture."

"There's been an error with the computer system," she said calmly, tapping into the keyboard once more, "On my list of overdue books it had a name but not an address. I simply went around all of the local businesses asking if they knew a Peter Vaughan."

"How do you know I'm Peter Vaughan?"

"Your boss showed me a photograph of you."

"Well I haven't had a library card since the age of twelve, and when I did have one I returned every single book that I borrowed."

She looked up at him again with questioning eyes, but Peter had nothing to hide.

"Alright then, you're free to go."

Peter forcefully nodded his gratitude and turned to leave, but his sight fell on the stairs rather than the door. Up those steps was a highly useful book that he had only seen two pages of, and it wasn't like anyone would have noticed he was gone.

He clambered to the second floor and slid the book out of the shelf, flicking to where he had left off as he carried it to a table. Taking a moment to prepare himself, he turned the page to see what new horrors waited. A page on the diet of Dragonkind was what greeted his eyes. He skim-read it, searching for the word that lingered persistently at the back of his skull and refused to wither away, and he found it.

In folklore, the diets of Dragonkind have often been composed of meat, one of the few exceptions being the Lambton Worm, who was fed on milk. However, the most unusual form of diet belongs to the aforementioned Malkonar, who is written to have fed on the psyche of other creatures.

Outspoken biologist Leopold Armstrong (1846-1894) was a firm believer in Dragons and spent many of the years before his death studying the species. He was particularly fascinated by Malkonars, and from the few surviving documents in his name he wrote that, through close scrutiny of the work of others, Malkonars fed on the minds of 'weak-willed' creatures. His theory went that Malkonars tapped into the minds of creatures and 'de-coded' the brain. Once done the Malkonar would feed on the intelligence of the creature, the loss of intelligence eventually killing the prey. Armstrong believed that the higher the intelligence of the victim then the harder their brain would be to de-code, hence his belief that humans could not be damaged as their intelligence was so great. Many leading scientists denounced Armstrong's work, leading to his retirement in obscurity and eventual suicide four years later, aged 48.

At first he said nothing, and he remained silent as he pressed the book shut. Head in hands, the new piece of information sucking away his sense of urgency, he spoke a solitary word.

"Shit."

He threw all of his mental strength behind not having a panic attack in public, but it was a tough fight. Was Malkonar eating his mind? Armstrong didn't think so, but it was in his nature to see the bleakest landscape. He thought hard about the possibility, and the longer he thought the clearer a lone word became: Armstrong.

He slapped himself. How the hell had he managed to forget about Armstrong? His name was the second or third key thing he had learned in this whole affair, and he had forgotten about him near instantly. Scorning his carelessness, he thought of everything he knew about him. Armstrong was a scientist and he had used the silo for experiments. He didn't know what for, but he was a believer in malkonars, and Malkonar wanted him to put the stone in the silo wall, so did that mean...

He chewed his lip. Surely Malkonar wasn't inside the silo? At first it seemed ludicrous, but the more he thought about it the more sense it made. The hole in the silo wall: a lock without a key, unable to open without the stone, and it didn't matter how long he'd been in there if all he needed to survive was the minds of bugs and beetles. And if the mind was his food then he could very well be his dinner.

He swallowed the vile taste in his mouth. Malkonar wouldn't feast on his neuroses when he specifically wanted him to take the stone to the silo, or would he? He checked his watch as a distraction, and was alarmed to find it wasn't long until lunch. Then they'd know he was missing. He had to go.

He wrote down his findings on a piece of scrap paper, replaced the book and made for the stairs, but his path was blocked by the Librarian, a look of curiosity etched into her dull features.

"Erm, hello," Peter said, "Can I help you?"

"Not particularly," she mumbled, "I'm just passing." Yet despite her just passing she didn't budge. Peter raised an eyebrow at her.

"You're curious, aren't you?"

"About what?"

"What I'm doing, running in here and running back out again every other day."

"Sort of," she said, "Every time you come here you rush in like a cheetah on steroids, read one page of the same book then dart out again. May I ask why?"

"I'll tell you some other time. I have to get back to work," he said, but she wasn't giving up that easily.

"You always get the same book on mythical creatures, why the fascination?"

"I just take an interest in that sort of thing."

"Why mythical creatures, though? Is it something to do with that malkonar thing you mentioned?"

Peter's body locked as she uttered that dreaded word. "Have you been spying on me while I read that book?"

She shuffled her feet. "A little."

"How can you spy on someone 'a little'? Why are you so interested in me and myths?"

"It's just...it's just that no one has ever taken such a compelling interest in such an unusual subject, and I'm curious that you're always in a hurry when you come here. Anyway, I really must be going, we have a new shipment today that I need to catalogue."

She shot past him before he could say another word, disappearing into the sea of bookshelves.

Though he was in a hurry Peter watched the shelves for a while. She had been spying on him and had taken note of his research, and that was far from good. How much did she know? Enough to suspect that a malkonar wasn't a mythical creature? Hopefully not, but he couldn't help but feel suspicious of her character, and as he made for the door he made a mental note to keep an eye on her.

He also withdrew his question sheet and jotted down another answer.

5. Why does Malkonar want me to return the stone to the silo wall?

To free him. He is trapped inside the silo and wants to be released.

ELEVEN

There was nothing Peter could do to soothe what lingered at the back of his mind. He lay with eyes clamped shut and arms resting over his slumbering companion, desperately trying to join him in the land of nod, but to no avail.

He tried to think of positive stories and fantasies to drag him away from consciousness, but everything in his mind had been invaded by Malkonar. The time he went to Wembley – Malkonar was sitting on the pitch. The time he went scuba diving in Polynesia – Malkonar was in the deep alongside him. That beach in Aruba where he had spent so much time getting sunburnt – Malkonar was lying next to him and biting effortlessly through the shells of coconuts. He didn't even know what he looked like, but his spirit was there, and that was enough to keep his eyes wedged open.

He breathed gently, muscles relaxing and body sinking deeper into the duvet. Then he felt a rush of blood to his head and his eyes widened, the blackness he once saw fading into blinding white. He tried to squint, but he wasn't sure that he could. Was he asleep? Was he awake? Or was he hovering in some unreality between the two?

He raised his arm to shield his eyes in time to watch an orange ribbon roll across the sky, shortly followed by another, then a third. Hundreds of ribbons unfurled in the air, transforming the white into an orange twilight sky. He rubbed his eyes, he had to be dreaming. The world he lived in was insane but it didn't do that, and it sure as hell wasn't as beautiful.

When he reopened his eyes he was no longer floating in an endless void of blinding white, but sitting in a boat. A rowing boat, the sort he would expect to see in nostalgic postcards, floating on a sapphire blue lake with a family of elegant swans swimming alongside him. Around the lake was a forest of grand pine trees which filled his nostrils with a beautifully fresh scent, all of this floating beneath the orange sky, watching over with a warm heart.

"Beautiful, isn't it?" a plain English voice spoke. Peter's heart soared up his gullet upon hearing he wasn't alone, and it crept even higher when he noticed who was perched at the other end of the boat, staring into the calm waters with omnipotent eyes.

"Hi, Septimus," Peter whispered.

"You seem unnerved."

"'Course I am. You're in my dream and you can speak English."

"How do you know you're dreaming?" Septimus asked, moving to the centre of the boat.

"I've never been here before in my life. This is all too new and idyllic for the places I've been."

"How come? You've been to Polynesia and the Caribbean, all of this may be subconsciously based off something you've seen here and there."

"Then if it's based off things I've seen then I must be dreaming," Peter countered, grabbing the oars at his side and beginning to row, "And how come you know I've been to those places?"

"I'm a malkonar," Septimus replied, "I'm a mind reader. Well, sometimes."

"What do you mean 'sometimes'?"

"I can only read what is at the front of people's minds. What has been repressed can only be reached by the experienced."

"So how much of my mind can you read?"

"Most of it. You haven't really learned to shove things away as you're a human, and thus you have no need to protect your thoughts. The things I cannot see are more than likely dark thoughts that you want to avoid, but everything else is open to me. I can see what your questions are before you ask them, and before you do, I'm speaking English because this is indeed a dream, and in a dream anyone can do anything."

"So are we having the same dream?" Peter said, raising an eyebrow.

"What do you mean?"

"Well, in the real world, are you and I dreaming the same thing? Are we having this conversation in our heads at this very moment? Are you hearing me in your language like I'm hearing you in mine?"

"Most likely," Septimus replied, "I can deduce that you are dreaming, that much is certain, but there is a lot that is uncertain to me. Still, uncertainty is one of the great things about life, is it not? The things we don't expect are always the most delicious."

Peter smirked, "You're a very intelligent and philosophical reptile, you know that?"

"Indeed," Septimus nodded, returning to staring over the side of the boat, "It is only a shame you don't replicate that feeling in the real world."

Peter stopped rowing, stung by Septimus' criticism.

"Sorry?"

"You don't understand me, so you don't see me as particularly intelligent. You've discarded everything I've written because anything you cannot read is inferior; you lock me indoors because you do not trust me to look after myself."

"I lock you indoors to keep you safe."

"I live in the same world as you, do you think I do not know what dangers lurk outside your house?"

"Well, no."

"Exactly, but you lock the windows anyway, for no one trusts a dumb animal that speaks gibberish. This is not a rare occurrence: think about the colonists that went to the New World. The people they encountered did not speak their tongue, therefore they were dumb. It is a horrific example of how the world works, but it is truth, and truth can't be altered."

"Wow," he said slowly, beginning to row again but slower than before, "Sorry, I didn't realise I was being so rude. I won't be from now on."

Septimus beamed. "Apology accepted."

He turned his eyes back to the water, studying the depths with a keen eye. He raised a claw and flexed it, and in a shot thrust it into the water. The splash made Peter's heart miss a beat, and when his breathing returned to normal he saw that Septimus had a fish in his hand.

"Not bad," he said, killing it with a casual flick of his claw.

"Wow," he said again. This wasn't Septimus as he knew him. The Septimus back in Averton was little more than a domestic pet who spoke gobbledegook, but this Septimus was inspirational.

"Tell me, Feela, are you hungry?" Septimus asked, scraping the scales away from the fish.

"Yeah, I wouldn't mind a bite to eat."

"Very well, let us feast on this fish."

The background changed in a split second, and Peter saw they weren't on the water anymore. They were on the shore, not far from the gargantuan pines. He looked at Septimus, who was cut off from him by a pile of logs. He blew a small breath of sparks onto the wood and it ignited, the flames slowly transferring to the rest of the logs.

"What happened?" he asked, head turning frantically, "We were on the boat and now we're here."

"We're in a dream, Feela, anything can happen," Septimus soothed, "There are no such things as timelines in dreams. Action no longer leads to consequence and causality doesn't exist."

"How do you know all of this? If we're both dreaming then how come you're not as oblivious as I am?"

"I'm a malkonar, Feela, a creature of the mind. Because of my psychic abilities I have more power over my subconscious."

"So?"

"So I'm in control," Septimus grinned, "While humans have a dream chosen by their subconscious, I can choose what I want to dream."

"Surely that's not always a good thing, though. I mean what if you're worrying about something? That can leak into your dream and spoil it."

"That can happen, but it's not something exclusive to malkonars. That's something I've observed anyway."

"What does that mean?" Peter asked, but his question received no answer.

Septimus removed the fish from the fire and cut it neatly in two with his claws. He handed the tail end to Peter and took a generous bite out of the head, his monstrous teeth glinting as the light hit them. Peter took a tiny nibble from his half of the fish. It was perfectly edible, but Peter didn't find food with organs poking out of it particularly appetising. Septimus smiled a razor-sharp grin.

"Not hungry after all, are you?" he said, ripping one of the fish's eyes out with his claw and placing it in his mouth.

"Not really."

"Humans are so fussy," he smirked, "You'll only eat certain bits of certain things, and even then it has to be cooked to a certain degree. Most pieces of animal are edible, you know. Except for caterpillars, stay away from them. I ate a few once and I was vomiting for three days. Not much fun."

"I can understand," he replied, then took a bigger bite out of the fish. Septimus laughed.

"You're trying to impress me, aren't you? My little lecture on culinary habits has made you upset, and you wish to prove to me that you're not a fussy little human being."

"Be quiet."

Septimus chuckled again, then leaned forward and blew onto the fire. Small specks of ice flew from his mouth and onto the flames, dousing them in water and extinguishing the fire. Peter watched with awe.

"You're curious," Septimus said, "Remember the book? Malkonars can breathe more than just fire."

"Fire, Ice, Electric and Turquoise, whatever that is."

"And that's not all. In the past individual malkonars have managed to create all kinds of different breaths that do weird and wonderful things. I, however, can only manage flecks of fire and ice."

"Can you do that in real life?"

"Breathe fire and ice? Yes, but only to the extent that you have seen. I'm keen to develop them though as they can be quite useful out in the woods."

"The woods? How do you know about them?"

"Dumb animal again, Feela. You don't think I can't unlock the windows, do you?"

The colour drained from Peter's face.

"Yes, yes. I know you do not want me to be out in the woods, but I must get outside from time to time."

"Why, though?"

"I'd have thought that was obvious: exercise. Your apartment isn't large enough for me, and it's easier to stay hidden in the woods than in the city."

"Well..."

"Look, Feela, we're in danger. I forage out in the woods, meaning I kill animals, and the more animals I kill the better my technique becomes. I don't know if you've noticed but we are in a battle with a malignant power, and when everything culminates would you rather have a partner who knows how to fight or one who doesn't?"

Peter sat still, twiddling his thumbs and watching them clatter together. He weighed up the pros and cons in his head, and while his conscience leaned towards cons Septimus' demand for respect was fresh in his mind.

"Alright," he sighed, "But be careful when you're out, and no breathing fire in the house either. I don't want you causing me more bother than I already have."

"Worry not, your warnings are heeded."

Peter finished the fish with an unsatisfied gulp. As it shot down his gullet the sky suddenly changed, the orange subsiding into a rich, dark chocolate. The now subdued colours of the trees began to melt into the air, forming one complete mesh that Peter's straining eyes struggled to see through. He looked out to the lake, but couldn't see where it began or ended. Only its faded glisten.

"It looks like the end of this dream is nigh," Septimus said, his eyes acting as beacons in the night, "I think we've time for one last crusade before our time is up. Feela, pick any time, place or fantasy you've ever wanted to be in and I will take you there."

"But what about the randomness of dreams?"

"As long as I'm here, I can control its course. Only the ending is random."

Peter closed his eyes and thought hard, trying to think of a situation he had always wanted to be in, but when put on the spot he found himself struggling. It wasn't a problem he had to fuss over for long, though, as moments later he smelled burning.

His eyes shot open. They were on a small piece of grassland, wedged between a beach and a great volcano that was spewing thick black smoke into the sky. He screamed in alarm, his strength draining away and sending him to his knees. As he fell he felt something sharp dig into his shoulder, and a glance to his right told him that Septimus was perched there, his squint waning as the filth above blocked out the sun.

"An interesting choice," Septimus said, "I found it a fair way into the labyrinth of your mind. Perhaps a fascination from a young age?"

"Where are we?" Peter asked, shakily climbing back to his feet.

"The island of Krakatau, the year 1883, roughly twenty-to-eleven in the morning."

The volcano rumbled again, making Peter's ears sting and drawing another squeak out of his throat.

"You don't mean..."

"I don't mean what?"

"You don't mean we're about to witness the eruption of Krakatoa?"

"Spot on," Septimus grinned, plugging his ears with his claws, "And I suggest you plug your ears too, this will deafen you."

Peter stuck his fingers in his ears seconds before the volcano exploded. Shards of rock flew into the sky and molten lava erupted down the slopes, a fiery avalanche consuming everything in its path. Great plumes of smoke billowed into the air, removing what was left of the sun from existence and dropping the temperature to a fierce chill. The ground shook violently and he almost fell again, but he kept his balance. He would be vulnerable on the floor, but as he observed the chaos around him he wasn't convinced he was any safer when upright.

"Bloody hell, that was loud!" Septimus giggled, removing his claws from his ears and wiping away a streak of blood that was dribbling out. Peter removed his own, feeling the same warm trickle flood his canals along with a piercing ring that muted all sound, but that problem seemed minor as he watched fast-flowing lava tumble down the mountain.

"Erm, Septimus?" he said nervously.

"Yes?"

"Shouldn't we run away from that lava?"

"We're doomed regardless, Feela. This island will be underwater pretty soon, and numerous tsunamis are tearing through the Indian Ocean as we speak, but don't fret. This is only a dream, you cannot be harmed."

"That doesn't mean I'm not afraid!" he whined, squirming as the lava reached the bottom of the volcano, incinerating trees and shrubs as it grew closer to them, but Septimus didn't care for Peter's moans.

"Ten seconds to impact," he said calmly, "Just relax and take the hit."

"Sep…"

"Nine."

"Ti…"

"Eight."

"Mus!"

"Seven."

"Stop this!"

"Six."

"We're gonna get killed!"

"Five."

"Please!"

"Four."

"No!"

"Three."

"Run!" Peter cried, turning and sprinting as fast as his spindly legs would take him.

"Two."

Peter glanced over his shoulder. The lava was gaining.

"Help!"

"One!"

He could feel the searing heat on his calves. It had to be less than a metre away.

"No!"

"Zero."

The lava collided with them. Peter felt his legs ignite and turn to ashes, allowing his entire body to collapse into the inferno. Then the world went white, and what he saw next was the pastel-coloured ceiling of his bedroom.

"Bloody hell," Peter wheezed, inhaling great lungfuls of air to sedate his emotional trauma. He closed his eyes again, unable to look at the malkonar curled up at his side, and he only dared to do so once his uncontrollable trembling had decided he had suffered enough.

With slow, leaden movements he sat up and stared at Septimus, who was lying on his back peacefully, a grin of satisfaction etched into his face.

TWELVE

Christmas was only a matter of days away, but even under hanging lights and the glare of Cloverhill Department Store's window display Peter wasn't overcome with goodwill. In his mind Christmas cheer consisted of hanging a bit of tinsel from the curtain hooks and waiting more than two seconds before slamming the door on carol singers, but this year he didn't feel so charitable. Not when every intolerable day walking under his storm cloud was complicated further by frantic shoppers blocking his path and cluttering up public transport. The only way he could find to keep wearing his mask of sanity was to think of what he could study or research to ease his suffering, be it Malkonar, Armstrong, or the stone.

The stone had gone from rotting in the drawer to pride of place on the sideboard, but it spent a great deal of time in Peter's twitching hands. Staring at it had now become a daily activity in the hope it would bridge another gap in his knowledge, but no matter how he touched or turned or brushed it it was still a slab of stone with a blood-red helix in the centre. No hidden openings, no engraved messages, no secret codes, nothing.

He sighed again, the same way he did after every failed session of examining the stone, and replaced it on the sideboard.

"What am I doing?" he mumbled to himself, looking away from the object of his frustrations. It was a good point: what was he hoping to achieve? The stone had already given him an answer yet he was choosing to ignore it, and as he glanced up at the clock to see the wrong time he realised that he had once again been distracted from the work he was supposed to be doing.

He went over to his bedroom desk where Septimus was sat, scribbling furiously on a piece of paper. He had been like this since the dream: more inspired, more creative and more productive. The exact opposite of how Peter was feeling.

He peered over the malkonar's scaly shoulder and skim read his work. Elegant handwriting and perfect alignment, as always, but the words in print were still the uncrackable code that filled Peter with frustration. He didn't dare voice it, though, not after the dream.

"Pozzit," he said as brightly as he could as he slumped down in the chair. Septimus smiled warmly at him for the word in his language, but the glazed look in his eye told Peter that he knew what he was thinking.

He opened his laptop, booted it up and tapped the Start button, but nothing happened. He pressed it again, but still nothing. He stroked his finger over the mouse pad, but the cursor did not budge.

"Bloody outdated machine," he cursed as he dug a mouse out of the desk and plugged it in, but even then the laptop continued to freeze him out. "Oh, give me strength!" he snapped, slamming his fist on the desk. Septimus yelped, and while that would have normally drawn his attention and an apology Peter's eyes was fixed on something else. The cursor had moved on its own.

He looked to see if the mouse had suddenly decided to work, but the piece of hardware was lying still and the cursor was moving steadily across the screen. It selected the Start button and darted up towards 'Word Processor', and clicked it. The bright background of the word processor burned his eyes in an instant.

"Oh God," he said, staring with a look of dread at the flickering black line, and it didn't disappoint. It slowly began to cross the page, leaving a greeting in its wake.

Hello Peter.

His teeth sank into his lip. Only two people could take control of his computer in this way, and while everyone at work was a whizz with computers they didn't know rule one of hacking. That left only one alternative, and it was the one he didn't want to deal with. Gingerly, he leaned forward and spoke.

"Hello Malkonar."

He never did work out why he chose to speak to the computer, but to his surprise it understood, and the line dropped down the page and spewed more words.

You've been dreaming.

"Yeah, I have."

Our dreams are interesting, aren't they?

"Yeah," he said, glancing at Septimus. He had stopped scribbling now, his intrigue taken by this seemingly one-way conversation, "And I bet reading a mind is quite fun as well."

Indeed. I have been probing your thoughts for quite some time.

"That counts for nothing though, doesn't it? You might know what I'm doing but you can't do much to stop it."

At this present moment I am indeed operating at a fraction of the power I am capable of, but remember that situations can change very quickly. You're well aware of what I'm capable of so you had better keep your guard up.

"Well you're speaking to me through my computer and you're probably decoding my brain to either possess me or feed on me, so I'm not going to underestimate you."

You can find solace in that I won't feed on you, Peter. You're far more valuable to me than that.

"But possession isn't out of the question?"

Only if you refuse to give me your complete co-operation.

"Wow, that's comforting," Peter snorted, "Considering I haven't co-operated with you from the start, I guess we've reached the conclusion that I'm utterly stuffed. So go on then, how long have I got?"

It's more complex than that. Hacking into someone's mind isn't a simple process. It takes a lot of time and patience; time and patience is something I don't have.

"And easing my fears is going to help you gain time and patience?" he asked, raising an eyebrow.

I am busy. There is someone else, someone who knows more than you do. They must be dealt with first, but rest assured I will return.

"And I'll continue refusing to give you the stone," Peter ad-libbed, Malkonar's comment sticking to his mind.

If you continue like that, Peter, I'll pay you a visit and take it by force.

"Liar," he spat. "You're inside the silo in Edgeley Park, aren't you? I don't think you're going anywhere in a hurry."

Where I am is not of importance right now, Peter. You may be right, you may be wrong. The only thing I will say is that you don't know what the silo and the stone mean to me.

"And unless you tell me what they mean I won't trust you, and as long as I don't trust you you're not getting the stone."

The black line flickered on the spot, waiting to produce more words. Septimus was now staring transfixed at the screen, reading over what had been written. The words themselves were mere scribbles in his illiterate eye, but his ability to sense the mood of situations gave him the taut expression that Peter could see. Then more words appeared.

May I speak to Septimus?

Peter stared at the blue malkonar, and he stared back at him. He made a gesture for talking and pointed to the screen of the laptop, and Septimus nodded, fluttering his wings to blow away the sweat that was trickling from his brow.

He picked up Septimus and sat him in his lap, facing the screen. Words began to appear in Septimus' language, and Peter felt blood trickle out of his lip.

Sine waske prisken vor sine foltan!

"Denor," Septimus growled, grinding his numerous teeth together and making a sickening squeak, "Sine waske prisken vor sine torcrat, curt yiskta vissen hackt dint!"

Sine kinde! Sine aar feart, sine cron poss montalstroff.

"Sine nin feart," Septimus roared, "Sine concil full lite."

Haerean, sine et Feela aar kraus et simplischaucher. Sine waske prisken et veve noone sine kann!

"Denor!" Septimus said again, entranced by the hatred being exchanged.

More words began to type themselves onto the screen, forming another message in the mysterious language of malkonars, and after reading it Septimus turned away from the screen with a look of pure disgust on his face. Peter watched him climb back to his spot, pick up his pencil and started scribbling again.

"Well, that was interesting," he said, observing his uneasy expression.

Indeed. I have just warned Septimus of the consequences of not handing the stone over to me.

"And have you changed his mind? Will he now slash my throat, steal the stone and bring it back to you?"

No, so he will perish for his foolishness.

"You've got to get out of the silo before you can kill him."

What makes you so sure that I am in the silo? I may not be.

"Maybe not, but it's quite likely you are."

I am wasting my time. I have much to do and I'm not getting it done by quarrelling with you. I'm giving you another chance Peter: give me the stone and I will spare you unimaginable pain.

"No chance."

There was another pause, as if the reply had caught Malkonar by surprise.

Very well, if that is how you intend to think, then so be it. Farewell once more, Peter, and here's some advice before we part ways: sleep with one eye open. You can never be sure of what's waiting for you in the gloom.

The laptop shut down, the black screen and slight reflection of Peter's pale face replacing the stark white of the word processor. He breathed a sigh of relief and sunk deeper into the chair, but Septimus leapt up from his writing and waved his arms to grab his attention.

"Malkonar," he whispered, drawing a claw across his throat. Peter shivered at the threat, but there was something else on his mind to prevent it from creating too much angst. Malkonar had mentioned that he was busy dealing with somebody else, but was this person a friend or a foe? Were their intentions benign? Did they want to stop Malkonar or use him for their own gain? He tried to answer but a yawn interrupted his thoughts. He looked at the clock and raised his eyebrows. Ten o'clock. Time to sleep. Time to shut out his fear for another night.

He stood up and made for the bathroom, but stopped when he saw Pepper. The dog was curled up on the floor of the living room, one sharp hazel eye open and watching him. Peter eyed him tight-lipped, then changed direction.

Without a word he went to the sideboard and grabbed Pepper's lead, but not his usual one. Not the one with the retractable plastic strap, but the one his parents had sent him years ago. The one made out of a metal chain. He crouched down at his side and clipped it to his collar, tying the other end in a double knot around the leg of the sofa.

"Sleep tight," he whispered.

He stood up and disappeared into the bathroom, not looking back at his restrained pet. If he looked back he would have seen Pepper's eyes. His begging, red eyes.

THIRTEEN

Peter woke up in the dark and stole a glance up at the projector clock. It mocked him with the time of 02:15.

"*Another bad night,*" he thought, a low groan tumbling over his lips. In his head he heard the sneering cackle of its cause.

He threw off the bedcovers and strode over to the window, sliding the curtains apart. Unsurprisingly the streets of Averton were deserted, and it did nothing to lift his sunken mood. He felt alone, stranded in a sleazy, shadowy town with nothing but a dog and a malkonar for company. And, of course, somewhere out there was Malkonar. Waiting his moment, directing him down a path he wasn't sure he could see the end of. He pushed the window open and let the sharp air sear his face and chest. The cold burned his skin, but feeling properly his vulnerability, his delicate skin that was so far still unblemished, absolved him of his fear.

He turned and collapsed back onto his bed, taking care to avoid Septimus' spines, but anxieties still blocked the off-switch for his body. Malkonar had mentioned somebody else, someone who knew more than him, and he wanted to know more. Three questions were all that he wanted to answer: who, how, and would it be worth his while to pursue them? They could provide him with valuable information on Malkonar and that was undeniably tempting, but Malkonar had said himself that he was hunting this individual down, which meant that going to the effort of finding them could turn out to be a colossal waste of time.

He pulled the sheets over his body and settled down, hoping to fight his way out of his indecision through sheer willpower, but as a restless hour ticked by he begrudgingly admitted that tonight would not be that glorious night. If he wanted to sleep he was going to have to make a decision.

He weighed up the pros and cons of each option in his mind, mulling over every fine detail to get the best decision possible. Cons always outweighed pros in his head, but with Malkonar involved the pros grew to a towering height, and once again he realised he was going nowhere.

Frustrated, he clambered out of bed and grabbed a coin from his desk, resting it on his thumb.

"Heads I find them, tails I don't," he whispered, and flicked his thumb.

The sweet chime of fingernail on coin broke the silence of night. It spun into the air, shimmering in the moonlight as it reached the apex of its flight, and he caught it as it began to plummet and slammed it down into his palm. He felt weak as he raised his right hand away from his left. He was putting his next step in the hands of chance. What did that say of him? He was weak, he was clueless, and he was looking at the coin in his hand and accepting its choice.

Tails.

That was it, the decision was made. He felt a great weight fall off his shoulders. He was to leave the unlucky sod who had become Malkonar's latest foe to their fate. The right decision? He didn't care. It was two in the morning and he desperately wanted to sleep, and with his worry slightly defused he clambered back into bed.

He wasn't happy, but he was satisfied, and that was enough to let him drift off and forget the dire hand that Lady Luck had just dealt him.

* * *

Peter woke to noise, very loud noise. He whined as its ferocious sound split his head. Was it the fire alarm? No, it was still dark. Fire was bright, and fire alarms didn't sound that deep. They also didn't roar.

He rubbed his eyes furiously, trying to gain some control of his senses. His eyesight became clearer, and his hearing followed suit shortly afterwards. With each passing second the noise began to resemble something he recognised. What he was hearing sounded like furious barking, the sort of noise a rabid dog would make.

He looked up and screamed. Pepper was stood over him, a severed chain dangling from his neck, the remnants of a link lodged between his teeth.

"Pepper?" he squeaked. The dog's panting grew louder, spraying his face with saliva that burned with hunger. He cowered and lay as still as he could, but lying still didn't stop Pepper from sinking his teeth into his calf.

He shrieked and flailed his leg, but the Siberian husky clung on, leech-like fangs eager to have their fill before letting go. The shaking made the wound worse, tearing up his skin and spurting blood onto the bedsheets.

The sight of his blood everywhere drove his desperation, and he leaned forward and grabbed Pepper by the jaws. Agony filled his throat with a roar as he levered Pepper's teeth from his leg, revealing the bite. Between torn skin and throbbing muscle was blood, spewing in a stream like a grotesque water gun. It made his eyes shrink. His vulnerability finally exposed.

He quickly shoved him off the bed, but the dog only used the ground as a springboard to launch himself at Peter's face. He caught him mid-flight, arms outstretched to maximize distance between man and dog, but Pepper's momentum pushed him onto his back.

He howled more furiously than ever, showering him with droplets of spittle, but Peter's body trembled not from the noise but from the burning red eyes. Red eyes that speared his soul. Red eyes that were the signature of only one person.

His head shrunk into his shoulders and his pulse accelerated, spurting more blood out of the wound. His arms began to buckle under Pepper's weight, fear draining him of his strength, and he breathed three heavily strained and fearful words.

"But Malkonar said..." he cried, but that, like everything else Malkonar had said, had turned out to be a bear-faced lie.

Pepper thrashed more violently. Peter glanced from side to side, looking for help, and found it in Septimus, curled up in a tight ball and sleeping peacefully.

"Septimus!" he screamed, whimpers of despair pouring out of his mouth, "Help me!" but the malkonar did not stir. He felt his arms bend a little further, lowering Pepper closer to his face and making his screeches of contempt even more unbearable. "Septimus, wake up or you're gonna die!" he said hysterically, giving the malkonar a sharp prod with his toes. This time the deep blue eyes flickered open.

"Help!" Peter shouted once more as Septimus unfurled. He looked frantically between dog and malkonar in between prayers for malkonar to reach him first, but with his focus divided he didn't see Pepper notice the awoken reptile, and didn't expect it when Pepper leapt at him.

The dog smothered him and dragged him off of the bed, but Peter was the one who let out the loudest gasp of horror. He leapt up in an impulse to help, but buckled as his torn calf took his weight. His head smashed against the wall, making the world spin, but he was brought back to reality by the heavily bloodstained sheets draped across his face. He tore them from him with a scream, swiftly drowned out by a venomous hiss across the room.

Septimus was perched on the bedside table and Pepper on the floor, snarling at one another. In Septimus' side three angry wounds had been cut, each one trickling deep red blood onto the oak that no doubt inspired the fury in his face.

With a scream of intent and a flex of his wings he leapt at Pepper, but Pepper anticipated the move and leapt also. The two collided in mid-air, jaws snapping at one another in the hunt to inflict more damage. Peter stopped feeling the pain in his leg.

The two hit the floor in a heap and began tussling, and a canine howl ripped through Peter's ears as Septimus sunk a claw into Pepper's shoulder. His eyes shone with delight, but a pang of hurt slapped his stomach. Septimus asserting his dominance was what he had hoped for, but hearing his dog, his best friend of seven years, in pain was a sound that crushed his spirit. Another claw hit him, this time in the side. Another demoralising howl rang out, and he panicked. He couldn't watch Pepper get savaged, even in this state. Common sense begged him not to, but once again he ignored its plea, hobbled forward and yanked Septimus off of Pepper.

The malkonar wriggled and struggled and flapped his leathery wings in his face in a bid to get free, but letting go meant Pepper would be mauled.

"Don't kill him!" he begged Septimus, but his act of charity was lost on his dog. With a roar of intent he leapt up and clamped his jaws around Septimus' waist.

A nightmarish squeal filled the air as Pepper's sharp canines dug into his scales and closed tightly. The colour drained from Peter's face. He moved his hands to Pepper's jaws and pulled for all his worth, Septimus' screams growing louder with each second as the teeth closed in on his vulnerable spine. His arms ached as Pepper resisted, muscles and arteries bulging against his skin, but for Septimus' sake he didn't yield. Slowly the muzzle began to separate, and with one great heave of effort Septimus managed to wriggle free.

He dropped to the floor and limped away, moaning as he went, and with another furious growl Pepper turned his attention back to Peter.

"Don't," Peter whispered, raising his hands in anticipation, but Pepper leapt anyway, striking Peter's face with his jaw and cutting a gash in his cheek. He screamed and frantically shoved Pepper away. The warm feeling of blood trickling down his face made it hard to breathe, and as Pepper squared up to him again and he saw the primal leer on his face he barely breathed at all. He was enjoying this. He had embraced the murdering of his master, relishing the thought of cutting more holes in his feeble skin. One less ally in a world with so few.

Pepper leapt again, grin ready for more bloodshed, but that split-second of terror had filled Peter with adrenaline. Adrenaline that made him dodge Pepper's leap, grab him by his waist, throw him to the floor and pin him down with his body.

Pepper exploded. Jaws snapping, roars screaming his frustration to all of Averton, desperate to escape and maul his captor, but Peter held on. His arms throbbed from Pepper's relentless squirming and tears dribbled from his eyes as his paws battered his legs, but he didn't dare release his grip. He looked to the doorway and saw Septimus, his lower body covered in blood, crawling to the salvation of the living room. Another roar from Pepper. He had seen Septimus and was thrashing more desperately, eager to deliver the final blow. Peter tried to tighten his grip, but one almighty pounce broke it.

A nightmarish sting of panic shot through his chest, and with a speed he didn't know he had he grabbed Pepper's legs. His charge was halted, but bloodlust was a powerful fuel and with another roar, one that eclipsed all previous screams of intent, he pulled himself forward.

Peter felt the carpet burn his skin as he was dragged into the living room, but they were at the back of his mind as Pepper gained ground on a panicked Septimus. He threw out his good leg in the hope that it would catch on something and halt Pepper's progress, and salvation arrived as his foot snagged the leg of the sofa. With newfound strength he reached for Pepper's waist and dragged him backwards, giving Septimus time to flee in the direction of the kitchen. Peter felt a small twinge of relief as the malkonar disappeared from view, but his fear reignited as Pepper twisted in his hands, rolling himself over so that their heads collided.

Shock weakened his grip and Pepper broke free, and as he felt four tensed paws straddle his body the last of his hope melted away. He looked into the red eyes glaring down on him, and behind them he could see Malkonar laughing, but the sadistic reptile didn't compare to the bloodstained teeth that snapped at him. He jerked his neck to the side as the bite closed in, missing by centimetres. He attacked again, his snout brushing Peter's scarred cheek but causing no damage. As he withdrew his head for a third bite Peter saw the blood that soaked his lips, the blood that had once beaten around his body, and the thought of more of his blood taking the same journey ignited his survival instinct.

He drew his knees to his chest and kicked out, the blow catching Pepper square and sending him flying across the room. He leapt to his feet and hobbled as fast as he could, but his moves were too swift and his wounded leg jarred, sending him toppling.

He barely had time to sit up before a screaming canine leapt over the back of the sofa and landed with a thump on top of him, lunging at his face and scoring a blow just below his left eye. Peter screamed as he felt his skin tear, but unlike so many times before he didn't let his muscles seize up. He had to survive, he couldn't die with questions unanswered. The thought of that sheet, with all its expectant white space, gave him an invaluable burst of willpower.

He forced himself upright and gave Pepper a shove. It wasn't much, but it was enough to let him scramble to his feet and hobble into the relative safety of the kitchen.

He found Septimus perched on top of the fridge, cowering. It was a heartbreaking thing to see, but now wasn't the time for sympathy. He grabbed Septimus by the tail and pulled.

"C'mon!" he roared, hysteria melting his speech into a shriek of terror, "You have to help me!"

"Hourt!" Septimus whined as he dug his claws into the plastic, "Lest croat..."

He was cut off by a vicious howl. Two sets of eyes darted to the doorway where Pepper was now stood. Legs straddled, teeth bared. Ready to pounce, and pounce he did. But the will to survive was now in charge of Peter's body, and that priceless will extended his arms and threw the fridge door open.

Pepper hit the heavy door with a clatter and stumbled backwards, clearly concussed, and Peter seized the opportunity. He grabbed a roll of tape from one of the drawers and pounced on the dazed Pepper. He pinned his head to the floor and hastily wound the tape around his jaws. His legs got the same treatment, as did his front paws, and only once Pepper surrendered and lay still did he finally snap the tape.

With a painful, drawn-out whine Peter collapsed against the fridge, and not too long after he felt his muscles finally seize up and shut down. The fighting was over. No more thrashing and wounding would be done tonight, and with the need to survive gone he felt his older, more familiar self crawl back into the cockpit. He looked between dog and malkonar with watering eyes, exchanging mutual glances of shock, exhaustion and pain, but no one said a word. No one dared interrupt this new era of silence. At least no one who lived in the apartment, as seconds later an immense banging rang through the air.

"Peter!" a voice shouted, muffled by the door that separated them. "Mr. Vaughan? Are you alright?"

Peter rolled his eyes at their timing, but shakily clambered to his feet as another round of banging disturbed the night. He limped towards the door, unlocked it and flung it open to the sight of Malcolm and Julie Nesbitt, the elderly Scots who lived next door, blissfully unaware of the horror that was unfolding in the house five metres away.

"H-hi," Peter stammered, and the two Nesbitt jaws dropped. Only after a few seconds scrutiny of his gashed face, torn bedclothes and bloodstained leg did they find the words to say.

"Your face," Mr. Nesbitt gasped, his liver-spotted hand trembling, "What's happened to your face, man?"

Peter ran his hand down his cheek and observed the line of red across his fingers. The overwhelming desire to tell the truth weighed down on his throat, but his tongue only allowed him to speak lies.

"Yeah," he began, his conscience shaking its head in disgust, "Pepper's getting a bit rowdy, it's a phase he's going through. I tried to shut him up and he gave me this, but he's nice and calm now. I know the barking and stuff didn't sound too good but it's nothing to worry about. I'm really sorry for disturbing you, and I promise it won't happen again."

The Nesbitts glanced at one another sceptically, then shrugged their shoulders.

"Alright," Mrs. Nesbitt replied, a hint of doubt playing in her voice, "Do you need any medicine or anything?"

"Nah, it's just a few scratches. Nothing a plaster or two can't fix."

"Oh, okay. Goodnight then, and please try and keep that dog quiet."

"Yes, Mrs. Nesbitt," Peter replied, unable to prevent his voice from cracking, "Goodnight."

He quietly closed the door, and once he heard the Nesbitts' door close he collapsed to the floor. Tears welled in his eyes. He was a wreck. Covered in blood; skin and mind scratched and scarred; his best friend now one of his worst enemies. The peace of his old, pathetic life, the one justification for it he had clung to, had been mauled before his very eyes, and it wasn't coming back so long as its architect went unappeased.

He wiped away a stray tear, and his hand came back soiled with a smear of blood. The backlog of rage in his chest soared to his head. Weeping, he punched the wall with all the strength in his trembling arms.

"Malkonar, you bastard!" he screamed, landing another punch against the plaster that shook his body and sent his tears flying through the air, "When I find you I'm gonna tear you apart!"

He threw punch after punch, feeling not the pain of each blow as the plaster tore his skin but the immense rage Malkonar stirred in him. Delicious fantasies filled his brain and drove his fists further into the wall. Fantasies of stabbing him, shooting him, mutilating him, studying his blood smeared thick over his hands as he cried vain pleas for mercy. Fantasies that he put on hold in a heartbeat when he saw Septimus flutter into the room.

The beats of his wings were awkward, each flap accompanied by an agonised moan, and as he hovered over the coffee table he seized up and swallow-dived into the floor. He curled tightly into a ball and howled, and as the sound resonated through his ears his malice melted away. His friend was in need, and what was he doing? Guilt colouring his cheeks, he crawled across the room and scooped Septimus into his arms.

"Hey," he whispered, "It's alright. I'll help you get better."

Septimus unfurled as he felt the protective hold on his back, allowing Peter to inspect his wounds. Most of his waist was an ugly red, small channels of the shade reaching up to his stomach and side where teeth-shaped tears continued to bleed. His breathing was regular but strained, eyes flickering between closed and half-open. He extended a weak claw and brushed Peter's face. He could feel it trembling.

"Feela..."

"It's alright," Peter said again, cradling him a little tighter, "You'll be fine, now let's get you cleaned up."

He caught Pepper's gaze as he returned to the kitchen. His eyes were back to their blue and hazel hues, and with it came the personality Peter knew and loved. This personality didn't understand why it had been bound by tape, and though he had managed to free his front legs he pawed the sticky bind that kept his mouth shut with distress. Peter felt his anger growing again. It wasn't his fault that he had his mouth gagged. He was the innocent victim of someone else's scheme, and now that the plot had failed he was having to suffer the consequences in his place. He looked at the laboured Septimus, and then the traumatised Pepper. Injured, agonised and distraught, all because he wouldn't give that stupid creature his rock. His outburst of uncontrolled violence against the wall ashamed him, but this wasn't a swell of anger he would ignore.

He gently lay Septimus down on the kitchen bench and stroked his scaly head.

"It's alright," he repeated, "I just need one minute, then I'll see to you."

He turned on his heel and strode over to the phone, in the gloom the same colour as the blood on his skin. He picked up the receiver and heard the dull hum of an unconnected line, but he was beyond caring.

"Malkonar," he hissed, "I don't know if you can hear this, but I've had enough. I've been far too generous to you. I've picked up your calls, I've talked to you and tolerated your threats, but this is the last straw. I'm going to destroy the stone and end this once and for all."

Peter waited for a moment, then the hum vanished. A pant shot through his ear, followed shortly by the pristine voice that haunted the line.

"Don't lie to yourself, Vaughan, it damages the soul," Malkonar replied. His voice sounded strained, as if he had been winded, but the malicious edge that had become his trademark was ever-present.

"I will," Peter said, "I'll take it to the silo and destroy it there. You can watch me destroy your stone and there'll be fuck all you can do about it!"

"And if you do that, Peter, I'll make your life even more of a misery than it already is."

"How?"

"Why should I explain? If you intend to destroy the stone you'll find out soon enough."

"You're bluffing."

"Have I lied to you before?"

"Just before! You said you wouldn't harm me and look what you've done."

"But I haven't harmed you, Peter. You're breathing and your wounds aren't fatal. The only liar here is you."

"Maybe so," Peter whispered, "But don't you dare think for one second that I will let this slip by me. I will remember this day for the rest of my life, and one day I'll make you regret ever doing this. I will bury you, Malkonar, and don't ever forget it."

"We shall see, Peter Vaughan, we shall see," Malkonar panted, his speech broken by gasps for breath, "Anyway, I must go now...I'm feeling weak...I must...recharge..."

Another whine from the kitchen sent the receiver slamming back down to the base. He rushed to return to Septimus' side and found him writhing in agony on the table, but the sight of him seemed to ease his pain a little.

"I'm so sorry you had to wait," Peter said guiltily, "I really am. I just had to get something off my chest. But it's okay, I'm here now, and I'm not going anywhere until you're alright." Another wail broke his speech in two. "It's okay," Peter reassured, reaching for the first aid box and pulling out a tube of antiseptic ointment. He squeezed a globule onto his fingers. "Now, this is gonna sting a little, but don't worry, I promise it will make you better."

He distracted himself from Septimus' scream as ointment touched wound with thoughts of Malkonar. He didn't feel any anger this time. He had been as vile and loathsome as ever, but he was also noticeably tired.

Septimus breathed back his calm, but he heard it as Malkonar's pants of exertion, and he realised something. On the phone Malkonar's voice was strained and he'd admitted to feeling weak, and though he hadn't specified why the conclusion was obvious: possessing Pepper had worn him out.

He smiled triumphantly as he soaked a dishcloth under the tap and used it to sponge the congealed blood off of Septimus' body. Malkonar had a weakness, and it was now up to him to exploit it, but how? He looked down at Pepper, still struggling with his bonds, and an unwanted thought entered his mind. Should he? Could he? He shook his head. There was no choice, he had to no matter how much it would hurt him.

His stiff fingers wound bandages around Septimus' waist much too tightly. He felt a rocket of pain tear through his innards, but he also felt the balance of power shift in his direction for the very first time.

FOURTEEN

The house was quiet without Pepper. Not that he made much noise, but the lack of his presence seemed to drain the heat from the living room air. Each day Peter felt it bite him with raw intensity that he had no choice but to ignore. He was gone for good, and he was never going to see him again. Unless he went to Don's house.

He had initially been reluctant to take Pepper off his hands on account of his new job: the night shift in a small factory in the West Side, an area affectionately known to Avertonians as 'Slum City', but the money he was owed for winning the bet, the promise of continuing his dog-walking dowry and the general gratitude towards Peter for picking him up off the scrapheap eventually managed to persuade him.

The transaction had taken place a week ago, but he still felt awful. It was his best friend he had disposed of, the friend he had owned and loved since he was a puppy and had gone almost everywhere with him ever since, but it had to be done for the sake of him and Septimus. Don lived a mile and a half away, and if his hypothesis was correct the strain of possessing Pepper would get the better of Malkonar before he could direct him to his apartment. Assuming Malkonar didn't turn his attention to the potential hostage now sharing a house with his weapon of choice, but that didn't trouble him too much. All that mattered was finding time for their wounds to heal.

The persistent pain of inflamed skin had turned Christmas into a low-key affair: no presents or turkey, just low quality alcohol and the stinging of scars that removed all sense of festivity and sent him to bed with a deep sense of dissatisfaction. New Year was no different, sitting on the sofa and sipping whatever warm, flat muck was left over from Christmas while trying to shut out the roaring crowds as they brought in the next twelve months of misery. After that life went on as normal, if normal was regarded as hobbling to work, ignoring the enthralled stares of co-workers at your scarred face, feeling nothing but contempt for their ignorance, and hobbling back home again.

Even Septimus, arguably the most cheerful member of the household, was subdued. He skulked around with his head down, breathing laboured by the gashes in his waist. Everyday Peter returned home to find him scowling at the TV, watching reruns of forgotten shows in a language he couldn't comprehend, and for a while he wondered whether the calm was doing greater damage than the storm. But the passing of time narrowed his scar into a nick and turned his limp back into a stride, and the first morning he didn't wake feeling the dull sting of his wounds he decided instantly to break from depressing routine.

Averton City Library was his first stop of the day. The Librarian was there as always, cowering behind her desk and trying not to look at him as he approached. She was paler and thinner than when he had last seen her, staring gauntly at her computer screen.

"Hello," she whispered, not looking away from her machine. Peter raised an eyebrow. Her murmur was a far cry from the brash and obnoxious voice he was familiar with. "Can I help?"

"I need books on local history," Peter said, but the Librarian didn't reply. "Local history?" Peter said again, unnerved by her lack of response. There was another distinct and uncomfortable pause before she tapped into her computer, and an even longer one before she finally said something.

"Second floor, row 276," she said with the quiet wisdom of an oracle. Peter beat a hasty retreat onto the stairs, stealing a single glance over his shoulder as he went. She was now looking in his direction, watching him go through her bespectacled eyes. Her vacant stare shoved him onwards.

Row 276 housed a collection of books on Avertonian history. Peter had perused the section several times before, because of a rumour back in school that someone stashed pornographic magazines there, safe in the knowledge no one would accidentally stumble upon it. He checked between the books hopefully, and when that yielded no outcome he started hunting for works on the life and experiments of Leopold Armstrong.

He knew that he had paid the Mayor of Averton a handsome fee to let him perform some dangerous experiments using the silo in Edgeley Park; that one of them had gone wrong and that led to the silo being sealed and the stone being cut in the wall, but that wasn't enough. He had to know what that experiment was, and if it was, as he suspected, Malkonar, how he had come into contact with him. He was a scientist, he had to have documents left over and published somewhere, and given Malkonar's telling silence he had to know whatever it was he wanted to hide.

He prised a card-bound book titled *Great Avertonians* from the shelf, flicked open the contents page and scanned the various names on the list. His luck was in. He swiftly turned to Armstrong's page and began scanning the faded text for any useful information. Three quarters of the way down the page he hit the jackpot:

After humiliation in Birmingham, Armstrong retired to his hometown in obscurity in 1890, spending his first year in a deep depression that abruptly subsided for reasons unknown. In July of 1891 he began new experiments and sought the assistance of the then Mayor of Averton, Robert Fletcher. In his memoirs (published by Averton City Council) he writes of Armstrong:

"He was an eccentric man with grand ideas, and the day he came charging into my office with numerous sheets of paper under his arm, each covered with wild illustrations of his plans, I knew I could not ignore him."

Fletcher never outlined Armstrong's plans in his memoirs, but it is mentioned that they eventually accepted his proposals in February 1892. Fletcher's power in the city helped Armstrong greatly, as this meant he had access to all of the facilities within the city's boundary, and he appeared to have chosen the grain silo in Edgeley Park as his headquarters. Fletcher writes of this in his memoirs:

"We spent many a time walking around the city, talking of his methods and previous works. During one such walk we strolled by Edgeley Park, and I clearly remember the glimmer in his eye when he saw the grain silo. I quickly told him that the building was far too useful to be used in experiments, but the steely look he wore as I told him made me realise he wanted to use the building badly. Sure enough, a few days later I received a cheque for £300 along with a request to use the silo for his experiments. A sum of that quantity was far too substantial to turn down, so I reluctantly gave him the permission he needed."

From that point onwards there is little to no information of the actual experiments that took place, but the reaction to the experiments in early 1894 was made quite clear by Fletcher.

"He charged into my office and slammed his hands down firmly on my desk, his fingers trembling as they rested there. I looked up and asked what was bothering him. He told me we needed to seal the *silo immediately, that it was too dangerous and posed a great threat to the city. I told him that he was being ridiculous and that the silo posed no danger to anyone. Before I knew it, he grabbed me by the scruff of the neck and hoisted me out of my chair, screaming at me that the town was in danger and that we had to seal the silo immediately. Against my better judgement I gave permission for the silo to be sealed. When I went to visit the closure the next day I caught Armstrong removing a pentagonal slab from the silo wall, the piece of stone having a clockwise spiral daubed at its centre. He gave me no reason for this, but I was in no position to argue at that point."*

Armstrong died later that year aged 48, leaving his home at 29 Kildome Close to his sister, but taking his experiments and mysteries to his grave.

As Peter read the last sentence he felt his body tremble. He knew 29 Kildome Close well. Very well. As a matter of fact he knew it inside out, because 29 Kildome Close was his childhood home.

Gears whirred to life inside his head, bringing an ancient memory to the front of his mind. It was a memory of the attic, a room out-of-bounds to his young self on the grounds that it was full of 'old science stuff', as his father would say, but he had raided many times anyway. The place he had discovered the stone.

The gears whirred faster. Since that was where he found the stone the 'science stuff' had to be Armstrong's possessions, and bearing in mind his parents wouldn't touch the attic with a bargepole they would all still be up there, and hidden in amongst them might be something very useful indeed. Information on Malkonar or his experiments, perhaps? Or maybe machines or devices that could combat him?

Excitement bubbled in his stomach, but his desire to storm his former home and raid the forbidden room was abruptly extinguished as another, less uplifting memory crept into his mind.

His parents had moved to Spain five years ago, and while the attic hadn't been cleaned out when they sold it the house no longer belonged to his family, so if he wanted to go and claim whatever was there it meant he would have to break in.

He gnawed his lip, aggravating the many cuts already there. He couldn't. He knew he couldn't, but he also knew he didn't have a choice. If he wanted to shake off Malkonar for good he either had to find out the truth about Armstrong's experiments or give him the stone, and the latter was completely out of the question.

He replaced the book and stumbled towards the stairs, senses fuzzy under the weight of his morality. He hated crime, but answers squeezed harder, and now he was going to have to commit one in order to get them. Septimus entered his mind and his nausea worsened. What would happen if he got caught? Would he go to prison? Then Septimus would have to fend for himself, food-wise and Malkonar-wise. That was far from desirable. And what if he didn't find anything useful there? So much time and tension wasted. It was all a huge gamble, but it was a gamble he couldn't resist when the payout was so high.

He stood at the stop of the stairs, but before he could place his foot on the first step a flash in the corner of his eye turned him around. Behind the bookcase, peering at him unblinking, was the Librarian. Their stares intertwined for a moment, blinks the only exchanges they made in the cold silence, then Peter's eyes ignited and his temper followed.

"Hey!" he shouted, and the Librarian took that as a cue to run.

He shot after her, entering the vast maze of bookshelves on the trail of her cream-coloured shoes, only to be let down as he turned onto an aisle and saw nothing but a single book lying neglected on the floor. His eyes twitched. Where was she? And more importantly, what was she doing? He stalked down the aisle, peering through the bookshelves and hoping to catch a glimpse of her elusive figure, but to no avail.

He made it to the end of the row and looked around. There were two aisles to the left and another eight to the right, the stairs falling between aisles six and seven. She would probably make a run for those if she wanted to escape, and sure enough a flash of beige appeared in the corner of his eye. He turned to meet it and there she was, making good her escape down the stairs.

"Come back!" Peter screamed, charging off in pursuit.

Hearing his voice, she picked up speed, taking the stairs two at a time as he bounded after her. He leapt from the top of the stairs, landing on the mezzanine mere inches behind her, but falling in a heap as he did so. He picked himself up as quickly as his jarred limbs would allow and returned to the hunt, but his prey was now halfway across the ground floor and heading for a door in the back wall.

"Stop!" he cried, but his slip had given her too much of an advantage. She reached the door several seconds before he did and disappeared behind it, the click of a lock ringing in Peter's ears as he clattered into the wood.

"Open up, God damn you!" he shrieked, pounding on the door with his fist, but a solid minute of hitting drew no response from the woman lurking behind it. Frustrated, he gave the door a sharp kick then turned and headed for the exit, pushing over a bookcase as he went. That would take her an hour to alphabetise at least, and the thought of her slaving over it was delicious.

He stomped out the automatic doors but stopped as a gust of bitter January air rustled through his thin shirt, pressing a small object in his breast pocket against his chest. He reached in and pulled out the offending scrap of paper, and cursed his poor memory. His question sheet, his one source of guidance in the twisted world he was living in, and he had forgotten all about it.

He unfurled its discoloured folds and grimaced at the faded ink, but as he reminded himself of the unanswered questions he realised he had another answer to offer it. His mood somewhat improved, he thrust a hand into his coat pocket, retrieving one of the many betting pens he stored there, and made amends with the one ally he could wholeheartedly trust.

1. How did I end up in possession of the stone?

Armstrong lived in the same home as me and kept the stone in the attic, where I found it.

FIFTEEN

Peter woke to the sound of a sharp ringing. Rubbing the sleep from his eyes, he glanced at the projector clock overhead. 01:33. He scowled. His insomnia was getting worse, and another late night disturbance was hardly going to help his upcoming break-in attempt. The thought of it punctured another hole in his spirit, but it was drowned out by the infernal racket in his head.

He waited for his hearing to come into focus and listened more intently, and after a few seconds he realised that the noise wasn't coming from his head but from the telephone. Dismayed, he clambered out of bed. His head started to throb, a side effect of standing up too quickly, but he didn't notice. He was far too tired to feel anything, not even fear towards Malkonar.

With laboured steps he padded across the floor, reached for the phone and, stifling a massive yawn, held the receiver to his ear.

"What?" he said, holding himself up on the sofa's armrest.

"Good evening, Peter," Malkonar said.

"Evening? You're having a laugh. It's half one in the bloody morning."

"I know, but I cannot sleep. We must talk right now."

"You can't sleep? *You?*" he hissed, "I wake up every day

knowing I've only had about five hours kip, and you have the front to call me in the middle of the night and say you can't sleep? What is your agenda? Is keeping me awake in some way going to solve your problems?"

"Sleep deprivation is a useful weapon, Peter."

He yawned and ran a hand through his tangled hair. "Yeah, which is why I want to end this conversation as soon as possible."

"Well then, shall we delve into the crux of my contact, if that is what you wish for?"

"Cut the cryptic stuff and tell me things bluntly!"

"Now now, Peter, calm down," Malkonar comforted, but he couldn't sufficiently disguise the sharp edge in his voice, "You need to keep your head if you wish to break into your former home tomorrow."

Peter's eyes shot open, "How do you know about that?"

"Did you forget that I'm a mind reader?" Malkonar taunted, "I know everything about you: thoughts, regrets, successes. Anything that's stored in your brain is now in mine."

A bead of ice-cold sweat trickled down his neck. With Malkonar's somewhat subtle way of going about business it was easy to forget just how dangerous he could be.

"Yes, but..." Peter began, but stalled as his eyesight flickered, "But it doesn't matter whether or not you can read my mind. As long as you can't possess me or feed off of my mind I'm in no danger."

"Correct," Malkonar replied, "But you've seen first-hand what I'm capable of with other creatures. Who knows, I could arrange a few...accidents, shall we say?"

His sweating grew heavier. "But you won't kill me, you said yourself you need me for other reasons."

"Maybe so, but pain and death are two completely different things. I've kept a lot of people in risk-free agony for a very long time."

"So I'm not the first?"

"The first human."

"What do you mean by that?"

"Your lack of knowledge is showing again, Peter. There is a world of dragons and malkonars out there that you don't..."

Blood rushed to his head, strengthening his headache but also his judgement. "Dragons are real?" he exclaimed.

"They are, Peter, and I've done some very nasty things to them in my time. Things that would sicken a person like yourself, and I'm quite happy to inflict them upon you."

He gulped, feeling his damp bedclothes cling to his skin.

"Your threats are weak," he squeaked, "You never do anything you say, intimidation is your only weapon."

"Then what was possessing your dog and tearing a gash in your face?" Malkonar crowed.

"Err..."

"Exactly, and don't say I didn't give you a warning: I told you to sleep with one eye open."

"And thanks to you, I'm sleeping with two eyes open."

"Calm down, Peter, I thought you were a very civilised person."

"I don't think anyone is civilised at half one in the morning!"

"Calm yourself," Malkonar soothed again, "Stress is one of the leading causes of many life-threatening illnesses, and I don't want you dying any time in the near future."

"To be brutally honest with you dying seems like the best option at this moment in time."

"Dying solves nothing, Peter, it merely robs you of the satisfaction of solving your problems."

"This coming from the creature that tried to kill me with my own pet."

"Not kill, just lecture, and I believe I lectured you very well in what happens if you keep the stone from me any longer."

"I'm in no danger," Peter answered, "I heard you on the phone last time. You were knackered from the strain of possessing Pepper for just ten minutes. There's no way Pepper could get to my house in ten minutes."

"Trust me, Peter, it's not just you, everyone around you is a target of mine."

"It depends whether or not you can attack them."

"What do you mean by that?"

"I've had a lot of time to think, Malkonar, and as I was on the way home today I realised something. The book said you're capable of telekinesis, yet you've never used it, and given how desperate you are to get the stone I'd have thought that by now you'd have turned my house upside down. Now I realise that you can't inflict all of your abilities upon me because your brainwaves can't reach me. Basically, you have different brainwaves for each of your abilities: telekinesis, telepathy, mind eating and possession. Obviously telepathy and possession can reach me, but it looks like telekinesis can't. As for mind eating, I'm not quite sure."

There was another deathly pause. His throat was begging for a drink of water, but he ignored it. The next response was far too important to put on hold just because he was a little thirsty.

"Your logic is impeccable, Peter," Malkonar said eventually, a hint of respect hiding in his words, "And for the most part your theory is correct. As for the mind eating aspect of my brainwaves...I think you will find out soon enough."

"What does that mean?" he said, his stomach lurching.

"No clues, you will find out soon enough."

"I demand you tell me what that means, Malkonar!" he roared, slamming his fist down on the table.

"Calm yourself. If I told you right now it would completely ruin the surprise."

"Malkonar, I don't know much about you, but I know you well enough to know that this 'surprise' you have in store for me won't be one I'll particularly enjoy."

"Ahh," Malkonar said, giving Peter an image of him smiling an extremely toothy smile, "You have learned, little one, the question is have you learned enough?"

"Little?" Peter smirked.

"Little by my standards," Malkonar sniggered back down the line. Peter ran his hand through his mattered mane again, squeezing his skull to fight the immense tension in his mind.

"Alright," he breathed, "You've made your point. You've woke me up and given me a scare, now would you be so kind as to sod off so I can get some rest?"

"There is just one last thing I ask of you."

"What's that?" he sighed, tiredness setting in once more, "Are you going to ask me to give you the stone again?"

"One hundred per cent correct."

"Well please refer to my second-last statement," Peter began in a cheery, sarcastic voice, "Namely the words 'sod' and 'off'. I believe that is all the information you need."

"Sarcasm is the lowest form of wit, Peter."

"Well at least I've got a sense of wit, unlike some."

"You can be rather stubborn and rude at times."

"I've got no choice. I've got some nutter with psychic abilities on the phone to me every other night and I've also got another one of your kind sleeping in my bed. I've got to keep myself sane somehow."

"Hopefully the one sleeping on your bed will be sleeping forever before long," Malkonar hissed, making Peter's skin tingle.

"What is your problem with him?" Peter growled, "What has he done to you that's made you like this?"

"He escaped from me, and that's all you need to know."

"Expand."

"No. You know too much already."

"I know too much about something that can't talk to me? What planet are you on, Malkonar?"

"Listen to me, Peter," Malkonar snapped. He froze, it was the angriest he'd ever heard him. "I've had enough of your stupid little games. I'm going to say this once and once only: give me the stone or die!"

"Never," he replied, grinding his teeth, "And as a matter of fact I've had quite enough of you as well for making threats that are as hollow as your demands." His voice reached a crescendo, "I might as well hang up now to save myself from your whining!"

"Well go on then, put the phone down, you coward!" Malkonar roared, "But I know you won't, I've seen inside your thoughts. You're too..."

To Malkonar's surprise, as well as his own, he slammed the phone down. The plastic shattered at the force of the blow. Pieces of lethal red shrapnel embedded themselves in the table and the floor, but most of them sliced their way through Peter's hand. He panted and squirmed as the pain took full effect, pinpricks of blood oozing out of the wounds. His heart was all but broken, beating at an unhealthy speed and only accelerating. He felt the pounding in his head again, realising it had never gone away since he had woken up. His throat screamed for water, and his limbs began to shake. He felt sick, very sick, and the world slowly began to spin.

He quickly stumbled to his bed and clambered beneath the sheets. Now he could hear a voice: Septimus' babble, but in Malkonar's tongue. He pulled the duvet over his head but it still found a way through the barrier. He could feel Malkonar standing over him, trapping and crushing his arms, his laughter ringing in his ears. He shook his head violently and the noise disappeared, but he couldn't rid himself of his thoughts. He was scared.

He whimpered and pulled the sheets tighter against his body. He looked at Septimus, but he was sleeping. He was alone. Alone to face the monster that could match every move he made, that invaded every personal enclave and pushed him however he pleased. The monster he was still utterly powerless to fight. He closed his eyes to hide the oppressive world around him, and his backlog of stress and fear took this as a cue to send a wave of fatigue crashing over him. He felt himself slipping in and out of consciousness, standing on the brink of vulnerability, and he panicked.

"Septimus," he whispered, his body still but his head pounding, "Help me."

SIXTEEN

When Peter woke up he could tell that it was still dark. Though his eyes were shut he had lived through enough sleepless nights to know when the sun wasn't lurking in the sky. He began cursing his inability to sleep, but paused when he felt a gentle breeze wash against his skin. Confused, he opened his eyes and saw not a white ceiling but a dark, chocolate sky.

"Welcome back to dreamland," a soothing English voice said suddenly. The shock of the sky and the voice made him sit up with a jolt, and what he saw locked him upright. He was in a tattered coracle, its wooden struts cracked and eroded, and on the crossbeam stretched across his legs sat Septimus, eyeing him with a gentle curiosity. "How do you feel?" he asked.

"Not good," Peter groaned, rubbing my greasy hair, "I feel ill."

"Well hopefully you'll be better in the morning. You can hardly be worse."

"What do you mean?"

"I woke up to the sound of you shouting," Septimus said, leaning closer to Peter's face, "You were asleep again by the time I finally checked on you, but what I saw told me something awful had happened."

Peter's throat tightened, "What did you see?"

"You were so, well, frigid. You were sleeping, but your body was locked like an animal in rigor mortis. I never could have imagined anyone would sleep with such...intensity. What ever in the world made you become like that?"

Peter looked Septimus firmly in the eye, and though he had no mental powers of his own the message transmitted, and Septimus asked no further questions.

Peter turned away, focusing his gaze at the world around him to distract from the now heavily subdued Septimus, but felt spikes of fear drill through his spine at what surrounded the coracle. This was not the dream world he knew. The sky was dark not because it was getting late, but because a thick wall of cloud was blocking out the sunlight. The mighty pines that formed a wall around him were charred black, wispy trails of smoke rising from some of their remains. The shore was overgrown with weeds and the family of elegant swans had been replaced by scraggly ducks that quacked menacingly as they swam by.

He looked back at Septimus, who was staring down into grey water. He reached over the side and ran a claw through the tainted slime, and as he brought his arm up a trail of rotten seaweed and fish skeletons followed, clinging to the points of his claws.

"The water is not as pure as it once was."

"You can say that again. What's happened here?"

"The landscape has become tainted, and considering this landscape is shaped by your psyche..."

"My thoughts are tainted as well," Peter finished, swallowing a lump in his throat.

"Indeed. Your recent actions have filled your head with impure ideas and destroyed the sanctuary within your own mind."

"In English?"

"You have angry thoughts, and consequently they have given you bad dreams," Septimus said impatiently.

"Right. So if this is a nightmare, how come it doesn't feel like one?"

"Nightmares don't always begin as nightmares. Something will happen soon which will change the course of this dream, and because this is your dream I'm powerless to stop it."

Peter furrowed his brow. "But you said you could take control of dreams."

"Only the sequential side of things. You provide the setting and the events. The best I can do is alter the course they take, but in the end you have the final say."

"So my bad thoughts have made my dream world polluted and you're powerless to stop it?"

"Yes, and I suggest you put your mind at ease before it gets worse."

Peter rested his head in his hands, "This is just perfect, isn't it?"

"I understand, Feela, but I'm afraid you are the architect of this. Only you can repair what you have built."

"Aye, but you're not the one with so many problems it's near impossible to keep track of what's going on."

"Well name your problems and I will help you tackle them."

"Well, there's the fact that Malkonar won't leave me alone and that he's tried to kill me twice with my own pet dog, not counting the fact that he's infinitely more powerful than I could ever dream of being, and when you add in a librarian who's acting strange, a thief that stole nothing and you, a malkonar that speaks gobbledegook, I've pretty much got the perfect sitcom."

Septimus sat silently for a moment, then frowned.

"I resent the implication that Carcratian is unintelligible drivel."

"Carcratian?"

"The language I speak in the real world."

"Your language has a name?"

"Of course it does, what compelled you to think that it didn't?"

"Nothing, I..." He saw Septimus' unimpressed gaze and hastily changed the subject. "So where does the name originate from?"

"Well from what I know it began with a malkonar named

Carcrat."

"Go figure."

Septimus narrowed his eyes,

"Are you aware that you have a very bad habit of interrupting?"

"Sorry. Carry on."

"Thank you. Now, from what I know there was Carcrat. He was a malkonar like me and was the first of our kind to really explore languages. He thought that malkonarkind should have their own language and thus invented the tongue I speak. When news spread of a language for malkonars it grew in popularity, and soon the entire malkonar population was literate. When he died the language was named Carcratian for his great service to our kind."

"Seems fair," Peter said, glancing into the murky water as he sensed something move beneath the boat.

"The word Malkonar is Carcratian," Septimus added, "It means 'mind reader'."

"Figures," he shrugged, "So is Feela a Carcratian word as well?"

"Yes. It's the Carcratian equivalent of Peter, which is a Greek word. It's one of the few instances of Greek influence in the language."

"Carcrat took influence from other languages?"

"Don't all languages steal words from others?" Septimus asked rhetorically, "Think about English, which is a real mongrel language. There's examples of Greek, Latin, French, Dutch..."

"Dutch?" Peter said incredulously, "Give me some English words of Dutch origin."

"Well, there's Aardvark; Cookie; Dam, as in Amsterdam and Rotterdam," he began with a smug grin on his face, counting off the words on his claws, "Freight; Iceberg; Meerkat, need I go on?"

"Alright, point made," he scowled, "But how do you know all of this? You know way more than a creature isolated from human stuff should do."

"Well, you can work it out. What do you know about me and

Malkonar?"

"That you're both malkonars."

"What else?"

"That you escaped from him?"

"Yes, and what does that imply?"

"That he held you captive?"

"Correct," Septimus said, "And how does Malkonar feed?"

"He eats peoples' minds."

"Yes, and what does the mind contain?"

"Intelligence," Peter said, rubbing his chin as it became clear, "So he passed that intelligence onto you?"

"Yes," Septimus grinned, "Anyone he feasted on, from professor to truant, he took their intelligence and passed it onto me. Thanks to him I know many things, ranging from the basics of playing the saxophone to tips on repairing BMX bicycles."

"Wait. These people he feeds on, what happens to them? Do they just disappear?"

"A good question," Septimus replied, "I imagine you've read many newspapers in your life, so tell me: what is Averton famous for?"

"For being a post-industrial slum that no sane person would want to live in," he said instinctively.

"That is true, but in terms of statistics which field does Averton excel in?"

Peter thought, and remembered a damning newspaper article from many years ago.

"Highest number of suicides."

"Correct, and can you guess why?"

"Malkonar," he said gravely.

"Indeed, it's all Malkonar. Armstrong was right about his intelligence theory: the smarter you are, the better defence you have against him. The people he usually picked off were those of average or below average intelligence. First he would chew away at important facilities such as memory and response in order to drive them insane. In their insanity he would guide them closer to him, where his powers were stronger; drain almost all of their minds and finally force them to hang themselves from a nearby tree. A grim method of feeding, but an effective one: they die, he feeds and nobody suspects a thing."

"So how long would this process take?"

"Like I said he usually picked on the not-so-bright, but that doesn't mean always. Normally he could drive someone insane in about a week, but for those of a higher intellect he could take months, years even."

"So if he decided to pick me off, how long would it take him?"

"A while at least," Septimus said, "You have an IQ of one hundred and fifty-three. You're an intelligent man, and it's your intelligence that's keeping you alive."

"I beg to differ," Peter spat.

"Really? Think of the choices you made: rescuing me, researching the stone, giving up your dog. If you had ignored all of those signs you would still be at square one, but look at where your educated choices have taken you."

"Those weren't choices, they were instincts."

"Instincts that were produced by your intelligence."

Peter placed his head in his hands, confused by praise.

"Tell me one thing, though," he whispered through his fingers, "Why did Malkonar pass the intelligence he stole onto you?"

"That I will tell you, but not here," Septimus said as he scanned the gloom above, "Malkonar could have tapped our minds. It will be better for us if we're awake."

"But how can you tell me anything when you can't speak English!" Peter protested, "And you're not picking it up neither. No matter what I do you still screw your face every time I try and teach you to speak."

"And for your efforts I congratulate you, but a language is not something that can be taught in a matter of days." He saw Peter's downturned face, and his reserve splintered. "There is, however, a way to speed up the process," he added reluctantly, and Peter's head jerked upwards.

"What is it?"

"Well, malkonars communicate mostly through dreams, and we can use them to send large quantities of information to one another."

"So right now you could tap into my mind and take the English language?"

"Yes."

"So why didn't you do that the first time we shared a dream?"

"With non-malkonars the process is slightly different," Septimus said, an awkward look playing on his face, "Malkonars can give and receive with minimal fuss, but with non-malkonars it requires a process called mind-bridging. On a technical level it is difficult to describe, but it takes place during dreams where the process is much simpler. Basically, during a dream the malkonar places his hand on the non-malkonar's forehead to create a bridge which lets information flow, but from what I know the rapid transfer of such a large amount of information to or from the brain of a non-malkonar hurts very badly, and I didn't want to put you through that ordeal without your permission."

"Try me, I've lived through a lot of pain..."

"In your nice house in Kildome Close with your stable family."

"You're interrupting now," Peter countered.

"Touché, but in all seriousness I don't want you to go through with this. When I say it will hurt I mean it: mind-bridging is not comparable to a stubbed toe, more having your foot amputated. At least that's what Malkonar shared with me."

"Well Malkonar's a liar, so I'm willing to take a chance. Septimus, could you take the English language from my mind and put it in yours?"

"Do I have your consent?" Septimus asked cautiously.

"Yes you do."

Septimus reached out a sweating claw, but hesitated centimetres from Peter's forehead.

"Are you absolutely sure?"

"Yes, Septimus, I am. Now do it."

With an uncertain breath he made contact, and Peter screamed as an intense pain ripped through his skull. He jerked his head free from Septimus' touch and grabbed his forehead.

"Jesus," he panted, feeling his pulse rocket.

"This is why I was reluctant to mention mind-bridging," Septimus said, "I understand why you are a keen but it's really not necessary. What I have to say can be told through gestures and..."

"Try again."

Septimus blinked. "Pardon?"

"Try it again. I was unprepared last time, but now I know what's coming I can brace myself for it."

"Feela..."

"I need to know what you know, Septimus. Do it!" Peter ordered, and Septimus reluctantly placed his hand back on Peter's forehead.

Tears of pain trickled from his eyes as the intense migraine returned, but he let him keep his grip. Every bad memory that lingered at the back of his mind tore through his head. The time Don punched him in the face and broke his nose. The time his father hit him for something he didn't do. Every single time he had been bullied at school. Being punched, kicked, scared, mocked and humiliated, every last piece of sourness brought forward for him to savour. His teeth ground together, threatening to shatter. Random words flew through his thoughts.

Mischief. Gambling. Separation. Betrayal. Flames. Shatter.

The stinging grew more intense and the feeling in his arms and legs slipped away, but he was only aware of more pointless words in his mind.

Sibling. Inferno. Massacre. Radio. Crown. Treachery. Love. Hate. Art. Atonement.

Atonement? How the hell did he even know that word? He tried to dwell on the mystery as a distraction, but his wonder was cut short by what felt like a knife ripping through his brain.

"Ah!" he screamed, heart thumping like an industrial machine. The dead tree background had long since disappeared from his sight, replaced by angry reds and oranges that bounced off his pupils. Nausea crept up his throat, but he choked it back down as he hyperventilated. His head was spinning in inexplicable ways, but still Septimus' scaly hand stayed clamped to his forehead.

His eyes began to flicker, the oranges and reds fading along with what little of the world he could sense. He was going to black out and wake up, back in reality, in his cosy bed with the duvet pulled up to his mouth. His sickness worsened, he was going to fail, and the answers he so desperately needed would continue to evade him. He wanted to lash out in fury, but he was too weak to do even that.

Another flicker of darkness rolled over his eyes, and he started to cry. He could feel himself slipping between realities, the world rapidly switching between bed and boat, but boat prevailed when the reptilian hand pulled away.

"Done," Septimus said, and Peter managed a weak smile before he collapsed.

For a moment his senses failed him, but when they returned he found himself flat on his back and covered in a thick sheen of sweat. The dream world was back, the pines and sky and weeds visible, but a dull throb in his head and stomach drained away any sense of elation.

"Are you okay?"

"No," Peter whispered. He began to shiver, curling into a tight ball to conserve what little body heat he had.

"Here, let me help," Septimus said, and Peter felt a warm coat wrap around his body.

"Wha..." Peter mumbled, "Where did that coat come from?"

"Dreams, Feela. If you want something you can have it without fuss."

He snuggled into its thick fibres, but then his body began to itch. He reached over and scratched, but that only brought more itches to plague his pale skin. He scratched harder, digging his nails deep into his skin and tearing the epidermis, but anything he did only brought more and more itches until it became unbearable.

"Urgh!" he screamed. He tore off the coat and flung it overboard, scratching his exposed skin desperately, daubing his fingers in blood, but as the garment slipped under the polluted water he felt his itching subside.

"Strange," Septimus said, his smile turning as the coat was tugged down and out of view by whatever lurked in that filth.

"That coat," Peter said, teeth chattering as an icy wind rocked the coracle, "What the hell was with it?"

"I'm not sure, but what I do know is that you are still cold. How about something else to warm you up?"

"Go on then," he shivered, and a mug of hot chocolate appeared in his hands. He sipped from the mug gratefully, but his gratitude collapsed as a vile taste hit his throat. He gagged and spat the drink into the water.

"Not nice?" Septimus asked, watching the liquid spread like an octopus unravelling its tentacles.

"Vile."

"Another bad sign," Septimus said, eyes darting across the lake, "First the coat, now the drink. Something that is supposed to be good..."

"Has turned bad."

"Indeed. These are strange waters we're in and make no mistake."

A ripple rolled across the water and tilted the coracle, and without a moment of hesitation Septimus stuck out his thin tongue and lifted a claw into the air. Peter was about to question the bizarre ritual when the malkonar looked at him with fearful eyes.

"The omen is coming," he breathed, "I can sense it." Before Peter could respond he scuttled over to the edge of the coracle.

"Wait here," he instructed, and dived into the water.

Peter scrabbled to the side of the boat. What on earth was he doing? He stared into the depths, looking for any signs of him and the creature he had definitely seen. Surely he wasn't going to fight it? This was a dream, and dreams didn't obey normal conventions. If he killed it a million more would probably appear, regenerating over and over until it was he that perished. He stiffened at the thought of Septimus leaving the dream and leaned closer to the murk. Was he okay? For his own sake he hoped so, but his faint hopes were dashed as Septimus surfaced.

"Help!" he screamed, thrashing at the water like a non-swimmer out of his depth. Peter grabbed him by the hand and yanked him back into the coracle, and nearly died of shock. Septimus' legs were gone, bloody stumps of flesh and broken bone where they should have been. Blood gushed onto the deck and over Peter's legs, and as the warm liquid pressed against his skin he couldn't stop himself from vomiting.

"I think this is where my dream ends," he croaked, silver tears trickling out of his eyes.

"What's down there?" Peter asked, wiping bile from his lips.

"Satan, Lucifer, Abaddon. Call it whichever name you like," he breathed, then closed his eyes and dissipated into nothing.

Peter stood up in the coracle, peering at the shore in the hope that someone was there. The boat swayed, making his stomach turn. The weight of expectation made it difficult to breathe. He wanted to wish himself away from this place, but without Septimus he was at the mercy of his twisted psyche.

He narrowed his eyes at the trees, and as he caught the sight of what looked like salvation something below the water slammed into the boat.

He wobbled and fell to his knees, the crossbeam shattering under his weight. Water began to seep in through a small hole and he started bailing with his hands, but then another blow to the coracle arrived. Peter shrieked and grabbed the edge to steady himself, and shrieked again as he saw the much larger hole that was beginning to tip the vessel to the right. He looked into the water, hoping a fish would save him, but saw instead a knife-shaped fin, a scowling eye and three teeth, patiently waiting for their dinner to descend into the drink.

He began bailing again, fright spurring his muscles, but the flow was outstripping his efforts. The edge of the coracle touched the water and Peter leapt to his feet, using his weight as a balance. The fin saw its chance. It barged the coracle once more and Peter fell backwards, tumbling towards the water and screaming all the way.

The second he hit the lake a row of teeth sank into his midriff. He roared, but was silenced by a mouthful of fetid water. He scrabbled for the surface, but what little light he could see soon disappeared as he was dragged further beneath the waves. In desperation he grabbed at the jaws around his waist and pulled. To his delight they released, but within seconds of making a break for the surface the same teeth embedded themselves around his neck, a brief bout of pain shocking him before his head was ripped from the rest of his body.

He woke with a start, sitting up with a flail of his arms and calming only when he recognised the pastel walls of his bedroom and the sodium glow of his bedside lamp. He groaned and rubbed his head, feeling a dull ache in the back of his neck.

"That was a bad dream," he said.

"It most certainly was," a strangely familiar voice chimed back. Peter froze, but then took a breath and looked over to the other side of the bed. He smiled.

SEVENTEEN

Kildome Close hadn't changed at all in the six years since Peter had fled its gold-plated nest, which made him feel even more out of place as he stood on the street corner, mentally preparing himself for the ordeal ahead. The kitbag full of tools was unhelpful to begin with, but the tattered jeans and jacket that had clearly seen better days were what he felt singled him out as an outsider to this cornucopia.

They had been chosen at the insistence of Septimus, on the grounds that they were ideal for blending into a crowd should he be involved in a chase, and he had accepted his advice silently. Partly because fear had taken away his voice, but mostly because hearing Septimus speaking in English was surreal.

He didn't say a word throughout breakfast, simply listening to Septimus describe the pleasures of hunting in the lush forests of Northumberland. He had nodded along, knowing he was trying to distract him from the massive burden he was about to place on his conscience, but it only spurred him with fears of Septimus getting hurt while out in the wild. That fear had infused with numerous dormant others with each step closer to his time, melding into the sickening sensation he now felt as he stood on the corner of

Kildome Close, waiting to make his move.

With a nervous step he began to pick his way down the street. Kildome Close was a row of Victorian terraced houses, a title that did no justice to their grandiosity. Each house was at least twice the size of a standard terrace, complete with vast bay windows and a terracotta chimney pot that prodded the permanently grey sky. Outside the polished doors were weedless gardens, and on the driveways shining new cars built by brands he could only dream of affording. It was hard for his adult eye to digest. Had he really lived here? It was neat, proper and very expensive, everything his scum-stained apartment wasn't. A street of suits with solid silver cufflinks and suave ties, that would give the residents all the more reason to suspect the urchin walking down the path would try to break in.

Shoving back his paranoia, he locked his gaze on the path ahead, counting off the house numbers in his head as he walked along.

"*37, 35, 33, 31...*"

He ground to a halt at the next house, eyes widening. That wasn't 29 Kildome Close. 29 Kildome Close didn't have whitewashed windows and an overgrown garden, and it most certainly didn't have a 'For Sale' sign sat in front of the door. He smacked his lips disdainfully, then with a stiffened hand retrieved his mobile phone from his pocket and called the estate agent's number on the sign.

"Hello, Austin Estate Agency."

"Hello," Peter whispered, voice subdued, "I'd like to enquire about 29 Kildome Close."

"What would you like to know?"

"How long has it been on the market?"

The sound of tapping filled the line, then the voice returned.

"29 Kildome Close has been listed for five years now. Is that all you want to know?"

"Yes, thank you. Goodbye."

He slid his phone back into his pocket, then kicked the sign over. His parents hadn't sold the place! They'd just boarded it up and left it to rot! He hissed his contempt for them at the faded brickwork. He'd been against them selling up in the first place, but this...this was an insult. This was how much he meant to them. Almost his entire life had taken place under that roof, and they'd left it to die with little more than a shrug. Breaking in now would just be piling more misery onto this sad relic, but he stormed up to the door anyway. He had fought too many personal demons to turn back now, especially now that the job had been made easier. No one would have interfered with the contents of the attic in the last five years, so his prize was definitely up there. With that knowledge safely in his mind, he rammed the door with his shoulder and punctured a hole in his ethics.

The rusted lock snapped with ease and he stepped inside. He saw the hallway, faded with neglect but still the same as always, and the memories flooded back. He shook them away, now wasn't the time for nostalgia.

He ducked under a cobweb and crept up the first flight of stairs. His eyes fell on the door of his parents' bedroom, and he quickly looked away. A trip down memory lane would only slow him down, but the temptation was gnawing at him, yearning to relive one last time something that was now so clearly dead. He ran up the next flight of stairs, not daring to look back, but hit another roadblock as he remembered what was on this floor: his bedroom.

He jerked his head away, but it was too late. He had glanced at his bedroom door and seen the dent in the wood, the one made by an infant Pepper when he galloped into it. More repressed memories and a touch of guilt screamed for his attention, but he pressed on, barely managing to ignore his sister's bedroom door before approaching the final set of steps that led to the attic.

He stopped, and all previous worries drained away. He had forgotten about these steps. They were ancient, wooden things that were probably as old as the house itself, and they looked it. He'd been up and down them several times before, but that was as a child. Would they take his adult weight?

He experimentally placed a foot on the first step, and an ear-splitting creak groaned its way across the house. The colour drained from his face, but the thought of what was waiting just one flight of steps away forced it back burning into his cheeks.

He dropped his kitbag to reduce his weight and placed his other foot on the first step. Another creak roared in his ear, but he held his nerve. He took another step, then another, and another. Each creak raised his pulse by five. He began to pant. He was on the verge of having a heart attack and there were still another six steps to go. He stepped a few more times, and as he perched on step seven he heard the unmistakeable sound of wood splintering.

He grasped the banister in blind panic. Fear killed his strength, tilting his head forward and letting him watch a few splinters of wood float down to the ground floor. He whimpered. If the stairs broke it was a one-way trip to probable death. He felt his legs go numb, but he couldn't stand still on a stair about to break.

He shut his eyes and took another step. The wood groaned but did not buckle. He clambered up the remaining five planks as fast as his tensed muscles would allow, and to his relief the aged wood held his weight.

He stumbled onto the solid landing and the small door to the attic loomed ahead, held shut with a rusted padlock. He rammed his shoulder into the door, but it held. He rammed it again, then again, and again, but it would not break. He cursed loudly. The kitbag of tools was on the landing, and though the crowbar inside it would be useful there was no way he was taking more than one trip on those death-traps that masqueraded as stairs. He slammed his shoulder into the door again, and this time the lock shattered.

He lost his balance and fell onto the attic floor, coating his clothes in dust. Choking, he forced himself upright and examined the room. A sea of cardboard boxes covered the floor, each one labelled with an outrageous handwriting that he recognised as his father's. In the far corner was a small table with a brass telescope perched upon it, and everything was weighed down by years of accumulated dust.

He waded over to the first row of boxes and read the labels. China and cutlery. Bedroom furniture. Dining room cabinet.

"*Great,*" he thought, "*Not only did they sell up, but they bunged everything into the attic and left it to rot.*"

He started to shove boxes aside, scrabbling towards the more degraded ones at the back, but each label was tailored to slow him down. A box full of ornaments and knick-knacks that had adorned the living room mantelpiece; a selection of comic annuals he had read as a child and, most tempting of all, boxes of his and his sister's childhood toys. He pushed them all behind him and didn't look back.

He barged his way closer to the back of the attic, and the further he went the less familiar the contents of the boxes became. Kitchen utensils and old suitcases gave way to thousands of pieces of paper, books and journals as thick as small tree trunks and rusted scientific apparatus filling damaged boxes to their brims. His eyes flickered hungrily across the scene. Where to begin? So much to read in so little time, and far too much to take home as well. Uncertain, he grabbed the nearest box, tore off its lid and rummaged through the contents.

Thousands of faded papers with swirly handwriting greeted his eyes, each document titled and dated. This one May 1893, that one November 1892, but none of the titles seemed to mention Malkonar. He skimmed through paper after paper after paper, but none of them bore the word he sought.

Frustrated, he grabbed another box and split it open, and a collection of books spilled out into the dust. He grabbed one and glanced the title. *The Theory of Mind Eating*. No use to him, but a promising start. He eagerly grabbed another book, one coated in leather dyed a deep and unwelcoming red, and opened the first page. Written in Armstrong's calligraphy and underlined neatly were the words *Malkonar Experiment.*

He read it with a maniacal grin spreading across his face. Perfect. Absolutely perfect. This was Malkonar's story, the one the lizard had been trying to hide from him for so long. He flicked through it, seeing page after page of red ink, and his smile widened. With just one read of these pages his mystery would be redundant, but once again he had to resist temptation. This wasn't the place to read it, and now that he had his prize he had to get out.

He crawled through the dust and back towards the attic door, but paused as he spotted something familiar propped up against a beam: his father's old shotgun. He scowled at it, remembering his ill-fated shooting lessons. His father was a keen huntsman and was equally keen to pass on his shooting skills to his only son, despite the fact he knew he detested the idea of shooting an animal for sport. Nonetheless, every Sunday he dragged him out into the hills to shoot at game, but the sessions ended after the fifth Sunday when a dispute led to Peter pointing the barrel at his father. Now, seven years on, he was delighted to see that symbol of murder where it belonged: rotting, forgotten and…

"Focus!" he shouted, slapping himself with his free hand.

Cursing his weak will, he crawled out of the attic door and cautiously crept back down the rickety stairs, a chorus of creaks and groans following him down. He stuffed the book into his kitbag and swung it over his shoulder, his muscles beginning to relax, and made for the first flight of stairs, but stopped as his peripheral vision sighted his bedroom door.

He turned to face it, looking apologetically at its peeling paint. It seemed so neglected, even by the standards of the empty house. Unloved, even. Yearning for a visitor after six years of isolation.

"No!" he hissed, slapping himself again. He had what he wanted and now was the time to leave, yet the golden promise of seeing his old room, the room where he had plotted against his father on so many occasions, the room where he and Don had downed bottles of plonk on Saturday nights, seemed too much of a draw to resist. He eyed the dent in the door, the one made by the adorable bundle of fluff that was puppy Pepper, and his will finally broke.

"I suppose one little look won't hurt."

He stepped across the landing and pushed open the door. The contents of the room were standard for an abandoned house: filthy carpet, peeling walls, bookshelf that contained only dust bunnies, but he saw none of it. He saw his old green bedspread with a young Pepper napping peacefully at its edge; his bookshelf piled high with classics and various dull textbooks from his schooldays; the walls adorned with posters of bands he had idolised.

He sat on the bed, ignoring the protests of the bedframe. He was home again, back in the house that had forged the bulk of his life, and it was better than he could have imagined. Here there was no Malkonar, no stone, no Septimus and no Librarian. Just home-cooked food and a shoulder to cry on. He lay back and closed his eyes, basking in this superior world, but his revelry was cut short by a car door slamming.

He leapt over to the window and peered through the small gaps in the newspaper. There were now two cars parked outside. One a generic-looking convertible, the other a silver hatchback with a logo painted on the side. The logo of the estate agent he had called earlier.

He cursed loudly, not caring if the entire world heard. He grabbed his kitbag and charged down onto the first landing. There were only two exits, the front door and the back door, and both were on the ground floor. Could he make a break for it? No, as at that moment the estate agent and a middle-aged couple stepped through the door and looked around, disregarding the years of accumulated grime in favour of imagining the development the future would bring.

He cowered in the shadows, watching and squeaking a little as their glances turned in his direction. He was stuck, unable to move a muscle until they moved on. Hopefully they would stick to the downstairs rooms, but if they went upstairs...it didn't bear thinking about.

He watched as the party began to move, fearing the worst as they reached the stairs, but they carried on and turned into the kitchen. He took a breath to steady himself and began to creep down the stairs, each creak sending his heart up to his mouth, but the sound of the estate agent extolling the virtues of the house kept them from noticing the thief in their midst.

He carried on down the stairs, and with each successful step he felt hope. Five, four, three, two, one step remaining, and as his foot touched the bottom step his heart inflated with happiness, but it shrivelled again as his other foot hit the stairs and sent a groan of epic proportions roaring across the house.

"Please,no," he whispered, but he was out of luck. The estate agent stopped talking.

"What was that?" a female voice asked, and a male voice answered with the last thing he wanted to hear.

"I'll go have a look."

He panicked, turning in all directions in a desperate hunt for sanctuary. The stairs? No. That would only make more noise. The front door? No, they'd see him running down the driveway. Fear tightened his throat. Where else could he go? Only straight ahead into the wall. Was there anything there? No, of course there wasn't, but the sound of footsteps approaching the hallway made him look anyway.

He peered along the peeling wall in desperation, and his heart leapt at the sight of a metal grille poking out of the paintwork. Of course, the utility cupboard! Praising every God he could think of he stepped inside, pressing in amongst the cobwebs and rotting household appliances, and closed the door silently.

Moments later the investigator appeared, and Peter squeezed his lips together to stop himself from whimpering. He was not unlike him in appearance: stubbly, wiry-haired and carrying a henpecked expression on his face, but this man carried much more muscle than the puny adult cowering in the closet. Muscles that would be very good for manhandling him should he be discovered. He watched him place a hand on the bottom step and thrust his weight onto it, but the stair stayed silent. He repeated this process with the next two steps, both yielding no noise, then turned a hundred-and-eighty degrees to face the cupboard he was hidden in, staring through the grille into Peter's eyes.

He stifled another yelp and stood deathly still, holding his breath so that he made no sound. Could he see him? He didn't know, and his ignorance was tearing at his innards.

The man stared at the grille for a few agonising seconds, seconds that brought Peter's body to the point of collapse, then shrugged, turned on his heel and slinked off back to the kitchen.

"Must've been the stairs," he announced. Peter used the sound of his speech to mask his gargantuan sigh of relief.

He pushed the door open a crack, peering to check if the coast was clear. It was. Now he had a clear run for the front door, and he didn't dare hesitate. He threw the door open and sped out into the golden sunlight of spring, his coating of dust giving him the ethereal twinkle of a ghost.

He didn't look back as he shot off down the pavement. There was nothing about it he wanted to look at. That wasn't the house he knew and it wasn't the one he wanted to know. That was a pile of ashes, its treasures discarded like common waste by people who cared about no one but themselves. That was the truth, a truth about several things, he knew deep down, and it was a truth he didn't want to confront. Now, like everything else he had seen since Malkonar had appeared, 29 Kildome Close was just another thing he wanted to get away from.

EIGHTEEN

Peter ran his coarse fingers through his hair, letting the jets of water beat down upon his body and wash all the dirt and dust and lint away. It was a good feeling, one that massaged away the fear and tension that had racked his body for far too long and washed it down the plughole. The job was done, the journal was his and everyone was happy. Septimus included.

A warm feeling bubbled in his stomach at the thought of him. The second he'd seen the journal in his hand he had dropped the poem he was writing and bounced around like a child on Christmas Day, and he was still dancing across the apartment when Peter went for his shower. He'd laughed when he'd first seen it, but thinking about it again only brought him confusion. Why did Septimus care so much about the find? He seemed to know Malkonar inside out, so surely he already knew about the experiments conducted by Armstrong?

He stopped scrubbing his hair. What did he actually know about Septimus? Not that much. Three or four things, give or take, about his housemate of four months. Not great, but at least that was easily fixable. Septimus was now a fluent English speaker, and all he wanted to know was now just a question away. Life, hobbies, birthday, it was all within reach. Information about Malkonar, just an intonation away. One measly question from him and more of Malkonar's mystery would slither down the drain. He grabbed the tap, he couldn't wait any longer.

He hopped out of the shower, wrapped a towel around his waist and made for the door, but stopped as he caught a glimpse of himself in the mirror. He blinked at his reflection, and bit down on his scarred lower lip. He had lost weight, that much was certain. He hadn't been chubby by any means, but the fat he had retained around his waist was gone, replaced by an outline of his ailing muscles. His shoulders were slouched, draping his arms closer to his slightly knocked knees. The sharp brow and heckled expression that characterised his face remained, but his cheekbones were more prominent, poking through wafery skin coloured a clammy grey, and the caricature was completed by dark rings encircling his bloodshot eyes and pressing down on his eyelids.

"Who the hell are you?" he whispered to his reflection. A heavy sigh spilled out of his mouth, and he continued on his way with his stride reduce to a shuffle.

Septimus was sitting on the sofa with a long-forgotten tub of ice cream between his legs, a spoon gripped tightly in his hand and melted vanilla smeared across his mouth.

"Good day," he greeted, ramming the spoon into the tub.

"Enjoying that?"

"Yes, thank you. Having lived mostly off weeds and earthworms this is a very welcome change." He swallowed another spoonful, purring in delight as he did so.

"Well don't eat it all," Peter snapped, malice ringing in his voice, "You'll get indigestion or something."

Septimus paused, then ate another spoonful.

"What's yanked your chain?" he asked innocently, scraping the bottom of the tub for any creamy dregs he had missed.

"Look at me," Peter replied, gesturing to himself with weak hands, "I look terrible. You can see my ribs and my frigging eye sockets. I've disintegrated from a below average human to an even further below average human."

"Don't say that, Feela. I'll admit that you've lost weight, but that's hardly a pressing issue. Just have a good meal and stick to proteins and carbohydrates and your weight will return."

Peter feigned listening, and as soon as the lecture was over he disappeared into his bedroom. Just looking at his clothes reinforced his fears, and putting them on made bile rise in his throat. His jeans had never hung desperately to his waist like that before, nor had his shirt felt so loose against his skin. Another look in the mirror confirmed his dread as he saw a child playing dress-up in their parents' clothes. Thoroughly dejected, he slinked back into the living room and collapsed onto the sofa beside Septimus.

"Are you alright?" he asked worriedly.

"Why do you ask questions? You know the answers anyway," Peter slurred, drunk on depression.

"It's healthy to let people pour their emotions out. After all, a problem shared is a problem halved."

"Septimus, we've had a mutual problem since day one, and two people knowing about it hasn't made things any better."

"I know," Septimus sighed, "But two sets of hands are better than one."

"Aye, but Malkonar's in control." He sat up and looked straight at Septimus, intent behind his eyes. "Think about it. At what point would you say we've been on top in this whole thing? Never, as far as I'm concerned. He knows more than us and can do more than we can. We are losing, Septimus. I don't know if not knowing English has made you oblivious to that, but we are. He hasn't set foot near us but he's caused more damage than I ever imagined," his voice picked up, riding the red wave of anger, "So to answer your question: no, I'm not alright. I might be in the future now that I have Armstrong's Journal, but right now I'm not. I'm tired, stressed, paranoid and wasting away like a fucking corpse!"

Septimus bowed his head and pawed the upholstery. He seemed

to shrivel, muscles contracting to suck some of his presence out of the air.

"I-I understand," he whispered, an invisible vice crushing his windpipe, "This is a very difficult time for you and it would be naïve of me not to understand why. However, I believe your answer to my question to be rather extreme and somewhat hurtful."

Peter felt himself calm, and with calm came guilt. He sat silently, holding his breath and hoping Septimus' next words wouldn't scar his conscience forever.

"I asked that question as I believed it would help you to feel better, but evidently not," he paused to swallow a distinct lump in his throat, "And while I understand you are stressed I didn't expect such a verbal onslaught. But I could have tolerated that too, were it not for your accusation that I was oblivious to the fact that we are losing."

He looked up, a mixture of hurt and fury swathed across his eyes.

"I am well aware that we are losing," he snapped, "And I have experienced losing status first hand. It was a thoroughly unpleasant thing and I have been trying to repress it for the past four months. I asked that question to try and help you feel better, because we need to keep our morale up. Especially my own, for though you accuse me of naivety I am suffering more than you could ever imagine."

He looked away, staring out of the window and across the fading Avertonian skyline.

"The claustrophobia," he shuddered, "The darkness I could live with, and the dirt, but there was no room." He turned back towards Peter with eyes clenched shut, his body shivering at the memories flooding his mind. "I would kick and scream and shout but no one would hear me die."

"Septimus," Peter said uneasily, but was silenced as his eyes shot open.

"And then you saved me." He turned away once more, crawling over to the window and perching on the ledge. "I am in debt to you for that," he said, peering into the incoming gloom, "I am frustrated with you right now, but I know you have done me an immeasurable kindness. Not just rescuing me, but giving me a roof over my head too," he shot him a thin smile, "I am touched by what you have done and continue to do for me, and now that we can communicate I feel I must repay you. I don't have much I can offer in return but I do know of one very apt way of repaying your charity, as not only will it help me to heal but it is the single most damaging thing I can do to him: I'm going to tell you everything I know about Malkonar."

A small shiver ran down Peter's spine. He sat up straight, ready to listen to whatever vital wisdom Septimus was about to impart. The malkonar leapt back down from the window perched himself on the sofa, sitting in his usual manner: legs apart with arms holding his body up between them. The sitting position of a small child, but a knowledge that far outstripped his own hiding away in his brain.

"Malkonar is...well, a malkonar," he began, his eyes now sporting a steely glaze, "You've probably wondered why he shares his name with my species, but to explain that you need a bit of context. Malkonar is part of one of the earliest families of malkonars. His lineage stretches back very far, back to the earliest records our kind has made. This family was founded by a reptile by the name of Malkonar, or Malkonar the First if you prefer. In families names are often passed down, and since the name Malkonar carries a lot of pedigree it has been used many times. The Malkonar you are familiar with is Malkonar the Eighty-Fifth."

"Eighty-Fifth?"

"I did say he has a long lineage."

"Jesus. So I take it that means the family was around at the time of Carcrat?"

"Indeed they were. The legend goes that Carcrat was friendly with Malkonar the Thirty-Fourth, and because the Malkonar family commanded a lot of power at the time he was integral in spreading his language across the globe. Some say that Carcrat slipped the definition in as a small message of thanks. A rumour, of course, but definitely a plausible one."

"So what did you call yourselves before then?"

"Wyrms," Septimus shrugged, "It's a word that's older than you think. Nowadays it's a word for dragons, but it wasn't always."

"Fair enough," Peter nodded, itching to proceed, "So go on then, tell me about you and him."

"Well, you know already that I had contact with Malkonar, and while you could describe us as close we certainly weren't as tight-knit as you would expect from people with our type of relationship."

"Why? What sort of relationship did you have?"

"Father and son."

For a brief moment Peter felt himself cease to exist. He lost all feeling in his body, from the hair follicles dotted across his head to the ridges of skin coating his toes, and his brain melted and dribbled out of his skull. He smiled uneasily, a small giggle tumbling out of his mouth. This docile, friendly reptile that a small child would want to squeeze the daylights out of was the son of that...*thing* in the silo.

"Seriously?"

"Yes. Malkonar is my father."

Peter nodded dumbly, and his surprise quickly morphed into horror as he remembered why Septimus was here.

"Please don't tell me he..."

"Buried me alive?" Septimus grimaced, "Did you not guess beforehand?"

Peter sat deathly still. "Oh my God," he breathed, his brain freezing into a solid, useless block. "Your Dad, your own Dad, tried to kill you? And in that way as well?"

"Yes, and that is one of the reasons why I resent him."

"One of them?"

"Indeed. He showed no affection or interest in me other than when I could be used for his own gain," he pawed the sofa again, stealing a glance at Peter's somehow gaunter face, "In the few times we ever did sit down and discuss things he would keep himself to himself. He never disclosed his origins to me and I would get into immense trouble if I ever attempted to read his mind, but he did share with me a handful of his exploits. Unfortunately he didn't share anything about his life outside the silo. Whenever I raised the topic he would grow agitated and snap his refusal at me, and he showed a particular resistance to talking about the females he had courted."

"Knowing how psychotic he is I doubt any girls went near him," Peter sneered, relieved at the chance to lift his strangled spirits, but his leer evaporated as he saw Septimus lower his head.

"I suppose you're right," he said, his voice reduced to a whisper, "Malkonar is certainly psychotic and it probably did render his advances useless, but the fact remains that at one point he did conceive a child with my mother. I am glad that you find the concept of him having relations with a female amusing, but unfortunately the joke is not shared, as his silence on the topic of relations means I have no idea who my mother is."

"Oh," he said, his shock being joined by a generous measure of hurt, "I'm sorry, I had no idea."

"It's alright," he shrugged, though he could see it certainly wasn't. "Anyway, at one point malkonars were one of the most prosperous species in the world."

"Were?"

"Yes, were," Septimus replied, "The early malkonars set about creating more malkonars, as you do if you want your species to survive, but over generations of creating life the creation process got, as evolution dictates, a little bit skewed."

"In what way?"

"Think about it this way: the human DNA is made up of twenty-three pairs of chromosomes. These chromosomes program what you will look like. Your eye colour, height, hair colour, and so on. Of course we know through genetic diseases that the formation of DNA can go wrong, and when it goes wrong..."

"You get mutations."

"Exactly. For roughly every ten malkonar hatchlings there was one 'dud' malkonar. These duds were physically identical to malkonars, but they had no mental capabilities. A genetic mix-up had created dragons."

"Dragons," Peter said quietly.

"Yes, dragons. Unfortunately we developed quite a dislike for the dragons and stopped them from breeding with malkonars."

"Nasty. I'm going to take a wild guess and say Malkonar didn't like them either."

"Not at all, and since he's been alive for a surprisingly long time I worry he has been corrupted further..."

"Hang on," Peter said, "You say he's been alive for a long time, and correct me if I'm wrong but you're implying he's lived longer than the average malkonar. How old is he exactly?"

"Well, he is quite an age," Septimus said, "He's over a hundred and fifty years old."

"Hundred and fifty!?" Peter shouted, "That's impossible."

"Apparently," Septimus shrugged, "Because the lifespan of a malkonar is not much longer than that of a human."

Peter choked on his own saliva. "What? How?"

"Because he knows something no malkonar other than me and him know," Septimus said, deliberately adding a dramatic pause, "How to cheat death."

"Oh God," he whined, placing a hand across his face, "Please tell me you're making that up."

"I'd like to say I am, but I'm not. It's what he has done for the last few decades."

"Go on then, how does he do it?"

"Let's go back to DNA," Septimus said with a small gesture of his claw, "Another feature of your DNA is that it chooses your lifespan. It decides when your body has to start degrading and wither into nothing. Malkonar essentially discovered the secret to immortality through eating peoples' minds."

"Go on," he coaxed.

"To get the intelligence he feeds off, Malkonar mentally extracts certain parts of the mind, usually those containing memory. However, sometimes his aim was off and he would end up flooding his mind with the data from body cells. He thought they were useless at first, but as his intelligence grew from taking the minds of people he gained an understanding of DNA. He now knew that DNA controlled your lifespan, and as he aged he thought back to the body cells he had stolen. Since certain chromosomes within the DNA of the cell contained lifespan, what if he could extract those chromosomes from the cells of a younger, fitter animal and use them to replace his ageing ones? He gave it a go and forced all of his cells to accept the new chromosome, and it worked. Every time he feels his joints going he repeats the process. He could die eventually of a disease, but he's the closest thing to immortal."

"Bloody hell."

Peter's shoulders slouched like Atlas had dropped the weight of the world onto them. Septimus shot him another reluctant smile.

"Shall I move on?"

Peter silently nodded.

"Alright then. The dragons were reproducing as well as malkonars. We shared the land and began to hide from the humans as their appalling treatment of the world around them became known to us. Both of us became very much underground species, but we had our language and a vague sense of co-operation so we thought we could manage."

"And now for the big 'but'," Peter grimaced.

"Indeed. As I've already said the dragons were never treated kindly by the malkonars, and their frustrations came to a head towards the end of the 19th Century. In 1890 there were mass dragon protests all over the world, demanding better treatment, and the malkonars reacted brutally. Many dragons were slaughtered for protesting, and Malkonar was part of the mobs that did such a thing."

"What happened then?" Peter asked, leaning forward in his seat.

"War," Septimus said, his eyes widening, "The dragons decided enough was enough and took up arms against their oppressors. Obviously the malkonars were better armed for combat, but the dragons were better trained. They were often used as soldiers in those days in order to protect 'pure' malkonar blood, and as a result the malkonars were beaten within months."

He paused for a moment and stared out of the window. It was beginning to grow dark, much the colour of the thoughts of war and killing that were plaguing their minds.

"The Conflict officially ended in mid-1891, but the actual conflict was far from over. Having not been content with drilling malkonarkind into the dust, the dragons decided that it was time for us to suffer, and thus came the rise of Dragon Assassins, or Drassins for short. They went around slaughtering the remaining malkonars, and they've been doing so ever since."

"And I take it Malkonar's a big target for them."

"Yes, and not just because he was a catalyst for the Conflict. During the war itself he killed many dragons. If I remember rightly he boasted killing over three hundred in just one battle, and he is infamous for it among Drassins. They all want him dead, and I can guarantee the remaining Drassins in the world will still be looking for him. It's been over a hundred years since the war began but I'm pretty sure they'll only believe he's dead once they've seen his rotting skeleton."

"And you," Peter whispered, squeezing his knees with white hands, "You're his son. They'll want you too, won't they?"

"Oh no, they don't know I exist. I was born after all of this and was merely told these facts in the many dreams Malkonar and I shared."

"Wait, how could you have been born after this? Malkonar's

obviously been in the silo since Armstrong's day so that would make you at least a hundred odd, and you certainly don't look it."

His reptilian smirk returned. "And this is where another feature of malkonars comes into play. After eggs have been laid the hatchlings inside can lie dormant for a very long time. The heat of being incubated by a parent spurs on our growth and development, but if that heat is absent we go into a state of hibernation. Obviously there is a cut-off point where the hatchling begins to decay, but that point is decades away from the moment the egg leaves the womb."

"So won't that make you a hundred-odd years old?"

"No. While an egg is dormant the hatchling does not age. The ageing process only begins once incubation takes effect, so even though my egg entered the world in the 19th century I didn't start ageing until I became incubated."

"Ah, so how old are you then?"

"Twenty-six."

Peter recoiled. "Twenty-six?" he spluttered, "You're two years older than me? How the hell does that work?"

"I understand your confusion," he grinned, "Our average lifespan is ten to twenty years longer than a human life, so naturally our growth cycle is a tad longer too. Our bodies begin to mature during our late twenties, and we finally reach full adulthood around age thirty-one."

"Right," Peter nodded, placing a hand to his temple, "So where do you come into all of this? This stone and Malkonar business, I mean."

"Now we get to the interesting bit," Septimus said, licking his non-existent lips, "I was born two years before you, that we have already established. My place of birth was the grain silo in Edgeley Park..."

"So Malkonar is inside the silo!"

"Yes, that interrupting thing really needs to be worked on," Septimus snapped, "Now, when Malkonar finally started incubating me my egg had probably been in existence for about ninety years, which is often past the point of no return for a dormant hatchling."

"What took him so long?"

"I don't know, maybe he was preoccupied, but at least he got around to it. Anyway, I am a child of the Malkonar family and the first of Malkonar the Eighty-Fifth. The first and also the last."

"How do you know you're the last?"

"Malkonar spent a lot of time meddling with DNA to keep him alive, but it came at a cost. Species are defined by which creatures can produce offspring with one another and which cannot, and by filling himself with foreign DNA he ruined his reproductive system, among other things. Even if he is lucky enough to get out of the silo and find another malkonar he can't make an egg."

"Alright, so no more kids for Malkonar. What about your life with him, then?"

"Not particularly fun. He brought me up in the cramped and dark confines of the silo, and I don't need to describe just how tedious that was. He raised me and taught me and fed me the minds of his prey, but as I grew older I began to grow suspicious of him."

"How?"

"He was always talking to himself, mumbling mostly about an Armstrong fellow and a stone and dragons with such malice and anger in his tone. Occasionally they became full-blown conversations. I would listen to them intently – it was the closest thing I had to entertainment, you see. All of his conversations were in Carcratian so I could understand what he was saying. They were almost always angry diatribes against one of the above, which was interesting but not fascinating, as I never really understood what he was doing. But then he started talking in a language then unknown to me."

He stopped, and Peter understood which conversation he was referring to, but neither could bring themselves to admit it.

"That night when I dreamed I heard the conversation again, but this time it was in Carcratian and could understand it perfectly, and through that conversation I finally realised he was actively seeking a way out of the silo, and what he would do if he got free."

"What did he have planned?"

"He wanted to exterminate the dragons, hunt them down and destroy them like common vermin. Restart the Conflict, basically. I knew already he had murdered dragons – he'd regularly boast about it in graphic detail – but I'd always thought his angry rants were just frustration from a lost war. The fact that he wanted to restart it terrified me, and since I knew Malkonar wouldn't give up after you had said no I had to stop you before you caved and handed the stone to him."

"Why did you want to stop me? You're a malkonar too, surely you would want revenge for the deaths of your brothers and sisters?"

"There is no revenge in murder," Septimus said, "Revenge is not repeating an act with reversed roles. Revenge is making your opponent bow to your superiority," he looked to the floor, scowling at an imaginary dragon kneeling at his feet. "And, much more importantly, psychopaths do not care where blood comes from so long as it is spilt. Once the dragons were dead he could very well move onto humans, and I fear humans are too hesitant to effectively deal with him. He's a dangerous creature, and any opportunity he has can only be detrimental to us all."

"So how did you try and stop Malkonar from getting the stone?"

"I tried to telephone you by means of my mind like he did," Septimus said. "But my mental powers are inferior to Malkonar's, what with me being younger, and I couldn't telephone you out and out without fainting. Instead I did the best thing I could manage: I broke into your answering machine and left you a message. *Cron asken nin jakov.* Remember those words?"

"Yeah," Peter said, stroking his stubble-laden chin, "That was the message."

"Indeed it was, and it means 'don't answer the phone'. In reflection it seems a futile gesture considering Malkonar had already called, but it felt like the right thing to do at the time. It didn't when Malkonar discovered what I had done, though."

Peter slid his hand over his mouth, "What happened?"

"Well, suffice to say he wasn't pleased. He built me a coffin out of the stones that littered the silo floor and shut me inside it," his voice softened, "He knew I would stand in his way so he left me to die a horrible death."

Peter looked to his feet, hunting for words to say. He never found them.

"Over the many years he'd been inside the silo he'd managed to dig quite deep under the surface, and after sealing my coffin he dug a little nook in the mud, stuck my coffin in there; sealed it and left me to die."

"Wait a minute," Peter snapped, raising an eyebrow, "If Malkonar can dig holes why doesn't he just tunnel his way out?"

"He is too weak to dig a hole large enough for his great body, and that is why he needs the stone."

Peter clasped his hands together in anticipation. "What does it do?"

"Well, did you notice anything on my coffin when you dug me up?"

"Yeah, a spiral on the lid, like the one on the stone but anti-clockwise."

"Precisely, and that spiral is very important. Do you know what the spiral is made of?"

"No."

"Well let me tell you: malkonar blood."

"How do you make it fall in a spiral?" Peter asked, unsurprised at the revelation. Everything malkonarkind did seemed to be cast in blood, sweat, tears or death.

"It is commanded to fall one way or the other. You need a series of incantations to do it and it can only be done with certain kinds of stone. Limestone is definitely one of them though, as that is what the silo is made of."

"Right, so what does it do?"

"It enhances or kills your strength, but only if it is the blood of another malkonar. A clockwise spiral grants you greater access to the subliminal world of a malkonar's mind. The blood gives you the power of the malkonar it came from to add to your own, so you can reach further with your mind and feed more easily. You also get a portion of their physical strength. Anti-clockwise spirals, however, absorb all of your powers. Rather than reaping the gifts of the blood it takes yours away from you. You become a dragon, essentially, and a very lethargic one at that."

"So the stone." Peter stood up and grabbed it from the sideboard, "Is it powering you right now? I mean, are you getting...upgraded by this?"

"Sort of," Septimus nodded, "A spiral's power is limited to the size of its host. The stone is no bigger than a plate and thus doesn't have much of an influence. That said it does give me enough strength to read human minds comfortably."

"So that means if the stone makes it back into the silo..."

"It'll become a very dangerous thing indeed."

"Yeah," Peter said uneasily, then quickly changed the subject, "So Malkonar put an anti-clockwise spiral on your coffin to stop you from escaping?"

"Yes, and it would have worked had he not meddled with his DNA. Because of his meshing of human DNA with his own he is in effect a hybrid, and that means his blood is not exclusively malkonar anymore."

"So the spiral couldn't fully shut down your mental powers."

"Precisely. Rather than have my mental abilities completely removed they were only weakened, and because of that I could penetrate the coffin and send you a distress signal. It caused me unimaginable pain to keep that signal going, hence my fainting, but as you can guess it was most certainly worth it."

Peter looked back to the stone and turned it in his hands like he had done so many times before. At long last he knew its secrets, but he felt no relief, only panic as he felt another worry arrive to replace the one that had departed. And another, and a third after that. Multiple realisations stacked up in his head, squeezing against the confines of his brain and sending shockwaves of confusion and paranoia searing through his head. He put the stone down and looked back at Septimus, his thin smile somehow growing thinner.

"So Malkonar wants the stone because it has a clockwise spiral," he said, struggling to pick his words.

"Indeed. The power it will provide will let him escape from the silo with ease. He is very weak – he has gone over a century without fresh meat and his body has suffered. Only mind eating is keeping his body from outright decay."

"He can live without eating?" Peter whined, another worry cramming its way into his mind.

"Malkonars can live their entire lives without eating. They'll have skeletal bodies and be almost too weak to move, but they can."

"And that's why he can't dig his way out."

"Indeed."

Peter fell silent again. The sun had gone long ago, cast aside by the unrelenting darkness of an Avertonian night. The city lights were difficult to pick out amid the reflections of his apartment, driving his growing sense of isolation. He caught Septimus' glance, he was frowning at him.

"Are you okay, Feela?"

"Yeah, I'm fine."

His frown strengthened, "You took an awfully long time to answer such a simple question."

"Yeah, I'm just thinking."

"What about?"

Peter paused again, twiddling his thumbs and making small noises to buy himself more thinking time. He couldn't navigate his head, skipping through it aimlessly and trying to avoid the murky residue smothering its walls.

"The silo," he said eventually, cutting the awkward silence with his sharp Avertonian accent, "Malkonar couldn't have put the stone there or he wouldn't be getting anything from it. Where did the blood for the stone come from?"

"I don't know, but I believe that's something Armstrong's Journal will provide," Septimus answered, nodding towards the dusty book that lay on the coffee table, "But maybe we should save that until tomorrow."

"Yeah," Peter whispered, "But what about the stone? I think I can guess now why Malkonar wants it, so shouldn't we destroy it?" And though he was used to surprises he didn't expect Septimus to leap on top of the stone.

"No, no, no, no, no!" he screamed, shielding the slab with his body, "We can't, not now!"

"But you..."

"That was then. This is now."

"But why?"

"Your second phone call with Malkonar, the one where I spoke to him, remember?"

"Yeah," Peter said quietly, remembering how Septimus had cried.

"His words made me cry for many reasons. He said many hurtful things, but he also detailed what would happen if the stone ever were to be damaged, and frankly you don't want to know."

"Tell me."

"Feela..."

"Tell me."

"If I told you what Malkonar had said you would never sleep again. The stone is our safety net, Feela, and it would be very silly indeed to walk on the high wire without it."

Peter opened his mouth to argue, but he caught Septimus' glare and deflated. He wiped his sweating palms and rested them on his knees. He was too lost in his newest fear to notice them trembling.

"Maybe you should go to bed," Septimus said, "You don't look too healthy."

"It's only eight o'clock."

"I know, but you're shaken and I think you should have a lie down. Believe me, you could do worse than have an early night."

"Like what?"

"Sit up all night worrying like you usually do," Septimus shrugged, clutching the TV remote and flicking through the channels.

"Fine, I'll go," Peter sighed, rising unsteadily to his feet, "Just turn the TV down, don't make too much noise and don't stay up too late."

"Understood," Septimus smiled, snuggling into the cushions as he settled on Channel 4, "Goodnight, sleep tight."

He felt his head cloud over as he staggered away. War; persecution; attempted infanticide, just what had he been roped into? He had always assumed it was an internal affair between him, Malkonar, Armstrong and Septimus, but that couldn't be further from the truth. The spectrum was far wider, encompassing entire species. Species that could and would kill him. He rubbed his temple in despair. With each passing day he was growing further and further out of his depth, not that his head had been above the water in the first place.

He reached into his desk drawer and pulled out the question sheet. Half asleep, he grabbed a pen and scribbled down an answer to one of the questions.

6. How significant was the scrambled phone call in relation to the call made by Malkonar?

Very. Septimus made the call as an attempt to warn me not to give the stone to Malkonar.

He shoved the sheet back into the desk and clambered into bed fully-clothed. Dark and murderous thoughts circled his vulnerable mind, but all he felt was numbness and nausea. The violent world in which he lived was more violent than he had ever imagined. So much killing and hatred, it was barbaric, but then he didn't know conflict. He had only ever seen it on the TV, safely tucked away in his living room while equally safe, naïve people argued over it from afar. But now he was caught up in one, and from this new vantage point he could see the uncertainty that came with each day. The one that pondered if that day would be his last.

    He snuggled into the sheets and fell asleep within minutes. Partly because he was tired after a backlog of bad nights, but mainly because he was struggling to digest the horror of his reality, and that made him too ill to worry anymore.

NINETEEN

Breakfast that morning was held in absolute silence. They sat at opposite ends of the coffee table, pecking at the continental breakfast Peter had prepared without a word. Septimus had snubbed his usual fare of dead woodland creature in favour of human cuisine for a change, but he was only nibbling at the array of food in front of him. Peter didn't blame him. He looked pale and unwell, his eyes drooped and his scrawny shoulders fixed in a shrug. Much the way he looked.

He sipped his coffee. It seared his throat and ordered him to choke, but he stopped himself before he could. Choking would attract Septimus' attention, and once he did that the conversation would be inevitable.

He took a bite from a piece of toast, the crunch sending a chill through his mouth, and used the opportunity of having his mouth full to steal a glance at Septimus. It was a disturbing sight to see, the malkonar that always seemed so composed looking like he was about to drop. Shaken, he swallowed and went to take another bite, but stopped as Septimus reached out to grab his mug of hot chocolate. His claw was trembling, and as he lifted the mug it trembled too, splattering the table with drops of scalding cocoa.

Peter put down his slice of toast. That was too unnatural and concerning for him to ignore.

"You alright?" he said innocently.

"No," Septimus mumbled, "Couldn't sleep."

"I told you not to stay up too late," he said in the fond hope that his fear was misplaced.

"It's not that," Septimus said inevitably, and Peter did his best not to deflate.

"What's up then?"

"I think I reopened raw wounds during our talk last night," he paused to stifle a yawn, "Raw wounds that made me tense and allowed unfriendly thoughts into my mind, thoughts I could usually ignore, and as a result I am very," he paused again as his eyelids flickered. "Very tired," he finished with an unenergetic flourish.

"You should go back to bed."

"Don't want to," Septimus slurred, swaying back and forth in his seat.

"Why not?"

"Malkonar."

"Malkonar's in the silo and Pepper isn't around. You'll be fine," Peter lied. Septimus raised an unsteady eyebrow.

"Feela, if you didn't have the same dream as me last night I'll be amazed."

The choke from the coffee finally caught up with him. As he sat gasping for air Septimus narrowed his bloodshot eyes.

"I assume that means yes."

"Yeah, I had a dream last night, and it wasn't pleasant. I've been awake since about four and I haven't stopped thinking about it."

"Indeed. I woke up around about quarter to three and I spent the next four hours trying to get back to sleep to no avail."

"Sounds rough."

"Not as rough as what I dreamed. What did you see? Just so I can compare."

"Volcanoes and lava. You?"

"The same, but Malkonar was there too."

"So the thing that came out of the volcano was Malkonar?"

"Big, red and reptilian with a crooked right horn? Yes."

"That was Malkonar," he said, staring at the carpet, "The reptile who's brought me so much trouble. That was him? That thing is what's hiding inside the silo?"

"Yes." He placed a claw on the table to steady himself, "So we were both in a wasteland. Rich orange sky, tall volcanoes with smoke belching out of them and pools of lava everywhere. Am I right in saying you saw that?"

"Yeah, then Malkonar burst out of one of the volcanoes and started screaming at me."

"Ditto. What did he say to you?"

"That I would die a horrible death and stuff like that."

"And then what happened?"

"He started shooting fireballs at me, and I ended up running into a pool of lava. Then I dissolved for a bit until I woke up in a cold sweat."

"I was mostly the same, except I flew away from a fireball only to have the second one fry my wings and send me tumbling into the lava below."

"So in essence we had identical dreams."

"Indeed, and I think we can guess who was responsible for them."

He leaned forward to sip his hot chocolate, and for a moment he looked like he was about to collapse into it.

"He's doing everything he can to make us cave in. As each day passes you learn more and more information about him, and that's the barrier that's standing between him and success."

"What difference does knowing stuff make? I've never had much intention of giving him the stone."

"Pressure and stress do weird things to people, Feela, and you would have succumbed to them last night were I not there."

"Oh, yeah," Peter said, flecks of shame painting his cheeks as he remembered Septimus' passionate defence of the stone.

"It is important not to let him play with our minds. So long as we know he is playing games we are fairly safe, but when other forces press down upon us the line between knowledge and ignorance blurs, and then we are sorely tested. For the most part you have been steadfast in your commitment to keeping the stone, but last night proved that you can be swayed. As I said, pressure and stress do weird things to people," he shut his eyes in a vain attempt to ward off his tiredness, "Much like fatigue is doing weird things to my head."

"You should go back to bed. You're going to keel over and scald your face in hot chocolate."

"Maybe you're right."

He looked straight into Peter's eyes and Peter looked into his. The glistening azure hue of his iris was gone, the blue faded and miserable, bordered by blood-streaked white.

"I think I am," Peter said, and he plucked Septimus from his chair.

He carried him to the bed and tucked him in under the sheets. The malkonar snuggled into them gratefully.

"Thanks, Feela," he said, shutting his eyes.

"No bother, mate. If you're feeling better when I get back from work we'll have a look at Armstrong's Journal, and while I'm out I'll pull in at the library and see if I can find out anything useful about Malkonar there."

"Alright," Septimus whispered, his voice almost inaudible.

"Sleep tight," Peter whispered back, and Septimus drifted away.

He couldn't help but fawn over Septimus as he fell into comatose with a gentle smile playing on his lips. Even after the torment he had suffered both past and present, there was still an optimism emanating from his baby face. It made him smile, and it stayed with him as he cleared away the dishes and made for work, even enduring the Spring nip that lingered in the air. He felt uplifted, raised by the knowledge that someone was immune to Malkonar's games, that they could find rest when lying on a rough surface. It gave him hope, and hope gave him his smile, and four hours later that smile was brutally ripped from his face.

* * *

Averton City Library was not the most welcoming place even at the best of times, but Peter was struck by the gloomy ambience as he strolled through the groaning automatic doors, so much so that he stopped dead.

The place was deserted, and while that was nothing new even the Librarian was absent, her desk empty and reduced to a shadow by the faint light. He took a few suspicions glances across the room, then slapped his hands on its oak surface.

"Hello?" he called, "Librarian, are you there? It's the one you like to spy on!" There was no answer bar the echo of his voice. "Hello?" he shouted again, "It's me. I want to read books about mythical creatures again so you'll want to know I'm here!" but still no one appeared.

He peered up to the higher floors to see if she was watching from above, but there was no sign of her business suit and aged glasses.

"Hello?" he called for a third time, but still no one answered. The only sound was the dull hum of the air conditioning, and that was a sound he'd never heard in this building. The library was far too quiet. Normally he would hear the shuffle of feet and the scuffing of paper as it was placed back on a shelf, but those noises had gone with the Librarian. Now there was just the ominous rumble of air blowing around the floors. A familiar sensation gripped his stomach as he scoured the building again for life, and it began to strangle as he noticed the patch on the floor.

It was small, coloured a dark-red brown, and splattered across the beige carpet. Alone it worried Peter, but then he saw another, similar stain. And another. And even more after those two, all forming a chain towards the door the Librarian had escaped behind the last time he had been here. He sunk his teeth into his lip like he had done so many times before, then followed the line of blots to the door. It was ajar, and he opened it just enough to let him slip through.

He weaved his way through the catacombs, following stains that grew progressively larger. His stomach rumbled in repulsion, but he continued to tail them onto another corridor where a lone door stood, all flaking paint and discoloured hinges, and from two rusted screws hung a small sign with smaller, chipped script:

Jennifer Green
Head Librarian

"Jenny Green," Peter muttered, "My stalker."

He reached for the handle but stopped as he noticed a larger stain beneath the door, way larger than any of the stains he had seen before. It was a different colour too, more red than brown, and the light caught it in such a way that it shone. His pulse spiked.

"What the..." he whispered, bending down and brushing his hand over the discoloured patch of carpet. The smooth liquid clung to his hand. He raised it to his face to see his fingers were a contrast of red, his print outlined in a rich scarlet above the pale of his skin. "*Very much like...*" he thought, but silenced himself before he could finish. Surely not? Heart thudding, he extended his tongue and placed his finger to it. He tasted iron. His eyes widened. Blood.

He threw the office door open, and he screamed. Inside was the Librarian, her throat crushed by a noose made of computer wires. He felt his legs go and quickly placed a hand against the wall to prop himself up, but that didn't stop him from vomiting.

He stopped after two convulses, bile dripping from his mouth, and slumped to the floor, pulling his knees to his chest and clamping his eyes shut. The Librarian was dead, the one prevailing mystery in his life gone, but leaving an even bigger and horrifying mystery in her wake. A foul taste gathered on his tongue. He had tasted her blood. The blood of a corpse, a dead and lifeless thing. Like his soul.

He forced an eye open and let it stare at the dangling corpse of the Librarian. Her face and arms were covered with slash marks. Some mere nicks, others yawning sores that wept congealed blood. Beneath her feet lay a craft knife, its dull steel edge streaked with blood. Uncertain, he stood up and approached it. Why would a murderer leave his weapon at the scene of the crime for all to see? He shook his head, the murderer was the one dangling from the noose. This was suicide, and the realisation urged him to vomit again.

He took uneasy strides around her corpse, examining her various bloodstains and injuries for any other evidence. His stomach groaned with unease as each weeping sore met his eye, but the churning settled as he spotted a crumpled letter sitting on her desk.

He snatched it up and unfurled its tattered folds, and the first thing he saw was a blotch of blood at the bottom of the page. He swallowed another upsurge of bile then, eyes straining, began to read.

Dear Peter,

I don't have much time, so I'll keep this letter as brief as possible even though I have much to say. I wish to explain my actions that have caused you so much frustration, and I hope what I'm about to tell you will prevent you from making the same mistakes.

I'm going to tell you something you probably didn't expect: I know about Malkonar. I've known about him since long before you first came into the library. I discovered him and his species in my teens through a very old book my mother gave me, one full of legends about dragons with the occasional mention of malkonars. I was never convinced they were myths though. The world is filled with images of dragons, and these images are so diverse. No other legendary creature has so many different looks – there aren't a hundred variations of the Minotaur or Medusa. The fact that so many cultures had seen the same creature convinced me that dragons must exist, and because of their similarities I suspected malkonars existed too. That excited me: malkonars interested me far more than dragons, but while I longed to search for them the details I had were so scarce I didn't know where to begin.

Then you arrived. From the moment you asked about malkonars you intrigued me. I didn't expect anyone else to know about malkonars, let alone ask for books on them. I was curious, and when I questioned you about it you intrigued me more by telling me it was none of my business. I knew then that you were hiding something, and with my favourite creature involved I did not dare to let you get away that easily, so as you left the library I secretly followed you to your office, and from there to your home.

I set up a regular watch on your apartment. I was convinced you had something in there, if not a dragon or malkonar then something that would lead me to one. Then my chance came: I saw you leaving your apartment block one afternoon with a friend and your dog, and I took the opportunity to break into your house.

I read your papers and learned about the stone, Malkonar and the grain silo, and I also caught a glimpse of Septimus as he ran across the kitchen. I yearned to grab him and take him with me, but I was scared of handling him and wary of staying too long in a house I had broken into, so decided not to risk it.

It was a thrill to finally have my suspicions proved right, but I was *not satisfied. Your papers on Malkonar and the silo were intriguing so I paid it a visit, and there I got to speak to Malkonar.*

He made me climb up the silo to a small hole in the surface and told me everything. His past; his present; how his species worked and so much more. He told me of how the dragons had slaughtered his species and how he wished to avenge them, and all that he needed to do so was the stone that you possess. He then went off on a tangent, asking me about myself and my plans, but I knew that he was trying to persuade me. I informed him of this, and he told me that I was an intelligent person, and that we could form a powerful alliance against you. He promised me power and success if I brought the stone to him, but I refused to accept unless I could have Septimus once he was free. He told me that was impossible, so I refused to assist, and he begrudgingly bid me farewell. All of this took place back in November, and I had no idea of what was to come.

Malkonar had told me about how malkonarkind fed, but I didn't realise humans were his prey too. After our meeting he decided I knew too much and set about dismantling my brain, and because I live on the estate behind Edgeley Park he had access to my mind almost 24 hours a day. Over the next month I could feel my intelligence decreasing. I knew I needed help, but the only person I could consult was you, and if I did that I'd have to tell you that I had followed you around, broken into your house and tried to make a deal with Malkonar. Instead, I faked a problem with an overdue book to lure you back to the library. You took the bait and went after your book again, and I spied on you, hoping that the books you were looking at would help me. When you confronted me over my spying I tried to use my questions as an attempt to draw information out of you, but my scrambled brain meant I didn't do a very good job and I had to escape before you became too suspicious.

Time passed and I became more and more helpless. I was losing energy and my ability to speak, but my sleuthing around the library's pages found nothing that could help me. You appeared at the library again and I spied on you in the hope that you would reveal something, but you saw me and chased me away. I looked through the books you had sought out but they were of no relevance to me. My time was running out, and now that March has arrived it finally has.

As I write this I can feel Malkonar taking over my mind, consuming the last of me. I would cry if I had the bodily control to do so. I have made a series of terrible mistakes, one after the other, and am now paying the price. I only pity my own naïvety. I thought malkonars were just another animal, but they're not. They're miles above us on the food chain. They're the hunters and we are the hunted, and I'm about to become their latest prey.

I owe you a thousand apologies for everything I've done, and though I don't have the time to make it up to you I can say this: whatever you do, do not let him out of the silo. He will do anything to get what he wants, but don't cave in. Don't trust a single word he says and always look over your shoulder, you never know what he is planning to sap your morale with.

Now I'm out of time. He knows about the craft knife in my desk and is making me reach for it.

The letter concluded with the signature of blood, but a few extra words were written in minute print at the bottom of the page.

Hello, Peter. Meet the person you chose to neglect on the toss of a coin. The one who, like yourself, knew too much. If I can do this to one innocent human without feeling regret, how many more do you think I can do it to?

Malkonar

Peter slowly folded the letter. One fold, two folds, three folds, and when the paper could fold no more he shoved it into the breast pocket of his shirt. The whole process appeared to be done in slow motion, but it was the fastest speed he could manage. What had started as a weird phone call had descended into murder, and murder of the innocents at that. He vomited once more, but only streaks of bile dribbled out of his mouth.

He forced himself to look at her dangling corpse again, and shame clouded his vision with tears. What was he thinking, telling her that it was none of her business? Saying things like that only made people more interested. And making decisions on the flip of a coin, really? His throat tightened. He could have done something if he'd used his instincts instead of a scrap of silver, but not now. The Librarian was dead and that was that. She was deceased, finished, departed. Gone from this world and never coming back no matter what he did.

Choking on his breath, he slid his mobile phone out of his pocket and dialled 999, each press of the button lasting an eternity, and raised the phone to his ear.

"Emergency, which service?"

"Police, please," Peter whispered, a lump in his throat making speech a chore. The line went silent, then a different operator spoke.

"Hello, Police."

"Hi, I-I've found someone dead, I think they've committed suicide."

"Alright, where are you?"

"Averton City Library."

"Okay, we'll send a team over. Just stay where you are and don't touch anything."

"Okay, thank you."

He slumped lower into her chair, diverting his eyes to the faded carpet. His stomach growled, bile burning his gullet, but a numbness in his chest rid him of any pain. He pushed his phone back into his pocket, and with a staggered blink he closed his eyes, and cried.

TWENTY

The last three hours were a blur to Peter. He only remembered the Police saying he had been ruled out of the investigation and being offered a cup of tea. He may also have been in a station and he may have taken a ride home in a Police car too, but he didn't know and he didn't want to know. It was all secondary to the intense sickness that clogged his stomach.

He fumbled his key in the lock four times before the door finally yielded. He stepped inside to the sound of music, and the thumping of an upbeat rhythm against his head pulled on his nerves even more. Plugging his ears, he made his way forward and found Septimus curled up next to the stereo, eyes closed and swaying his head to the music trickling out of it.

"Septimus," he grunted, but it didn't rouse him from his ecstasy. Temper frayed, he jabbed the off button and the apartment returned to silence. Septimus opened his eyes.

"Oh, hello Feela," he said, "Have you had a good day?"

Peter scoffed. "No I haven't," he said, rubbing his forehead as his eyes glazed over with helplessness, "I've had the worst day of my life, and that isn't a figure of speech. So far I've taken dodgy phone calls, had voices in my head and nearly been mauled by my own pet, but this tops all of that," a maniacal grin grew on his face, "I saw a dead body today."

Septimus' euphoria withered in an instant. "What?"

"Yeah, today I saw a dead body, and it was horrible. More horrible than anything I've ever seen before, even more horrible than the time Don broke his leg and the bone came through his skin. This day has been burned into my memory for all eternity. Even when I am dead I will see this day over and over again in my non-existent mind. So no, I haven't had a good day, and the sound of Crowded-fucking-House isn't going to change that!"

He took three erratic steps backward and collapsed onto the sofa, burying his head in his hands.

"This is bad," he cried, "This is very, very bad."

"What?" Septimus asked again, hunting for words to say, "How? Why?"

Peter stuck his hand into his breast pocket, grabbed the Librarian's note and flung it at the Septimus. He read it, then he read it again. Then again, and again. With each read his facial expression dropped from curious to neutral to concerned and finally angry. By the time he was finished he was gripping the note so tight puncture marks from his claws were covering the paper.

"And now he murders," Septimus hissed, brow narrowed and his monstrous teeth bared. "This has got to end soon. He's out of control and causing more and more damage by the day."

"So what do we do to stop him?" Peter whispered.

"That's the problem. We can rule out giving him the stone as that brings no good to anyone, but after that I have no other ideas. The solution is not obvious but one certainly needs to be found."

Peter slid his hands up, revealing moist eyes. "So where do we find one?"

Septimus pondered this, then clicked his claws.

"Armstrong's Journal," he said triumphantly, "We were planning to do that anyway, and even if it doesn't give us the answer we want right now it will still give us something useful."

He grabbed the book and thrust it into Peter's sluggish hands, and with an awkward motion he opened it to the first page. Through watered eyes he could barely read the flicks and swirls of Armstrong's writing, but with a laboured voice he began to read aloud.

Feb. 17th, 1891
Today marks a significant day in my own personal history as I, Leopold Armstrong, have found the answers to the questions I have been puzzling over since I first learned of the creature known as a malkonar.

After extensive research of the Weymouth Parchment, considered the only reference to malkonarkind in history, I am confident I have found the way to lure a malkonar to a location of my choosing. For this I require a vial of malkonar blood, which I have managed to acquire from a gypsy woman who claims to have taken it from a mass grave of the species, its location she refused to reveal. While I am sceptical of the truth in her story I am confident the liquid is genuine. The only other thing I need to pursue my goal is a location in which to conduct my experiment.

I am fairly certain a previously undiscovered creature suddenly appearing will cause some unrest among Avertonians, so I will need a base of solitude. Unfortunately I am not in possession of such a location, so to acquire one I will need the help of a third party. Hopefully a certain Mayor of Averton.

"Hmm, interesting," Septimus said, placing a claw to his mouth, "1891, that's three years before Armstrong died."

Peter only nodded, and he quickly flipped to the next entry to avoid unwanted questions. It was dated almost a year after the last, but Peter didn't raise this concern and continued reading.

Feb. 3rd, 1892
I have managed to acquire the use of the grain silo in Edgeley Park for the experiment I told of in my last entry. Mayor Fletcher needed some convincing to allow me to use a prosperous structure in this town, but a financial incentive has finally managed to turn his head.

A few more preparations are needed before I can begin, namely preparing the spiral with which I will lure the malkonar in. According to theory a clockwise spiral should lure a malkonar to its site due to the power it generates, and if my research is correct an incantation is needed to turn the blood. While I am not certain I believe the correct chant is 'Rotaro yar balas'. Naturally I am nervous as this is my only chance to get it right, but my research has never led me astray so far and I will trust its verdict.

"Rotaro yar balas..." Septimus thought, "That's not Carcratian as I know it. Perhaps classical, perhaps a different language entirely."
 Peter grunted in approval.
 "Not feeling very talkative?" Septimus asked sympathetically. Peter grunted again. "Do you want me to read it?"
 Peter shook his head.
 "Are you sure?"
 He nodded.
 "Alright then, if you insist. Now do you care to read on?"
 Peter grunted again, then brought his strained voice back to life.

Feb. 15th, 1892
After years of research it is with great pride that I write that as of today my experiment has officially begun.

I finished my initial preparations the previous evening, namely taking a pentagonal slab from the silo wall and performing what I have dubbed the 'spiral ceremony'. Much to my relief the ceremony was a success, the blood forming a perfect clockwise spiral at the sound of the chant.

I then replaced the slab into the silo wall, and what happened next took me by surprise. As I pushed the stone into place the mortar holding the rock together glowed a golden shade so brilliant I had to shield my eyes. I presume this occurred due to the enhancing power of the spiral slab coursing through the structure, but I cannot know for sure. One thing I am certain of, however, is that those three seconds of illumination are three seconds I will never forget.

Hopefully the silo should now act as a beacon, luring malkonars to feast on the power it offers. Unfortunately the only thing I can do for now is sit and wait and hope that a malkonar is drawn to its powerful flame. I only hope Mayor Fletcher's patience will last until that day.

"So Armstrong deliberately lured Malkonar to the silo?" Septimus asked. He received no answer. "Do you have any thoughts on that entry, Feela?" he coaxed, but Peter's glare forced him into retreat. "I believe he did," he said quickly, "I can't picture any other malkonars being drawn to the silo."

Peter grunted his approval again, and turned to the next entry.

Feb. 27th, 1892
It has worked. Today at four minutes past eight in the morning a malkonar arrived at my beacon. I had spent the last twelve days keeping a vigilant eye on the silo, day and night, for any activity, and the day I have pined for has finally arrived.

I ran to the Mayor's house, woke him and we set off to inspect the silo, barely fifteen minutes after I had initially sighted a dark figure landing beside the turret. When we arrived we saw through the half-light that the door to the silo was gone, loose stones that once belonged to the wall littering the floor. We knew at that point that the creature we were dealing with was of a substantial size, and when we peered inside the silo with our lanterns we were not disappointed.

In the centre of the building was a battered and malnourished malkonar, curled into a ball with his wings covering his face and body. I called to him and asked him his name, and he replied 'Malkonar'. I asked him if he needed any assistance, and then he decided to sit straight.

With limbs outstretched he covered at least three quarters of the silo area comfortably, but he was thin and poorly fed. His ribs and other bones poked through his discoloured scales and his wings had numerous gashes in them, some of which were bleeding. In his arms he held a small blue egg that he clasped with intensity, but that was his only baggage.

He requested that we bring him food and medicine, and we obliged. He didn't say anything as we fed and doctored him, answering our questions with grunts or nods of the head, and when we left him seven hours later he hadn't said a word at all.

It is hardly a promising start to this experiment, but what I have longed to see has finally been seen, and this day is a day I will never be able to forget.

"And this is where it all begins," Septimus said, "I'm even there as well. Albeit as a dormant egg, but there nonetheless. So, what happens next? Please..."

"Hang on," Peter said. He stopped shortly after, surprised at himself for feeding his curiosity, and the blue reptile perched on the coffee table was just as shocked.

"Yes?" he encouraged, and Peter folded.

"Why's Malkonar malnourished?" he asked, raising his head just enough to look at Septimus, "If he's as good a killer as you said why is he like that?"

"It's 1892, Feela. At this point Drassins are running rampant and he's in hiding, and if you hide in the wrong place food can be hard to come by."

"Why's he hiding from the Drassins?"

"Killing three hundred dragons is easier when you have an army behind you. Here he's alone and starving with an egg in his hands, and even he isn't so hubristic as to pick a fight in that condition. Now, do you care to read on?"

"Okay," Peter nodded, relieved to turn his eyes back to the book.

Jun. 15th, 1892
In the four months I have tended to Malkonar his health has improved drastically, but his temper is fiery and non-negotiable. Generally he is polite if somewhat monotone, but if I ask him too many questions he will hiss at me or give me a verbal warning, and if I persist he will grow violent and slam his claws into the silo wall. The worst I can do is attempt to relieve him of the egg, which, despite his neglect of it, he will defend with his life. With every visit I see he leaves it abandoned on the floor, but if I even move in the direction of it he unleashes a mighty roar. This egg, however, has led me to a significant discovery.

On one occasion I suggested taking the egg home with me to see if I could encourage it to hatch, and he responded by blasting me with a jet of turquoise-coloured fire. I lost consciousness soon after, and when I rose from my slumber he informed me that I had been asleep for five hours. The 'multicoloured fires' concept was one I was initially sceptical of, but now that I have witnessed it with my own eyes I am a reformed man. I only hope he does not unleash fire as we humans know it upon me.

"Curious," Septimus said, "Malkonar appears to have acted very broody around my egg, but why didn't he choose to incubate it until some eighty years later?"

His question was a valid one, but Peter's scrambled mind was elsewhere.

"So turquoise fire means instant knockout?" he asked, voice low and barely audible.

Septimus raised an eyebrow. "So you want to talk after all?"

"Answer the question!"

"Presumably," he spluttered, "My knowledge of fire is limited, and turquoise is not one I have examined in great detail."

"Can you breathe it?"

"No."

Peter grunted and turned the page of the journal, but Septimus wasn't content to let him lapse back into silence just yet.

"I can breathe fire and ice," he said, but Peter didn't reply. "Aren't you curious about that at all?"

Peter shook his head.

"Want to see me breathe them?" he tried.

Another shake.

"It looks amazing," he protested, but Peter wasn't interested. Unfazed, he sat up straight and took a deep breath, chest bulging unnaturally as he did so. He made an unusual spitting noise with his tongue and a thin jet of fire shot out of his mouth and dissolved shortly after. Peter wasn't watching. He coughed to grab his attention then quickly repeated the process, but this time he emitted a streak of light blue fire. It glinted in the light, very much like an icicle, and a shot of cold air burned Peter's pale skin and froze the apathy on his lips.

After his second performance Septimus turned to face Peter, smiling.

"Cool, eh?"

"I told you not to breathe fire in the house," Peter said curtly, and as Septimus' head sunk in despair he started to read again.

Nov. 3rd, 1892
As the end of the year approaches I have found that the Malkonar Experiment has been largely fruitless, but at the same time it has still wielded some useful information. Such as today, for instance, where Malkonar finally spoke of what had drawn him to my beacon.

His story is fascinating, and to save the burden of writing it out in full I shall summarise it thus: dragons do exist and are descended from malkonars, and a few years ago there was a war between the two species. The dragons were victorious and have spent the time between now and then hunting down the remaining malkonars.

Malkonar is naturally very bitter about his past, and I worry his violent thoughts could leech into his actions. On the positive side, I reiterate the point that he is polite and civilised at the best of times, and so far he has not objected to me taking notes on anything he says, but I don't find myself trusting him completely. Then again, I get the impression that Malkonar doesn't entirely trust me either, judging by the way he stares at me with narrowed eyes whenever I am around. Still, I have managed to document some useful information, so a strained relationship is fine for me as long as it provides me with knowledge.

"That sounds worrying," Septimus said.
"What does?"
"Armstrong's obsession with knowledge. I think being mocked for his belief in malkonars made him determined to prove that he was right, and this made him oblivious to just how dangerous Malkonar is. He says himself that they had a strained relationship, and as someone who lived with Malkonar I can tell you that he

doesn't enjoy tolerating people."

"Knowing him he has a strained relationship with everyone."

"Sadly, you're about right. It's all a question of how long it is before that strained relationship becomes no relationship."

"Not very long," Peter mumbled, "That last entry was November 1892. He has just over a year to live."

"Well let's see."

Septimus nodded towards the Journal, and Peter flicked to the next entry and began to read.

Jan. 19th, 1893

The Malkonar Experiment is nearing its first birthday and I fear human-malkonar relations have become rather strained. Mayor Fletcher has ceased to visit Malkonar on the grounds that he is a dangerous creature and poses a health risk. Personally I am glad to be shot of him – I am grateful for his finances but so far he has served only to hold me back. He asks the wrong questions at the wrong times, so to hear the sound of silence on my right is nothing short of a relief.

The reason for our strained relationship is what I believe to be Malkonar pining for freedom. Though he doesn't speak much he has made the occasional hint at leaving the silo and stretching his healed wings. In my mind it is too risky: this entire project has been covert and I intend to keep it that way. He has argued and I have argued back, but so far I have had the final say. As an expert in these matters I am confident that he will not desert the silo, as he relies too heavily on the power of the stone. Very much like a child without its mother, Malkonar without the silo will be very vulnerable indeed.

"And he calls himself an expert," Septimus sneered, "I'm sorry, but give Malkonar a source of power and a year to stockpile it and he will become a very dangerous creature indeed."

"But there's still no divide," Peter snapped, a flashback of the day's horror spurring him forward, "The page is dated 1893, so Armstrong has about a year left. Something has to happen between now and then."

"Indeed. Keep reading, there can't be much more now," Septimus said, and Peter obliged.

May 24th, 1893
It is with great sorrow I report that human-malkonar relations have hit a new low, a product of a conflicting opinion that cannot be avoided.

Malkonar has spent the last three months threatening to leave the silo on the grounds that being cooped up indoors is bad for his health. I informed him that he is an important part of my research into malkonars and that he can go free after I have presented him to the scientific community, but his response was to hiss and roar and demand he go free immediately, saying that he was no exhibition. I attempted to soothe him, but that only made the situation worse. He told me that he was no one's pet and that he was only staying inside the silo because he had nowhere else to go. I calmly asked for his co-operation and he begrudgingly agreed to stay inside the silo, provided I ask fewer questions about his life.

I am now worried that my own subject is on the verge of jeopardising this entire project, but I have worked long and hard at this and am not prepared to let him sabotage my plans at this stage. He is a strong creature with an equally worthy intellect, but I am a man, and a man is the strongest thing on this planet. No man will be bested by a creature. It always has and always will be that way.

"Oh no," Septimus sighed, covering his eyes with his claws,

"Armstrong, you foolish, foolish man."

"Yeah."

"Human arrogance," he mumbled viciously, "Smart enough to build a machine but dumb enough to ignore it flaws."

"Yeah."

"Are you going quiet again?"

"Yeah."

"Don't you have an insight you want to share? You're doing well."

"No."

"Are you sure?"

"Yeah."

"Okay then," Septimus nodded, his voice cracking in defeat, "Well, I just hope that their ignorance hasn't given Malkonar something that endangers us. Do you want to read on?"

"Yeah."

Jul. 4th, 1893
Today the United States of America celebrates the day it gained independence from the British Empire, and very much like my ancestors from the year 1776 I find myself struggling with an unruly subject.

Malkonar's behaviour is becoming almost unbearable: he sits for hours on end curled up in a ball, thinking hard, and throws tantrums of epic proportions if I speak at the wrong moment or ask the wrong question. The silo is beginning to show the strain of his rages – the last time I visited a lot of the mortar on the inner walls was crumbling and the stones were scratched and scarred, and what frustrates me is that I have no idea how to deal with such mood swings. My only idea as to where his violence comes from is that it could be derived from his anger for the war in which he lost so many of his brethren.

While I have sympathy for his losses his persistent anger and lack of consideration for myself is driving my patience to bursting point. I am a scientist and I have a presentation to prepare, and I refuse to let an unruly malkonar stand in my way.

"With an attitude like that he's asking for trouble," Septimus mumbled, gazing across the silhouetted skyline of Averton, "But nothing has happened that would make Armstrong want to seal the silo."
"Yeah."
"So what will happen between now and his death?"
"I don't know."
"What do you think might happen?"
"I don't know."
"Nothing?"
"No."
"Okay," Septimus said, "Could you read on?"
"Yeah," Peter said, flicking to the next entry and reading once more.

Dec 31st, 1893
I know I do not update this experiment log too often, but what has happened today has shaken me to my very core, and if I should die tomorrow I would be satisfied to know that I have recorded this for someone to find.

It began this morning when I went to give Malkonar his breakfast. I was feeling rather pleased with myself as I approached the silo, as I had had Cook make a Christmas pudding especially for him to act as a peace offering in our troubled relationship. However, as I drew closer to the silo I heard conversation, which I immediately recognized as Malkonar's. Probably due to years of isolation he has developed a habit of talking to himself, and listening to what he was saying scared me in unimaginable ways. I drew a pencil and paper from my pocket and recorded what he said, and I have transcribed his exact words below:

"I hate this silo. So barren, so isolated. I'm so alone, even with that imbecile and his cowardly friend around. I can't win, can I? I've had my species murdered by those deformed atrocities, and now they want to kill me for daring to stand up to them. When was respect taken out of the equation? I let them live and they repay me by trying to kill me. Well no more. I'll destroy them, I'll destroy them all. I'll tear them to shreds, make them beg for salvation while annihilating them. I'm stronger now. I was dying before, but I'm healthy again thanks to that fool and his experiments. He knows I want out of this silo and believes I won't leave, but I'll prove him wrong soon enough. Once I'm done with the dragons and the Drassins I'll go for him. Actually, make that the human race. I'll reclaim all of the land they stole from us, make them our slaves. I'll repopulate the malkonar species and make them the dominators of the Earth. They might have guns, but they'll pose little threat to us. They're scared of fighting because they're so puny. In fact, I bet a newborn malkonar could destroy a human. They rely too heavily on intelligence. It wasn't brutality that got them to the top of the food chain, just being smarter than any other creature around them. I cannot believe we surrendered to those smears. They will die, but the dragons must go first. I must bide my time. I am almost strong enough to kill, and a lot of killing is what I must do."

I then gave Malkonar his food, praying that he wasn't reading my mind and seeing my horrified thoughts. He accepted the pudding with a smile, but by this point I could see behind his warm grin and deep into the dark, ruthless void known as Malkonar.

I am trembling as I write this, as I simply do not know what to do. Seeing the faces of my mocking colleagues as I unveil Malkonar to them is a day I yearn for, but I fear the threats he made are all too valid. He has shown nothing but disdain towards me since he arrived, and I think it is obvious that he is staying only for the power source he feeds off. I am torn in a moral battle: disregard the issue and risk having myself and every other human killed, or remove the spiral, seal the silo and wave goodbye to scientific exploits. I need time to decide, but this is a decision I will have to make soon.

"And there's our answer," Septimus said, "And to be honest, it's worse than I thought it would be. Looks like Armstrong did us a bigger favour than we realised." He paused to allow Peter a word which never came. "Please finish the Journal, the tension's killing me."

Peter nodded and began to read, the anticipation welling up inside him.

Jan. 5th, 1894
It is with much disappointment that I inform you that the Malkonar Experiment has finally come to an end. After a few days thought I finally decided that it would be best to seal Malkonar inside the silo, as he is a danger to everyone in Averton and Britain herself.

I managed to persuade Mayor Fletcher to let me seal the silo for good yesterday, and today I convinced Malkonar to take a nap, during which I had the door to the silo sealed with thick concrete. Mayor Fletcher finally decided to show his cowardly face as I was removing the spiral from the silo wall, which should sap Malkonar's strength enough to keep him in there. Thankfully he didn't ask any questions.

Now I can only hope that my plan has worked, and start again on ensnaring a friendlier, less ruthless malkonar.

"So that's it then," Septimus said, looking relieved to have an answer, "Armstrong sealed him in there and he's been there ever since."

"Uh-huh."

"Well, we've got a couple of answers from that. They might help us in the long run."

"Wait."

"What?"

"One more."

"Is there?"

"Yeah."

"Curious. I can't see where the story goes from here, but I suppose anything else is a bonus."

"Yeah," Peter said again, and began to read for the final time.

Jan. 16th, 1894
This is the final time that I will write into this journal, and I guess it is fitting that it will stretch onto the final page. Malkonar is still inside the silo after eleven days, but that hasn't prevented him from exacting his revenge.

I am angry at myself for overlooking this point, as it was on this matter that I gave my ill-fated talk in Birmingham. I'm talking, of course, about mind-eating, and Malkonar's mind-eating will be the death of me.

The basic idea of my theory is that the more intelligent a life form is the harder it is for a malkonar to 'decode' the brain. Once it has been 'decoded', however, the victim is consumable. I have been in close proximity to Malkonar for the best part of two years, and I think it is obvious that he has been gnawing at my brain since the experiment began.

Right now I can hear him inside my mind, screaming at me to die, to throw myself into the fireplace and let myself burn, but I must write this before he gains complete control. I wish I could turn back the clock, stop the beacon ever being created and let Malkonar die of starvation like he deserves, but I saved him and made him stronger, and though I realise my mistake it is too late. At least he is inside the silo where the damage he can cause will be minimal, but people will still die to satisfy his hunger, and it appears I will be the first to appease his stomach.

My hands are trembling, he's trying to make me stop writing, but I must finish. He's telling me to climb into the attic, go through the window and jump off the top of my house, and soon he will make me perform his request. If anyone finds this, tell my sister May that I love her, but don't dare mention Malkonar to her or anyone else for that matter. He needs to stay hidden to Averton for the rest of time, and if anyone finds the stone they risk dooming us all.

Now it is time for me to go. He almost has complete control of me, and I will not go out kicking and screaming as that is what he wants. I will die quietly and with honour, and as a result I hope to earn my reward in Heaven. Goodbye, planet Earth, I pray Malkonar will leave you alone.

Peter slammed the journal shut as if hoping to squash Malkonar between the pages like an unlucky fly. He said nothing, but the scowl on his face told a story for the curious. Septimus only stared to the floor.

"Ah," the malkonar said.

"Yeah."

"He consumed Armstrong too."

"Yeah."

"Indeed."

More silence bar the picking of fingers and claws at upholstery. Septimus covertly studied Peter's angst several times before daring to say something substantial.

"Now that Malkonar's intentions are clear to both of us," he said experimentally, and finished the sentence when Peter didn't react, "We need to ask ourselves how we handle him. Do you have any ideas?"

"No."

"Come on, you must have something."

"Don't ask me questions."

"But you're insightful."

"I don't have the answers."

"You don't know that."

"I haven't known them before."

"You might this time."

"I don't."

"Not now, you might later."

"I never will."

Septimus groaned. "Do you not want to talk to me?"

"No."

"Why not?"

"You ask too many questions."

"You just want to think about it on your own?"

"Yeah."

"Yet you complain you never have the answers."

"I don't."

"So why think?"

"To find them."

The reptile groaned again. "This is futile," he whined, "Look, Feela, if you don't want to talk to me then talk to your question sheet. You know more than you realise, and if I can't convey that message to you then maybe that can."

Peter didn't acknowledge the suggestion with words, but he did stand up and shuffle over to his desk, sliding open the drawer with frigid fingers and pulling out the discoloured bank of knowledge he depended on. Picking up a pen, he examined the list, and filled in the answers he knew.

2. What did Armstrong do that caused the silo to be sealed?

He lured Malkonar to the silo as an experiment, which backfired horrifically. Technically he did nothing to cause the silo to be sealed: he overheard Malkonar discussing his plans and decided he was too dangerous to be free.

4. Why was a hole cut in the side of the silo when it was sealed?

To remove the spiral stone: a tablet producing the power that was helping Malkonar to grow stronger. The absent power has successfully kept Malkonar inside the silo ever since.

He surveyed the sheet with a twitching eye, and among the smudges of ink he found a realisation which sent his voice soaring back up his throat.
"Septimus."
"What?" he said, not turning around.
"I've finished my question sheet."
This time he turned.
"What?"
"All the questions have answers."
"The sheet is finished," he said, and looked down, "Uh oh."
Peter felt his body chill.
"What does that mean?"
"It means the anchor is gone."
"What?"
"The safety net has been removed," he breathed, and before Peter could reply he scuttled off into the bathroom, slamming the door shut behind him.
He lowered his eyes back down to his question sheet. His Bible, written in ink smudged and darkened by months of rot and grubby

fingers. He reread every question and answer, and found they didn't make any sense. They were correct answers that bore no relevance to anything, and he guessed why instantly. These questions were dated: they came from a time when he didn't know what he was up against, and the needs of yesterday did not apply to today. The enemy was the same yet different, and the sheet had taught him precisely nothing about him. He smirked helplessly. Human arrogance: he had spent six months mindlessly chasing answers he wanted to know, not what he needed to know.

He didn't sense himself rip up the question sheet, but as he tossed the fragments into the air and watched them spiral back down to Earth he felt more vulnerable than ever before.

TWENTY ONE

Peter didn't eat dinner that night, nor did he touch the cups of tea made for him by a concerned Septimus. He didn't speak either, his only noises being a defensive grunt when Septimus tried to interrupt the TV programs he was watching. He hated TV, but it was a welcome distraction from his incessant questioning and the corpse that lingered in his mind.

When twilight turned to dusk he retired to bed, but sleep was impossible. His sleep pattern was so erratic he had become nocturnal. He spent most of the daylight hours slumped half-asleep at his desk and the moonlight hours feeling completely wired, and what occupied his head served only to reinforce that.

He lay restless, and after much twisting and turning he cursed and sat up, flicking on the bedside lamp before cradling his head in his hands. The light stirred Septimus, and he sleepily rolled into life.

"What's going on?" he grumbled, "Has Malkonar escaped?"

"Go to sleep," Peter said, his first words in three hours.

Septimus' eyes opened, "Oh, you're talking again."

"Hmm."

"Or not."

"Maybe I am."

"Well either way you're making a considerable fuss over something as simple as talking," he said, sitting up alongside his human counterpart.

"I have reason."

"I'm well aware of that, but that's not the only problem you have."

"Hmm?"

"You worry too much."

"You don't say," he snapped.

"My point exactly. A side effect of your worrying is insomnia; insomnia leads to tiredness and tiredness to impatience. Hold onto something as destructive as anxiety and you'll cause yourself far worse problems."

He looked down at his skeletal arms. He felt the bones, his own bones, grate against his skin, and his veil finally dropped.

"Yeah," he whispered, slumping back into his pillow. "Look at what Malkonar's done to me," he said, a lump in his throat. "Look at what I was and what I am now. What's happened to me?"

Septimus leaned into his ear. He expected to hear comforts, but instead he heard, "You need to stop feeling sorry for yourself, Feela."

"Huh?" he exclaimed.

"I said you cause *yourself* problems for a reason. You have changed much since I arrived and it has all been positive, but this is the one vice that holds you back, and you need to break it before it causes yet more damage."

"W-well what do I need to do?"

"Just show some confidence, Feela. Do you want to defeat Malkonar?"

"'Course I do."

"Then let that motivate you. Treat that goal like your question sheet: don't shy away from any opportunity to advance it. He preys on the indecisive, and if you can't trust yourself to succeed when it matters you'll be little more than his plaything, and that's...that's something I don't want to imagine.

He turned away. "The idea of a victorious Malkonar sickens me. That rat, that bastard, that shameless, charmless bastion of all that is wicked about this world, dominant." Wisps of smoke trickled from his nostrils. "It's disgusting," he said, turning back to Peter with malice in his eyes, "And it can't happen. For the sake of all that is good we cannot let that grub prevail."

"You show a lot of resentment towards your father, you know that?"

"What father?" Septimus hissed, "He didn't do anything I would consider fatherly, so I refuse to bestow him with that title. The closest thing I have to a father is you, I suppose."

"Father?" He cocked an eyebrow, "What kind of father figure am I?"

"Well, not only did you save my life, but you've also shown me more love, care and respect in five months than Malkonar did in twenty-six years. If that doesn't make you better than him in your eyes I will be amazed. Now, I think you'd better sleep."

"Sounds like a plan, shame I can't," Peter groaned, pulling the covers up to his throat.

"Feela, just relax. I know you are bitter about the Librarian but there was nothing you could do. You didn't know until it was too late."

"Don't talk about the Librarian," he said, squeezing his eyes shut.

"Okay, I won't."

He lay down at Peter's side, and Peter promptly turned away from him.

"Feela," he said, "You won't make yourself feel better if you continue to isolate yourself."

"I'm sharing a bed with you, that's hardly isolation."

"Yes, but you're refusing to acknowledge me when I may be able to help your restlessness."

"Well can you?"

"If you turn back towards me you'll find out."

He lay still for a moment longer, then sighed and rolled onto his back.

"Thank you," Septimus said, "Now then, maybe this will help."

He felt a scratching on his skin, and he opened his eyes to see Septimus perched on his torso, curled into a ball and nuzzling his head against his neck. Rough scales and sharp claws cut into his skin, but with each brush of his muzzle he felt himself relax. He placed his hand over him and hugged him to his chest.

"Is that better?" Septimus asked.

"Yeah," Peter said, "I don't know why, but it is."

"That's good. A nice hug always helps me feel better," he said, his voice growing sombre, "They were a rare thing back in the silo."

"Oh."

"Well, you know yourself that he never had much time for me. That's why I wish I had my mother around." His voice softened even more, "Malkonar might have been tolerable then. She could hardly have been worse, but like everything else I've ever really wanted to know Malkonar has denied me the privilege."

Peter hugged him tighter and adjusted the duvet so that it covered both of them, anger bubbling in his brain. He had suffered for five months at the hands of Malkonar, but Septimus had endured twenty-six years, and seeing how unloved and neglected he felt drove the malnourished sense of determination lurking somewhere dark in his chest.

"I'm so sorry," he whispered.

"What for?"

"For taking so long to find you."

"It's okay. It doesn't matter how long the journey takes so long as you reach your destination."

Peter looked at him doubtfully. "But that's not true though, is it?"

"What?"

"An inner-city apartment, surrounded by humans and cut off from your own species? This isn't where you want to be. It's better than what you had before, but it's not a home for a malkonar and you know it." He cuddled Septimus closer, "You haven't reached your destination, have you?"

There was silence, a solemn roll of azure eyes, then a single word.

"No."

* * *

Peter spent the next working day suffering from an intense bout of PTSD, but despite his pale face and slack limbs his colleagues were oblivious to his suffering. That suited him fine, as he had no voice – the constant images of the Librarian he was seeing had snatched it away.

She was everywhere. On his computer, on the walls and on every note passed around the office. His twisted mind even imagined a spray-can image of her corpse on the concrete walls outside like some grotesque Belfast mural.

He didn't work. Concentration was far beyond his mental capabilities, but when lunchtime arrived he didn't escape his administrative hell. Going outside might tempt him into Averton City Library, and that was unthinkable. He began to tremble at the thought, which finally drew the attention of his coworkers.

He didn't answer their questions, nor did he speak when his boss came to talk to him, but when he was told he could go home to rest he was gone before they could even think of changing their minds.

He managed to unlock the front door at the third attempt and crawled into familiar territory, which quickly became unfamiliar as he realised something was wrong. He couldn't feel Septimus in the apartment. The living room was earmarked by a warm, musty feel that emitted from Septimus' presence, but it wasn't there. Even the smell of curdled milk that had become his trademark was absent.

He shuffled around the apartment, but didn't find him. A tinge of concern crept into his head, and it was then that his mind chose to drop the images of the Librarian and remind him he hadn't seen Septimus that morning either. He had woken up, eaten breakfast and left the house without catching a glimpse of the blue malkonar.

He whimpered and dropped onto the sofa. Where was he? He couldn't have been out foraging that long. Wait, last night, he'd been upset. Oh God, he'd upset him and now he was gone. His eyes jerked towards the window. Was he coming back? He had to, he didn't like being outside alone, but outside there was only open sky. He tore his eyes away before it tore into him.

"No," he scolded himself, "He's just gone foraging, he's fine. Just relax."

He watched TV, and only after two hours of tedium did he become aware of Septimus' absence once more. He ate a hastily made dinner to push down the acid churning in his stomach, eyes fixed on the window through every bite. The sky was now orange, but still he saw no small blue object fluttering towards him.

The sun went down and he pressed his face and hands up against the cool glass and examined every inch of Averton that he could see. Nothing bar the city lights, then his breath shielded the world from view.

He sat down and pulled his knees to his chest in time to catch the tears dribbling down his face. He was alone, no Pepper and now no Septimus. A boat with ripped sails drifting through the storm. He closed his eyes and sobbed, making no effort to silence himself. He wept with such intensity that it burned his chest and drowned out the outside world, which was why he didn't hear the noise until long after he'd run out of air to choke on.

He stopped crying when he heard it, and slowly turned to its source. Red, plastic and broken, but still making noise. Noise that was the calling card of the last person he wanted to hear from.

"No," he choked, "Not now."

He tried to shut out the piercing sound in his ear, but now it was in it refused to come back out. He persevered, but his efforts came to nothing, and with a heavy sigh and an intense feeling of worthlessness he resigned himself to his fate.

With a tear-stained hand he grabbed the receiver, squeezed the hurt out of his voice, and lifted it to his face.

"Hello, Malkonar."

"Good evening, Mr. Vaughan," Malkonar replied, "I hope you are in good health."

"Well I'm not, if you must know, and guess who's to blame?"

"Is it a certain malkonar who is seeking a certain stone?"

"Absolutely right. Why don't you just curl up and die, Malkonar? You'd be doing the world a favour."

"That would be no good, it means I couldn't drive you insane."

"So that's what this is all about? Driving me mental?"

"Reclaiming the stone is my priority, watching your collapse is a bonus."

"Well you'd better tell me what you want before my mind crumbles."

"To the point as always, Peter," he said, then spoke again with more relish in his voice, "I'm going to make you an offer, one I doubt you'll turn down."

"What's the offer?"

"Well, you may have noticed that Septimus has been absent for a good portion of the day, and I can confirm that he will be absent for a very long time if you do not give me your complete co-operation."

Peter's world slowed to about half its normal speed. He stood unblinking, tapping the phone's table with increasingly rigid jabs. He gripped the receiver tighter, and as the loose shards of plastic ripped his skin his calm ran out and he ignited.

"What the hell have you done to him?" he shrieked.

"Calm yourself Peter, he is fine for now."

"How?" he barked, "I want reasons, you scaly bastard. How'd

you get ahold of him?"

He heard a laugh ring down the line and drive a spike through his nerves.

"How?"

"It was so simple," he chuckled, "I'm only ashamed of myself for not thinking of it sooner."

"Reasons, now!"

"Calm yourself, my good man, your answers are coming."

Peter forced himself silent.

"Excellent. Now, I'm sure you're aware of how Septimus goes foraging every day," he said, his voice bleeding arrogance, "It's a risky thing to do given the situation you are in, and it's especially risky when you hunt in the same stretch of forest everyday. It's even more dangerous when you remember that your nemesis has a killer hound at his disposal."

"Oh God," Peter whined, sensing the ending to the tale.

"Yes, he was no match for your mutt. Once the jaws clamped around his neck it was all over," he laughed a little more, "He's mine now, Peter."

He collapsed to the floor and slapped himself until his cheek rushed with blood. What had he done? Why had he moved Pepper to Don's house and not a shelter where he could cause no harm? He slapped himself again when he realised the answer.

"Stupid!" he said, digging his fingernails into his skin, "Stupid! Stupid! Stupid! I'm so fucking..." Then he remembered where Pepper had gone. "Oh my God, Don!"

"Calm yourself, Don is quite safe. I have engagements more pressing than that wastrel."

"Oh God," Peter panted, "You could have killed him. You could have killed him and the Librarian within a week. Oh God, I could have had two people killed in two days!"

"Yes, your precious morals are in tatters," Malkonar cackled, "You're broken, Peter. You've no Septimus, no Pepper, no friends and now there's blood on your hands. I've won a devastating victory and I expect a tribute for my efforts."

"What do you want?"

"I would have thought that was obvious by now," he said, the slurp of licked lips ringing in his ear, "I want the stone, and if you wish to see Septimus alive I suggest you bring it to the grain silo at Edgeley Park tonight at half past twelve precisely."

"And what happens if I don't?"

"Then Pepper tears him into tiny little pieces," Malkonar said simply, "Pieces so small that an infant would have no problem swallowing them. If you think you've got it bad now you'll be horrified to see how life without Septimus is. It will be like having no immune system."

"Threatening to tear your own child limb from limb, some father you are," Peter said, disguising the panic in his voice.

"Don't distract yourself, Peter. I expect you to appear at the silo tonight, and if you don't bring the stone with you I'll make you very sorry indeed," and with that the line went dead.

The receiver landed with a thump on the body of the phone, but the thump of Peter collapsing onto the sofa was much louder. He lay there in a stupor, scouring his empty mind for any loopholes or get-out clauses, but his search returned no results.

He leapt to his feet and began to pace the room. Give him the stone or lose Septimus. Those were his choices and both were equivalent to signing his own death warrant.

He paced faster. What should he do? He couldn't abandon Septimus, not at this stage, but another side of his personality told him that freeing Malkonar was far more dangerous than losing an ally. No, he had to stop being a coward and go for the sake of Septimus, for the sake of what he perceived to be good, but then he would be endangering his own life. His head burned and he started to sweat as conflicting ideas battered his senses, and eventually he could take it no more.

He roared in anguish, strode into the kitchen and stuck his head into the freezer. Years worth of accumulated ice scratched his skin and sent intense throbs through his head, but the chill helped him regain some composure. He stopped hyperventilating, and with his breathing under control he returned to crying.

Numb streaks dribbled across his face, and the pain made him sob. Septimus was right: he was spineless and cowardly and would rather stick his head in a freezer and cry than save his best friend. He laughed bitterly. He was lost and helpless, trapped once again in a web of paralysing anxiety he had weaved himself, but then he saw the tub of ice cream and the pain paled into insignificance.

He blinked to clear his eyes and stared at it. A blue box with a yellow label that would have been worthless had he not seen it perched at Septimus' feet. He felt the cold drain away and saw the past. He was walking out of the shower and Septimus was sat on the sofa, eating from the tub with enthusiasm. He saw his undisguised joy, his sheer delight at finding something that made living among humans worthwhile. Something that had made his woeful life worth living.

Another tear fell out of his eye. His mind was made up, he was going to show some confidence.

TWENTY TWO

The world was a dark blur when he stepped onto the street. He didn't recognise Averton anymore, there was something out of place with everything. More or less windows than before, the paving stones arranged differently than they were a few hours ago, nothing was right. This wasn't the city he had been born and bred in, but a post-industrial labyrinth of shadows.

He began walking, the cold biting the hand that clutched the stone with a vice grip. Anything his body could have jettisoned had gone long ago, leaving an empty shell with nothing to do but retch and walk tentative steps all the way to 29 Kildome Close.

It was still abandoned, and by darkness it seemed even more daunting than before. He went inside anyway, climbing up every creaking staircase until he reached the attic.

He crawled in, flicked the light on and sat in the dust. The glare made him squint but he could still see what he had came for. Long and smooth, a stark contrast of wood and metal propped against the wooden beams. He picked it up and held it in his hands, a symbol he had shunned so many times before for its hand in sick entertainment. Not anymore. He scrabbled among the boxes, hunting for any packs of shotgun slugs he could find and emptying them into his pockets until they bulged.

* * *

The rusted gates of Edgeley Park warned with barred teeth of what was waiting for him, but he ignored its pleas and clambered over the gates. He stared into the gloom to steady himself, then took a step, gravel crackling beneath his feet. He kept his head down to keep to the path. He couldn't get lost, not in a blackened space surrounded by a fence. With Malkonar in it. He shivered and shuffled faster, riding the snaking trails into the nerve centre of Edgeley Park.

When he lifted his head again he saw the lake glistening in the faint moonlight, and to its side he could make out the outline of the silo's turret. He swallowed the foul taste in his mouth and crept towards it, each step growing progressively harder.

He placed a hand to the rugged stone and checked his watch. 00:28. He was early, but it only gave him more time to panic. He closed his eyes and felt his heart beat, each pulse rattling his ribcage, threatening to shatter the bones that kept his vital organs safe.

He breathed but it came out as a whimper, as did the next breath, but he missed the third as he heard Malkonar inside his head.

Good evening, Peter, I hope you have what I want.

"Yeah," Peter said, "Now where's Septimus?"

He will appear in time.

"That's not good enough. If you want this to work then we'll have to operate on a level of mutual respect. If you want the stone then bring Septimus to me, you're not getting anything until I know he's safe."

Very well, he sighed.

A set of glowing red eyes emerged from behind the silo. Moments later they were joined by a pair of white eyes with blue irises, silver tears clinging to the corneas. The eyes then became part of animals, whose shapes formed into that of a dog and a malkonar. The snarling red eyes belonged to Pepper, who was clutching the owner of the fear-glistened white eyes in his jaws.

There you go, he heard Malkonar say, *He's fine and well. Whether or not he stays fine and well depends on your actions between now and the end of this encounter.*

Peter stared at Septimus. He was on his side, Pepper's jaws clamped across his neck, lips curled to reveal the teeth that prodded.

Curious? Malkonar said.

"No," Peter replied, "I know what's happening. His mouth's around his neck and one of his canines is over the jugular."

Very good, Peter, and can you guess what happens if you don't give me the stone within the next minute?

"Pepper bites and he bleeds to death."

Yes, now hurry along. The clock is ticking.

He stared into the eternal eyes again. He didn't say anything, nor did he send a message directly to his brain, but the look in his gaze said *do it*. He did.

He took tentative steps up the small mound upon which the silo sat and caressed its rough surface with his fingers, slowly striding around the base like he had the first time he had been here, all those months ago when the Park Keeper had told his naïve self about Armstrong and his experiments. When he was blissfully unaware there was a murderer just inches away from him.

His hand descended into the silo wall and he felt another strand of sanity snap. Sweating, he turned to face the wall and, turning the stone so that it matched the shape of the hole, shoved it in.

The mortar glowed a brilliant gold that illuminated the entire park, forcing his eyes into a squint. The light swiftly faded and a rumble shook the air. He looked up, following the sound, and was rained on by flecks of mortar. He took a few steps back, and seconds later the spot he once occupied was filled with one of the silo's vast stone bricks.

He cantered back down the mound as another brick fell from the top, then another and a third soon after, each one sinking into the mud. A shower of ancient mortar rained down on him, some into his eyes, but he kept them open to watch the bricks fall and the hole in the top of the silo grow wider still. By the time the wall stopped tumbling the silo had lost a quarter of its height, and left a gap large enough for a monster.

A deathly hush descended upon the park, the lapping of water and the gentle rasp of Peter's breathing the only sounds, then the quiet was punctured by a cackle and a grateful sigh.

"Over a century," Malkonar said, this time verbally, "Over one whole century. Do you know how long that is, Peter?"

"Longer than most humans can live for."

"Exactly," he said, giddy delirium breaking into his tone, "I have been living in this prison for longer than you and your parents have been alive, and I've held my nerve throughout. I've been starved, frustrated and suffered many a nightmare leading up to this moment, but I did not break, and now my perseverance has been so richly awarded. Now, before I make my grand reappearance, how about a little lighting?"

A fierce jet of green fire flew into the air, rising high above the silo in one solid bolt before twisting to form a sphere, the flame swirling like electrons around an atom.

"Do you like it?" Malkonar said proudly. "Green fire is excellent for illuminating dark locations such as this."

"Don't you think an artificial sun will draw attention to the park?" Peter asked, shielding his eyes from the intense light.

"Who cares? I'm free and there's nothing anyone can do about it. Now brace yourself Peter, because here I come!"

A crimson hand with scratched claws rose from inside and grabbed the lip of silo, shortly followed by another, identical hand. The claws tightened their grip on the rock, and as Malkonar's head slowly rose up into view Peter's body crashed. Red scales, faded from a century without sunlight, a twisted right horn and a primal leer stretched across his lipless face. He pulled more of himself out of the silo to a chorus of sickening cracks as seldom-used joints screamed into life after years of inactivity. He was skeletal, bones jutting out of his slight frame at odd angles, but it didn't detract from the fear Peter was feeling as he perched on the rim of the silo and looked down on him with a wicked smile.

"Alright," he said slowly, swallowing every organ that had lodged itself in his throat, "You're free, now give me Septimus and we can all go home happy."

Malkonar responded with a snigger.

"Oh, Peter," he chuckled, "Oh, Peter, Peter, Peter. You didn't seriously expect you'd be leaving here alive, did you?"

He choked on his words. He looked over at Septimus, his terrified face reflecting his own, then back at Malkonar, and bit his lip.

"Why?" he spluttered, his whole body shaking, "Why do you want to kill me?"

"Because I have unfinished business with Armstrong."

"What do I have to do with Armstrong?"

"Armstrong had a sister named May whom he left his possessions and his house to. May had a daughter named Pauline, who had a son named Steven, who had a son named..."

"Peter," he finished, exhaling every last wisp of air from his lungs. "My great-great-uncle was Armstrong."

"Exactly, and who better to finish the business we had with than the latest generation of his family?" he lifted a claw. "Let's bathe in old blood, shall we?"

In an instinct Peter swung the shotgun from his shoulder and shoved a hand into his pocket.

"Oh?" Malkonar laughed, "So you went for the shotgun after all. That symbol of brutality you've spent so many years despising is your weapon of choice against me."

"Too right," he hissed, pulling two shotgun slugs from his

pocket and loading them into the barrel.

"Are you blind to what is wrong with you, Peter? You are broken and this is yet another sign of it. You're descending to my depths, the depths of murder, which is as far below your precious morals as you can get."

"Well you know what? You're right. I am broken. I'm not the same Peter Vaughan you called back in October. You have snapped and twisted me into someone completely new. Since you came into my life you have shown me just how fucked up this world can be, and frankly I don't care about ethics or compassion or any of that shit anymore. You have drilled any sense of morality out of me, and since I've been reduced to your level I might as well act like you," he snapped the barrel shut and raised it to Malkonar's head, "If you don't give me Septimus I'll blow your brains out."

"Oh, will you now?" Malkonar said, stifling laughter, "Well, as charming an idea that is I'm afraid that you're forgetting something."

"What?"

"I have the power of telekinesis, and it's perfectly usable at this range."

Peter's grip on the shotgun slackened.

"So?" he said timidly.

"So dance for me, Peter Vaughan."

An invisible force seized his body and hoisted him into the air. He screamed, dropping the shotgun as he rose to draw level with Malkonar's eyes.

"Feela!" Septimus shrieked, but he was cut off as Pepper tightened his grip on his neck. Peter looked at him desperately, but the feeling of warm breath on his skin turned his attention to the abomination perched in front of him.

"Did that take you by surprise?" he taunted, evil eyes burning through his soul, "It's been a long time since I've had a chance to do this, so I want to make this opportunity worthwhile."

"Oh God," he whimpered, the colour draining from his face,

"What are you gonna do?"

"Well Peter, what I'm going to do is make you sorry you were ever born."

Peter didn't have time to think before he was flung backwards. He screamed, turning turvey in mid-air until he clattered into a tree, spine creaking as he slammed against the bark. He fell into the mud and lay in a heap, silent and motionless, teeth ground to fight the wave of excruciating pain searing through his back.

"Well, that was fun," Malkonar laughed, "How about we do that again?"

He was back in the air before he could scream his protests, and his words finally came in the form of a roar as he smashed into another tree. A crack echoed around the park as his shoulder blades shattered, and the pain intensified as he tumbled through sharp branches and hit the ground again.

He whimpered and tears spilled from his eyes, but they stopped as he was flung again. He soared over the grass until he nose-dived into it, landing on his chest and fracturing his ribs, rolling until he came to rest at the foot of the silo.

He could barely open his eyes through pain and tears, but he could see Malkonar staring down at him with a grin on his face.

"Oh dear," he said, "Did I hurt you too much? Well, that won't do. I don't want you dying too quickly."

Though his vision was blurred he saw Malkonar breathe a jet of pink fire in his direction. He panicked and tried to move, but as the flames smothered him the sensation relaxed his muscles. Various scents hit his nostrils: melted chocolate; aftershave; roses and fresh-cut grass, all of the smells he adored. He breathed in the pink flames greedily, and felt an overwhelming surge of health as his back pain subsided. His shattered shoulder blades clicked into one, and the various muscles that had snapped against the trees slurped back together. When the flames gave way to the green light of the park he found strength in his body once more.

"Pink fire," Malkonar said sweetly as Peter rose to his feet, "A great healer. Something I created recently to deal with the arthritis I was developing." He watched as Peter staggered towards the shotgun and shook his head. "What, Peter?" he said, "You want the shotgun? Well, we can't have that. Anyway, that fire will have left you dehydrated. How about a drink?"

"Wait!" Peter blurted, but he was lifted skyward once more by Malkonar's vicious mind. He watched helplessly as he floated through the air until he hung over the rippling surface of the lake. "No," he breathed, but breathing didn't stop him falling from the sky and into the icy water.

Hands, feet, fingers and toes all went numb as he bombed into the lake, but he forced himself to flap towards the surface with every last ounce of his rejuvenated strength. It didn't work. He kicked and flailed and wriggled as much as he could, but he was sinking.

He found more effort from within and used it, stretching his body as far as he could to reach the surface that was growing ever further out of his reach. He gurgled in horror, air spilling from his mouth. What was happening? He swam harder, kicking with more force than he thought possible. Then he realised what Malkonar was doing, and as the horror began to sink in he hit the bottom of the lake.

The feel of the rough stones roused him and he pushed the ground, hands tangling in the water flora. His chest was hot and swollen and he needed to breathe, but no matter how hard he pushed he remained glued to the lakebed. He gave one almighty heave, but the pressure was too great and in the struggle he let a few precious bubbles of air escape his lips.

His heart hammered faster against his ribs, using up the last dregs of oxygen in his bloodstream. He tried once more to lift his ailing body from the lakebed, but his arms finally buckled and he lay still. His eyesight flickered, he was blacking out and could barely breathe, but he didn't thrash.

"*It's okay,*" he thought, his face crushed against the stones, "*It was going to end like this anyway. Drowning isn't a bad way to go really, it's very peaceful."*

With his lungs deprived of oxygen he began to slip away, but then he was pulled upwards with amazing force. An intense pain slammed at his stomach, but it faded away as he broke the surface and the immense taste of oxygen filled his mouth.

He tumbled through the air and landed at the foot of the silo, jarring his leg painfully as he hit the ground, but the pain was meaningless against the thrill of tasting life. He breathed in rapidly, retching as air he had never valued ripped through his lungs and resurrected him.

"Did you enjoy your drink, Peter?" Malkonar asked, grinning from horn to horn. Peter sat up, shivering and coughing up fetid pools of lake water, and looked at him with hardened eyes.

"I'd have preferred a coffee."

Malkonar chuckled. "Your wit is ever present, I see," he said, "It's impressive, certainly. I must say I admire your ability to stay calm in the face of death..."

"Well kill me then!" Peter shouted, "You've twittered on about killing me but you've spared me twice. Do you really want to kill me or are you just winding me up, you anorexic rat?"

"All in good time, Peter. In the grand scheme of things you're a mere hors d'oeuvre for what I have planned, I merely wish to drag this event out as long as possible. I haven't kicked someone around for the best part of a century so I'm going to bloody well enjoy it!"

Peter scowled and forced himself to his feet. His jarred leg protested fiercely, and throbbed harder as he took unsteady steps across the grass, but with the shotgun in his sights he had no intention of stopping for a rest. He had to get to it, he needed it to survive. That and Septimus. Oh God, Septimus.

He looked to the malkonar hanging awkwardly from Pepper's mouth and added another cut to his lip. He had to set Septimus free somehow, but his jarred leg meant there was no way he could react fast enough before Pepper's teeth ended him. He blinked. Pepper's teeth would kill. Pepper's. His heart shrivelled. His best friend of seven years had turned on him when he needed all the help he could get.

A spike of pain shot through his leg at a convenient time. Malkonar had eliminated all of his friends from the game: Pepper, Septimus and even Don. His heart fluttered at the thought of him. Was he really okay? He should have been on his night shift at the factory by the time Malkonar called and thus safe from Pepper, but Malkonar was a liar. A dirty, devious liar who spun his tales to inflict maximum pain. The thought of Malkonar lying about Don's safety made him grit his teeth in anger and spurred him onwards. He had been a dreadful friend by giving him Pepper and now he was going to repay him in the only way he could imagine.

He ground his teeth. No mercy tonight, Malkonar had to die. He had chosen violence and now he had to pay for it. For his own sake. For Septimus' sake. For everyone's sake. He scuttled on, and between painful jabs in his leg a vague plan began to form.

He knelt down and reached for the shotgun, groaning as his leg screamed its protests, but as his fingertips brushed the cool metal of the barrel he was lifted into the air again.

"Oh, for Christ's sake!" he snapped as he drew level with Malkonar's face.

"Indeed," Malkonar replied, "I like to halt my opponent's plans just as they touch the brink of progress. It gives them an illusion which is wonderful to see destroyed."

"Alright," Peter shrugged, contempt hanging on his tongue, "So what now, you scaly bastard? Beat my brains out against the mud, toss me into the silo and seal me in? Hit me with all of your different fires and watch as they make me explode like a firework?" he swung a fist at the air, "I'm sick of being thrown around like a fucking ragdoll! I'm sick of this stupid one-sided fight!" he jabbed a finger at Malkonar, "How about you let me have a shot for a change, eh? It's not like I can harm you!"

Malkonar cocked his brow at him, then nodded his head.

"Alright," he grinned, "You are right in saying that this battle has been one-sided, and seeing as you'll be dead in a few minutes I may as well let you get on the scoresheet," he lowered him to the ground and levitated the gun into Peter's numb hands, "Go on then, have a shot, but please don't get your hopes up. You said yourself you cannot harm me and you're quite correct."

Peter held the gun, lips squeezed tightly shut to hide the smile lurking inside his mouth. He wanted the free shot and Malkonar's inflated ego had granted him it, but it wasn't for him. The lone bullet was for his plan. One he had never thought he would have to undertake, but after five months of torment it didn't take a genius to work out that he was a liability. He was standing in the way of his survival, and that meant he had to go.

He snapped the barrel closed and raised it to his shoulder. Malkonar bent down to broaden the target, a smug grin painted on his face. Peter breathed and focused his sights on his head. This was it. One shot that he had to get absolutely right. If he did that stupid grin would evaporate into nothing, but everything hinged on basic shooting lessons nine years ago.

"Well, Peter?" Malkonar said, "What are you waiting for? Blow my brains out."

Peter tightened his grip on the trigger.

"Brace yourself," he said, and then he did what he had previously thought impossible. He turned the barrel fifty degrees to the right, steadied his aim, pulled the trigger and shot Pepper cleanly through the head.

With a painful whine the husky staggered and dropped to the floor, and Septimus quickly broke free of his grip. The look of horror on Malkonar's face as he realised what he had done was priceless to Peter, but the novelty quickly wore off as a painful pang of guilt rocketed up his spine and locked his muscles tight.

"You!" Malkonar roared, leaping down from the silo. Peter turned to run but stumbled on his sore leg, sending him to the ground. He scrabbled backwards, but a red hand slammed into the grass over his shoulder before he could make any ground. He looked up to see Malkonar towering over him, a furious leer on his face. "Curse you!" he hissed, "You've tried my patience one time too many, Peter Vaughan," he raised a claw, "And now it has expired!"

He closed his eyes before he saw the claw swing, but the hit he was expecting was replaced by an almighty roar of pain from the reptile above. He snapped his eyes open to see Septimus sinking his teeth and his claws into Malkonar's back, ripping two discoloured spines out of his back in an eruption of blood. He flailed violently and Peter scrambled away, scooping up the shotgun as he went, and as he broke away from the trap Septimus leapt from Malkonar's bloodied body. Malkonar lunged for him but missed, and as Septimus hit the ground and scrambled to Peter's side he screamed his frustrations and took to the sky.

Septimus wiped a trickle of blood from his mouth. "Thanks," he said simply.

"No problem."

"No really, thanks. I know that Pepper was..."

"It's nothing, just don't say his name."

"You're really okay about it?"

"I guess so," Peter nodded, unsure of his own emotions, "It feels like a weight's been lifted. I'll probably feel it in the morning though."

"If you make it to morning," Septimus warned, "The balance of power has shifted, but we're not out of the woods just yet."

Peter nodded and unsteadily climbed to his feet. He looked back to the silo to see Malkonar perched on the rim once more, a vexed look in his eye and his claws crushing the bricks beneath them.

"You will pay for that," he seethed at Septimus.

"I'm sorry Malkonar, but this never had to happen," Septimus said, "You could have let me go, flown off and we would have all gone home happy. Instead you chose to fight, and now you're going to feel the consequences of that."

"Really?"

Malkonar closed his eyes and Peter and Septimus flew up into the air. Peter grimaced and gripped the shotgun tighter, but the blue malkonar calmly looked at his father, not breaking eye contact for a second.

They rose to Malkonar's height and he dangled them in front of is face. "What shall I do now?" he said to himself, the edge in his voice betraying his malice, "Maybe I should just torch you with a bout of fire, or how about a fall through the trees? Smashed against the silo wall even? Decisions, decisions."

"Or how about you let us go free and lie down while we kill you?" Septimus asked, narrowing his eyes and grinning confidently.

"Maybe not. I think I'd prefer to annihilate you."

"Then you leave me with no other option."

He broke free of Malkonar's telekinesis, dropped and spread his wings, rising back up into the air and landing a sharpened claw between Malkonar's eyes. The shock of the attack broke Malkonar's grip on Peter and he hit the ground to a crack from his healthy leg.

"What?" Malkonar roared. He swung a claw at Septimus, but scratched only himself as Septimus leapt away.

"You're not the only malkonar around here!" Septimus cackled as Malkonar wiped blood from his face, "You of all people should know that. Deflecting your powers is easy from this range."

Malkonar responded only with a scowl and a grunt, then took to the sky, his vast wings blocking out the sun he had created. Septimus dived for the safety of the trees, but a vicious jet of fire from Malkonar's mouth took off in pursuit. He felt the searing jet scald his feet, but his head start meant he won the race by the narrowest of margins.

He landed in an inferno. The leaves and branches around him ignited instantly and stung his scales, but he was prepared. He launched a burst of light blue fire and spun on the branch, aiming at every flame he could see until his lungs ran out of air, and when he stopped to breathe he saw not flame but frost coating blackened wood and leaves. He admired his work with a relieved smile, but through the wintry scene he saw Malkonar's furious glare.

"Do try harder," he said. Malkonar screamed.

* * *

Peter couldn't feel his legs. There had been an intense fire in them that had given way to numbness, and now they wouldn't budge no matter how much he willed them to. Normally he would have panicked and screamed for assistance, but time was precious and the shotgun was out of reach, so with a grunt of exertion he slammed his hands into the mud and pulled himself forward.

His legs screamed as they were dragged along, but he ground his teeth and ignored it. No time to waste. A rush of fire soared overhead, but he didn't let himself get distracted. A roar of anger sounded out, a low one that sounded distinctly like Malkonar's. He relished the noise but didn't look to see why, he only had eyes for the gun.

He extended his spindly arms and pulled again. More pain which he ignored. He wasn't far now and he didn't dare stop.

The sound of flapping wings filled the air, closely followed by the crunch of claw on stone. Peter didn't look up, but he knew what it meant and he pulled himself faster, but it was too late.

"We can't have that," Malkonar said delicately, then indelicately flung Peter through the sky and into a tree for the third time.

He hit the tree face first. A shocking pain shot through his jaw, but it numbed under the weight of his broken leg as he hit the ground below. He curled into a ball and whined in pain, blood spewing onto his tongue. He spat it out and watched three of his teeth go with it. He blinked at them, then ran his tongue along the bloody stumps they once occupied. He didn't panic.

"Pain is temporary," he whispered to himself, curling his

fingers to find purchase in the mud, "Can't give up. Have to keep going," and to the protests of his body, he dragged himself onto hands and knees and began to crawl back towards the silo.

*** * * ***

Malkonar watched Peter crumple to the ground with great pleasure, but his joy was short-lived as moments later a jet of fire seared his shoulder. He turned his head in its direction in time to allow Septimus to land another claw between his eyes.

He swung his head to shake him off, but he was gone before he could do so. Furious, he wiped the blood from his snout and looked across the sky, but there was no blot of blue to be seen. Then a claw struck his thigh. He shrieked and kicked, but once again lashed out at nothing. He raised and primed his wings, ready to take to the sky, but then a light flash burst across his eyeline.

"Stay still!" he ordered, sending out a brainwave. Septimus froze under his influence and began to float towards him. He broke free but was trapped him again before he could make any serious ground. He tried again, flapping his wings faster, but drew the same result, and he didn't attempt a third as Malkonar floated him in front of his demented eyes.

"Septimus," he said, "I must compliment your fight. Swift, tenacious and damaging." He chuckled, "Well, you did learn from the best."

Septimus only regarded him with a steely gaze, but nothing could match the blind fury Malkonar had in his own.

"It's such a shame. You have so much potential, and it's being squandered for the sake of so little," he peered down at Peter, barely moving and leaving a bloody streak in the dew, "That is what you choose to defend? Your species crippled and vulnerable, and rather than take up arms to protect your brethren you instead alliance yourself with that feeble smear of an organism?"

"Shut up."

"Listen to me," he growled, "Every day you spend with Peter damages you. You're growing domesticated, like his dog. He feeds you his discards and expects you to obey his every command, and like a dumb animal you follow them in the hope of getting a treat. Pathetic!" He slammed a hand on the silo, shattering a brick. "I'm ashamed to call you my son. You're everything a malkonar shouldn't be, and while my patience has run out I'm willing to offer you one last reprieve." He leaned out, his nose inches from Septimus' face, "You have a choice, and you have five seconds to make it. Join me in defeating Peter and restoring the malkonar race and live, or remain with Peter and die like the waste of flesh and blood you are."

Septimus held his peace, and Malkonar began to count.

"Five," he began. Septimus did nothing. "Four...three....two...."

"I've made my decision."

Malkonar leaned in closer and bared his rotten teeth.

"Well?"

"Malkonar, if you are the driving force behind saving our species, then I hope we go extinct."

Septimus spat in his face, and that was the last thing he did before Malkonar shot forward and plucked him out of the air with his ragged claws.

* * *

He peered at the weapon with dreamy eyes, a beacon of hope against the gloomy shadows daubed on everything by Malkonar's artificial sun, but he took his time. He had to stay discreet, keep low to the ground so that Malkonar wouldn't fling him away again, and with him practically immobile already he couldn't afford to lose another limb.

He looked up and saw that Malkonar was still staring at Septimus. Good. He raised an arm to pull himself a little closer, but stopped at the sound of beating wings. He looked up again and saw Septimus in Malkonar's arms, the larger beast whirling through the air in triumph. He did everything to silence a scream, and plunged his hands into the earth. He was bruised, battered, battle-scarred and broken, but against his agony he dragged himself a little further forward.

He stopped to suck in air and looked up again. Malkonar was now perched on the silo roof with Septimus pinned to its rocky ring. His pupils shrank and he turned to the gun. It was still out of reach.

* * *

Septimus was stuck, pinned under Malkonar's powerful grip of which no amount of wriggling would free him, but that didn't stop him from trying. He writhed as much as his spine would let him, scratching at the air but landing only the slightest of blows, yet it was enough to flare Malkonar's temper.

"Stop squirming, you little brat!" He scratched Septimus' face with a flick of his claw, and the blue reptile yelped as blood trickled down his face. "You've caused me too much trouble since the day you were born!"

"So why did you hatch me in the first place?" Septimus snapped back, taking another swing, "Tell me. You've never told me anything about myself so tell me that."

"All I will say is that you were meant to be my successor."

"Well I'm not your successor and I never will be. I would rather have you kill me here right now than do anything in your name. You're a disgusting, shallow creature and an even worse father and I hate you!"

"Shut up!"

"I hate you!" Septimus screamed again, "You've never done anything for me. All you ever did was moan about others and the things you would do to them. You could have talked to me, made that silo a better home than it was, but no. You were so wound up in avenging the dragons you ignored your only ally, and now you've lost him. That's just as well really, as through ignoring me I've discovered what a loathsome being you are. I hate you!"

Another scratch sliced his cheek.

"Don't you dare speak to me like that!" Malkonar seethed.

"I'll speak to you however I please. I don't see why I should be polite to you anyway. You're abusive, violent and irrational and I hate you!" He looked up at his father, face pulled in a contemptuous smirk, and with one sentence cut through Malkonar deeper than any sword could. "And I bet Mum hated you as well."

Malkonar's eye twitched, and with a roar that severed the night sky he spat a vicious jet of fire at his son.

Septimus screamed and thrashed as the flames consumed him, and then there was nothing. Intense light then darkness, a vice grip on his chest then slack. He peered up at an insane grin with watering eyes, and then he felt pain. Unimaginable pain. He began to cry and the tears seared his tender scales. Blood began to weep from everywhere. Arms, legs, chest, all slowly dyeing him red. The colour of the maniac smiling down on him.

"There." He placed a claw to Septimus' mouth to silence his growing moans. "And any more words about her will make your ordeal far worse than I intend it to be."

"You..." Septimus began, but his cracked lips burst and muted any further words.

"Your insults have deserted you," he teased as Septimus' mouth filled with blood, "What a wonderful sound silence is. Words are the last refuge of the weak, so to see their one vice snatched away is most pleasing."

Septimus spat the poisonous taste of iron from his mouth. The bile only reached his lip and dribbled down his face, aggravating his scales more. He whined again and drew yet more laughs from the creature holding him down.

"Well," he said, examining Septimus' ruined body with an unmistakeable shine in his eye, "Those burns look pretty severe. I dare say your average human wouldn't survive them. How about some pink fire?"

Septimus nodded obediently, but Malkonar cocked his brow at him.

"Now now, my boy, that's not how you accept gifts. Let's try again: would you like some pink fire?"

"Wha..."

"Words, boy! If you're as fond of them as you lead me to believe then make use of them. Now, would you like some pink fire?"

"Yes." More blood trickled into his mouth.

"Yes what?"

"Yes plea..." he choked on the acrid bile filling his airwaves.

"Nearly there."

"Yes please," Septimus cried, but Malkonar only responded with a snicker.

"Well too bad, little one. You didn't have to interfere with my plans, but you did, and as a consequence I'm afraid all of my gifts are out of bounds to you," he paused to enjoy the horror on Septimus' face, "Now, onto Round Two."

He sunk his claw deeper into the scratch he had created in Septimus' face, peeling back the scales and flesh beneath. He screamed as his skull was scraped.

"Do you want me to stop?" Malkonar asked innocently.

"Yes."

"What was that, boy?"

"Yes!" Septimus raised his voice as Malkonar's claw moved across his face, edging towards his eye but instead veering off towards the corner of his mouth.

"You'll have to speak up, I'm awfully deaf."

"Yes!"

"I'm pretty sure there's more words than that."

"Stop it!" Septimus begged, but Malkonar cut through the last strands of flesh separating scar and mouth.

He stopped screaming as he felt the corner of his lip snap, and experimentally opened his mouth. Pain and blood, lots of blood. Spurting from his face and soaking his chin, his body, the stone and some even flying into the shadowy silo. He squeezed his mouth shut and began to cry.

"Oh dear," Malkonar said over the sound of his weeping. Through teary eyes Septimus looked at his father in hope, but the reptilian tongue sliding over his teeth shattered it.

"Your face looks very uneven, and that won't do. I'd better do the other side," he said, and to muffled shouts of protest he lowered another claw.

* * *

With fingers straining Peter brushed the barrel of the shotgun, but then he toppled. His eyes slammed shut and shot open again. He'd blacked out. He cursed under his breath. He was running out of time and energy, and having listened to Septimus screaming atop the silo blacking out wasn't something he could afford to do.

He pushed himself upright to the sound of another roar, and his head swelled with fury. He couldn't entirely see what Malkonar was doing, but whatever it was he wanted to do exactly the same to him.

He dragged himself forward another inch and grabbed the shotgun, turning awkwardly in the direction of the silo. He raised the gun to fire. His hand trembled, but it didn't bother him. A distraction would be enough.

Through weary eyes he aimed in Malkonar's direction, and as he lowered his claw he pulled the trigger. The slugs shot into the night and buried into his right shoulder, not far enough to cause serious damage, but enough to make him yelp and turn away from the lifeless lump he towered over.

"You'll pay for that," he yelled, glaring down at him. Peter held his ground.

"Give me Septimus!"

"Why should I? He's happy enough up here." Malkonar grinned, licking the blood from his claw, "I'm sure he doesn't want to leave."

"You've burnt him alive and cut him up, I'm quite sure he'd rather come back to me."

"Nonsense!" Malkonar chuckled, "Look, he's reaching out for a hug." He nodded to Septimus' arms, stretched out and weakly slashing at the air in a vain attempt to harm his deranged parent.

"I'm surprised you know what a hug is, Malkonar," Peter said, anger flaring at his behaviour, "According to Septimus you weren't the most affectionate father."

"He never deserved affection anyway." He stopped as one of Septimus' attacks brushed his arm, and he responded by blowing wisps of pink fire at Septimus that evaporated inches from his airwaves. "He never followed my orders," he continued over the anguished cries of his son, "Always disobeying, never obedient."

"Well put it this way, your crimes are far worse than his will ever be."

"What crimes?"

"What crimes?" Peter said incredulously, "Well, there's the fact that you've murdered, kidnapped, harassed, possessed and generally abused anyone who's been unfortunate enough to come across you."

"Those aren't crimes, those are just parts of my job."

"Part of your job? So abusing your son is your job then," Peter spat, "Neglecting him at an age when he needs his parents, refusing to tell him anything about his life, and now trying to kill him when he dared to disobey you. All just a job. I cannot believe how disgusting you are, Malkonar."

"Don't bother with guilt, Peter, that emotion is lost on me."

"At last, you're admitting you don't have a conscience." He looked at Malkonar with more ferocity, tears of desperation building in his corneas. "I presume love and sympathy are lost on you as well, and for that reason alone you should let me have Septimus. I mean, look at what you're doing to him! Your son, for Christ's sake!" His jaw slackened with passion. "If this is what you call winning then you've won, and since you've won you should spare the loser. Please, Malkonar, give Septimus to me. You can kill me after that, but if he dies at least let him die in the arms of somebody who cares about him."

Malkonar tilted his head from side to side like a metronome, tipping the balance from life to death and back again.

"Decisions, decisions..." he said, his delight undisguised.

"You've won, Malkonar," Peter said, and his hollow concession of defeat was enough to convince him.

"Alright, take him," Malkonar said, swiping Septimus off the lip of the silo with a powerful backhand slap.

Peter didn't breathe as Septimus fell. His charred wings struggled to catch the wind, and with one broken and one dead leg all Peter could do was watch until the inevitable arrived.

He hit the ground spine-first, a hideous click rising into the air as his bones broke. Septimus cried out in pain, opening his mouth and exposing his elongated smile that made him look as demented as the creature above him. Then he fell deathly silent.

"Septimus, are you alive?" Peter cried out in anguish.

"Yeah," the malkonar slurred. His eyelids flickered for a moment, but blood trickling down his throat made him retch and kept him awake.

"Oh God," Peter breathed, pulling himself to his side, "Don't worry, I'll get you a doctor. Doesn't matter if they're human, I'll get them and they'll make you better. You're going to live, don't you worry, I just need to finish with Malkonar..." But Septimus was too disorientated to listen to his babbling, and spat out the message he wanted to give.

"His mouth."

"Whose mouth?"

"Malkonar's. Shoot his mouth," he said, his Glasgow Smile

opening to its full extent and spurting yet more blood onto the grass.

"Why his mouth?" he asked frantically, his eyes darting between the two malkonars.

"Just do it," Septimus whispered, then his mouth fell shut and his body went limp.

"And then there was one," Malkonar crowed, basking in an imminent victory. He flapped his wings and the grass around him rustled, but Peter grabbed the shotgun before it could be blown away.

"Let's see what that one has then, shall we?" he retorted, loading two more slugs into the shotgun and snapping the barrel shut as loud as he could. He used the time to think about Septimus' cryptic message, and with fear sharpening his senses he quickly unravelled why he was keen to have him put a bullet down his throat. He smiled. Genius.

He looked at Malkonar and pulled the most confident face he could muster.

"So what have you got?" he taunted, "Are you going to be a coward and lob me into a tree again?"

"No," Malkonar said, hoisting him off the ground once more. His legs dangled helplessly in mid-air, but his hands gripped the shotgun tightly, "I'm going to make you pay for shooting me in the shoulder."

"How're you going to do that then?"

"Hmm, good question. How about some fire? Human flesh burns quickly and painfully. I imagine it will be a sight to behold."

"Be careful," Peter teased, squeezing away his delight at him playing into his hands, "Humans are delicate, too much and you'll kill me."

"That's what I intend to do, Peter," Malkonar said, opening his mouth to spit fire. "The games are over, and now it's time to extinguish your flame," he said, but his pause to speak gave Peter the time he needed, and without a moment's hesitation he aimed and fired straight into his mouth.

Malkonar snapped his jaws together as the slugs sliced through his oral cavity. He stood still for a moment, wide-eyed and taut-muscled, then his chest convulsed and he vomited up a great deal of blood. His body began to tremble as he lost control, and Peter hit the grass with a painful thud once again. He quickly looked up to see Malkonar shaking violently, his pupils dilated and his face fallen on one side.

"My...my..." he slurred, his speech hindered by the fact that only one side of his face was moving. "Br-br...brain...st-stem,"

"What about it?"

"Hit with...slu...sl...slug, dam...aged, need pink f-f-fire!"

His innards hissed as he tried to produce the fire that would heal him, but only worthless wisps rose from his bloodied lips.

"Dam-m-age has giv...ven me Bell's P-p-p-Palsy!" he exclaimed in a panic Peter never could have dreamed of hearing, "C...can't b-breathe pink fire!"

"What a shame," Peter sneered.

"I need m-more time!" he wailed, "Need...w-weeks to make e-e-enough fire!"

"Well you don't have weeks, do you? You should get out of here while you can," he started to load the shotgun again, "Because in a minute I'm going to finish you off."

"You sh-should go too," he hissed, "Every s-second y...you s-sp-s-spend here you are pre...venting Sep...Septimus from...g-getting tr-treatment."

He stopped loading and glanced across at Septimus, who was sitting in a pool of red grass. He swallowed his disgust. Killing Malkonar was a fantasy on the verge of reality, but Septimus dying was a nightmare in the same place. Malkonar could live now and die another day, but once Septimus was gone he was never coming back.

"Alright," he said begrudgingly, "You're right, I am wasting time, so I'm going to give you a chance to fly away. If you take it then you can have all the time you need to heal yourself and live on like the scum you are, but if you're too slow then I'll shoot you through the mouth again and you'll live on as a stuffed animal at Averton Museum. You have ten seconds Malkonar, so choose.

"Ten," he began, snapping the barrel shut. Malkonar said nothing. "Nine. Eight. Seven."

Wisps of sweet-scented smoke rose from his nostrils, and he tried to inhale them with little success.

"Six," Peter said, raising the shotgun to his shoulder. Out of the corner of his eye he saw Septimus convulse, and while panic crushed his throat he kept counting, "Five. Four. Three."

Malkonar was trembling now, the immense amount of activity his weakened brain was trying to perform overloading him. The grip his claws had on the silo rapidly switched from white-knuckle to loose. One wing rose while the other fell, and his left eyelid blinked half a second before his right.

"Two..." Peter said, taking careful aim at Malkonar's slumped mouth. "One..." he shouted, his finger tightening on the trigger.

"Alright!" Malkonar snapped, "I'll...go."

Peter didn't celebrate. The second Malkonar declared his surrender he dropped the shotgun and scuttled over to Septimus as fast as his hands and thighs would take him.

He was lifeless on the floor, his chest still. With gentle hands he scooped him up and placed a finger to his neck. Nothing. He frantically felt elsewhere, and on the fifth attempt he felt a bump against his fingertips. A slow, weak bump, but a bump nonetheless.

"Well?" Malkonar said. Peter looked back at him and narrowed his eyes.

"I thought you were going."

"Why l-leave be...before I've h-h-heard the fi...nal s-score?"

"He's alive," he said, "Barely, but still alive. Now get going, and if I feel his pulse go before you're gone I'll put those bullets through you anyway."

"Fine, just let me d-do one more t-t-thing."

"And what's that?" Peter asked, but then he was catapulted across the park and hit the silo face first.

"That," Malkonar whispered, grinning on one side of his face, "You m-m-may have w-w-w-won th...is fight, but I will...alw...ays have the final w-w-word. B-bye now!"

He spread his vast wings and flew drunkenly through the night sky, dipping and rising at wild angles with every beat. He flew further and further away until he became a figurine in the sky, which became a blob and then a speck until finally he melted into the gloom.

Peter watched him go through half-blind eyes as more and more blood poured from his head. He was broken beyond repair now, both physically and mentally. No legs, no blood, no mind. All gone; expired, like he was going to be if he didn't stem the bleeding. But he didn't care, he was happy. He had beaten Malkonar, he had made him flee from him, not the other way around. Besides, Septimus was running out of life, so what did it matter if he went with him? Without him he had nothing to live for, so maybe it was for the best that he was going to die here.

High above him Malkonar's artificial sun began to fade, its once glaring green trail now a mere smudge in the night. He watched the world dim a shade until blood filled his eyes and blinded him. He blinked it away, and as his eyelids flickered he felt himself fall numb, hovering on the verge of a sleep from which he wouldn't wake.

His chest convulsed painfully and his vision faded further, and in the darkness he saw everything. Malkonar, Septimus, Don, Mum and Dad, the phone, the Librarian and various other people and places he had encountered in his 24 years. He saw Heaven and Hell, both filled with lifeless entities masquerading as souls. Some dressed in white and some reddened by flame, but all carrying the unblinking glare and tight-lipped mouth of a corpse.

His mind shifted and he saw a man. He fell to the floor and morphed into a ball and came out in the shape of a baby.

Reincarnation. Was that what awaited him? What would he come back ask? A teacher? A priest? Maybe even a malkonar. He shuddered at the thought.

He watched the shapes bounce around his head until another sharp convulsion drained them away and brought him back to reality. He sucked in air to steady himself. He was awake, and he vowed to remain so until he passed. No hallucinations, no revelations, just life and then death. Now wasn't the time for dogma. Now was the time for him to lie back and remember that he had fought for Septimus, and that was all he needed for the journey to the next stop on the line.

Though he tried to resist he began to slip in and out of consciousness again, and in his bouts of wake he heard and felt things. First he heard feet pounding along the ground. Then a voice, but he could not tell whose it was or what it was saying. Next he felt hands on his chest, pushing firmly against his ribs like a mallet beating a drum. Then he felt the hands again, one under his knees and the other across his shoulders. There was something in his lap too, but what it was evaded him, and when he closed his eyes for the final time he still hadn't worked out what it was.

When he picked up the phone on the 29th of October the day that Peter Vaughan reached his end was merely waiting to happen. But today was not that day.

EPILOGUE

Sunlight streamed through his left eye, blinding him with its harsh rays, though judging by the lone plane of sight he saw through it was doing better than his right. But he could see nonetheless, and that meant he was alive.

He gave a sigh of elation, but he sucked it up again when he tried to sit up and his wounds reminded him of their presence.

"Take it easy," a gentle voice soothed, a voice he knew but could not place. Hands gently pushed him back down onto his pillow, but he couldn't quite see who they belonged to.

"Septimus?" Peter croaked, his throat burning.

"Don't worry about him. He's in a bad way, but he's alive."

More elation. They were both alive. They had made it through Malkonar's madness.

"Dr. Ananth has seen to him. It'll take him a while to heal, but he'll be fine."

"Who's Dr. Ananth?"

He heard a surprised smack of lips. "He's the bloke who lives directly above you," the voice said, "Don't you know anyone in your building?"

"Mr. and Mrs..." he began, thinking of his two Scottish

neighbours, but their surname evaded him. "I don't know," he said dejectedly.

"Well you will soon. The entire apartment block's been talking about what you've been up to and it's only half past one."

Slowly, Peter's eyes began to adjust to the intense light. He was in bed, his broken leg held firm in a cast and his head swathed in bandages, the linen covering his right eye and blocking its sight. He turned his working left eye to see the rest of his body, dotted with various plasters and stitches where twigs and branches had poked and pierced. Then he looked up and saw a head.

Human, with bloodshot eyes and thick stubble coating the lower half of its face, greasy hair and uncontrollable sideburns too. A head with an unmistakable stench of alcohol that was the trademark of only one person.

"Don!" he said, shooting upright amidst protests from his body, "Erm...er...well...this is a surprise."

"Welcome back to reality, Pete," Don said calmly.

"Yeah, that Septimus person I mentioned, just ignore it. I was talking in my sleep again," he babbled, but Don wasn't fooled.

"Don't bother Pete, I know everything."

"Everything?"

"Yeah. Malkonar and Septimus and all that, I know about it."

"Oh," he said, feeling deflated as he watched his hard work come undone. "How?"

"You got me a job, that's how."

He frowned. "What?"

"Yeah, if you hadn't told me to get a job, I wouldn't have been on the night shift. If I wasn't, I wouldn't have been walking past Edgeley Park last night and I wouldn't have seen the green fireball in the sky. Because of that I wouldn't have scaled the fence, wandered into the park and watched the entire thing, and once the whole affair had finished I wouldn't have carried both of you back to your apartment and got Dr. Ananth to treat you, and then I wouldn't have found out about all of this Malkonar business. So yeah."

"Wow," Peter said, stunned, "Thanks, man."

"No problem. Sorry I didn't do more to help, but I was kind of shitting myself at seeing a giant dragon...thing."

Peter gave a reluctant laugh. He thought back to last night and tried to think if he had seen Don lurking behind in the trees or hiding in the bushes, but as he searched an unwanted memory flooded his mind and he let out a scream.

"Pepper!" he cried, "Is he alright?"

"He's dead, mate," Don said sadly, "You shot him through the head with a shotgun, and not many get up from that."

He slumped forward like his spine had been erased. "Oh."

"I buried him in my back garden this morning, made him a gravestone and everything. You're free to visit him at any time."

"Cheers," he mumbled, rubbing his head only to stop when a pang of pain shot through it, even though he felt no scar there.

He fell back into his pillows and watched Don take a drink from a bottle of water. His eye twitched, had his face fallen?

"Septimus regained consciousness a couple of hours ago and told Dr. Ananth everything," he said spontaneously. He was looking away, but Peter could see his lips stretched tightly across his face. "And he passed the info onto me. Malkonar, the phone calls, the dragon-malkonar war and so on. Everything from the last five months, I know all about it now." He turned to face Peter. Now he was scowling. "Thanks for not telling me that your dog was going around savaging people."

"Yeah, about that," Peter grimaced.

He forced himself to look Don in the eye, and his glare tore through him. He had just survived the most harrowing ordeal of his existence, but his guilt made this ordeal feel so much worse than anything a mad malkonar could do to him.

"I don't think I can say anything other than sorry," he began, voice heavy with sincerity, "I could make excuses but I'm not going to, it was a stupid thing to do and I wasn't thinking of your safety whatsoever when I handed him over. That's my entire defence, I guess. I'm incredibly sorry for what I've done and knowing how you dragged my near-dead self out of Edgeley Park makes me feel so much worse. There, that's it. If you want to storm out the door feel free to do so. It's certainly no more than I deserve."

Though discomfort burned he kept his eyes locked on Don, watching and waiting for him to get up and leave, but the seasoned drinker remained in his seat and the tightness melted from his face.

"You know," he said, "In any other circumstances giving me a killer dog without me knowing it would lead to you getting a few fists in the gob, but today I'm gonna make an exception. You put me in danger, and don't get me wrong, I'm pissed at you for it, but you did it to protect someone you care for so much you would take on a giant psychic dragon-thing to stop them from getting killed, and having watched you get thrown around and have your bones broken for an hour for the sake of keeping him alive, I'm willing to let you off this once."

"Oh thank God," Peter breathed, making Don laugh.

"Yeah, I'm still your friend. I might be a bit self-centred at times but I know a good deed when I see one." He smirked. "One thing I've got to say, though: way to dive in out of your depth, Pete."

"Don't blame me. Malkonar was the one who started it all, I just dived in and hit my head against the bottom of the pool."

"Well, at least he's gone now."

"He'll be back," Peter said firmly, chewing his lip in anguish, "He's not dead and he can dope himself up on pink fire until he's well again. Then he can start a war with the dragons, and that's something I'll probably end up being roped into."

"Will he though? I saw what you did to him. I doubt he'll be in any hurry to start a war with dragons if you of all people can knock him down."

"What do you mean 'me of all people'?"

"You're the most mild-mannered bloke I've ever met," he

laughed, "The only other person you've ever raised your voice to was your dad."

"He got what he deserved, as did Malkonar." He grabbed the bottle of water from Don's hand and took a swig. It soothed his throat instantly. "But at the end of the day he's still out there and he will cause trouble, and I fear the dragons will be an even bigger problem."

"You worry too much."

"Tell me something I don't know."

"No really, you do. Instead of celebrating the fact that Malkonar's gone after torturing you for half a year you decide to worry about what will happen next. Just relax for a change, it feels good once you get the hang of it."

"You've said that to me about twice a year since we were nineteen."

"Well maybe this time you should listen to me. Treat this as a wake-up call, Pete. No offence but you're a wreck, and if you're going to get back on your feet after this then you need to learn when to take a step back and breathe. Will you do that for me?"

"How am I..."

"Think of it as making it up to me for giving me Pepper," Don added quickly, and Peter's protest dissolved.

"Alright, I'll give it a go," he sighed, collapsing back into his pillow, "Anyway, where's Septimus? I can't see him anywhere."

"Still at Dr. Ananth's, he's worried about his wounds becoming septic. I can't believe anyone would do that to him, like, not even a psychopath," he drew lines across his face with his fingers, and Peter knew what he meant.

"That's a crash course in Malkonar for you," he said, "And don't think that's the worst he'll do either." He shook his plastered leg. "Do I have any crutches? I want to go and see him."

"No," Don said, snatching back the bottle and taking another drink, "Didn't figure you'd need any, it's not like you'll be going anywhere in a hurry."

"Well I'm going upstairs to see Septimus whether you like or not."

He awkwardly pushed himself out of bed and Don rushed to support him.

"I'll take you," he said, clutching his arm, "Anything to stop you killing yourself on those stairs."

"Cheers," he replied, but as Don shuffled forward he didn't move. "Don," he said, looking down at his body, "Why am I in my bedclothes?"

"Someone had to, and by the way: no, it's not the same as your foot size. Now let's go."

* * *

The journey was only two flights of stairs long, but they didn't make it far before the neighbours began to swarm. Mr. and Mrs. Nesbitt were the first, asking if Peter was okay and if the 'little dear' was too, and from that point onwards they could hardly go two steps without being approached by some curious person wanting to know what had happened. Half of them he didn't actually know, faces he had seen but never talked to, yet they greeted Peter like an old friend before launching their curiosities at him.

At first he tried to politely skirt the questions, but as more neighbours swooped down on them Don lost his patience. He lifted Peter off the floor and used him as a battering ram to shunt his way through the crowd and up the stairs.

Dr. Ananth was waiting in the doorway of his home, and he quickly ushered them in before shutting the door tightly behind them.

"Hello lads," he greeted in a rich Indian accent, "I can guess why you're here."

"Aye," Peter nodded, "How's he doing?"

"He's stable. I've been awake since five treating him, and while

I can only do so much right now I've got him under control. He's going to be here for a while but I'm certain he'll recover."

"That's great," Peter smiled, but he couldn't disguise his wince at the apron he was wearing. It was a typical cooking apron, worn cloth in pastel colours that had clearly seen its share of kitchen nightmares, and by the bloodstains that Peter could see it had recently experienced a completely different kind of horror.

"I know," he said, holding his hands up in apology, "It was a messy job. I had to perform minor surgery to deal with some of his injuries, and the sheer extent of his burns meant he began to bleed pretty badly."

Peter stared at him with a mixture of anger and hurt. He wasn't sure if he meant it, but it had the desired effect.

"Do you want to see him?" Dr. Ananth said, wilting under Peter's hostility, "He'll probably still be asleep, but he'll be happy to know you've been."

He didn't wait for an answer, turning on his heel and striding away before Peter could even think of speaking. Don grabbed him and they followed his path, meeting him at a closed door with a piece of paper bearing the message 'Be Quiet' tacked to it. He gently pushed it open, took a quick look in to see if anything was amiss, then ushered them inside.

The room was dimly lit, drawn curtains shielding almost all of the light and emphasising the delicate Indian patterns that adorned them. At the foot of the curtains was a bed swathed in rich blue sheets, with two women sat either side of it.

One was dressed in a graceful light-blue sari, gently singing words under her breath and stroking the quilt delicately. The other, much younger woman in Western dress held a bowl in one hand and a spoon in the other, letting the creature who was sat upright in the bed lap at its contents. Peter knew it was Septimus, though it was hard to recognize him through the swathes of stitches and bandages that covered his body.

"Hello, Peter," the older woman said, "I'm glad you're awake, you looked in a bad way when I last saw you."

"Thank you, erm..."

"Mrs. Ananth, or Darshana if you prefer."

"Thanks," he said again. They nodded back respectfully, but a lone word didn't satisfy his gratitude. "Thanks, all of you, I really mean it. You've already done loads for me and him and you hardly even know us."

Darshana beamed at him. "Don't worry," she said, "My husband saves the lives of strangers for a living, so what's two more?"

"It's common decency to help those in need," the younger woman added.

"Ah, yes," Darshana said, gesturing to her, "This is our daughter, Anahita."

"Hey," Peter said, but his eyes remained on Septimus.

"There's no need to worry," Anahita said, blowing on the spoon, "He's in safe hands. He's got good medical care and this warm milk is doing wonders for his mood." She spooned more milk into Septimus' waiting mouth, the warm drink coursing through his frail body and making his eternal eyes light up. "Well, I'm out of milk," she said, rising from her chair, "I'd better go get some more. Why don't you have my seat while I'm gone? You look like you're struggling to stand."

Though her offer was voluntary Peter found himself being ushered into her chair, and as Don and Anahita forced him down he knew exactly why.

He looked at Septimus, his bandaged body in touching distance, and the malkonar's eyes turned to him. He read several emotions in his gaze: anticipation, surprise, relief and something else which he couldn't place.

"Hey," he said softly. He placed a hand next to Septimus, not touching but close enough to feel his warmth.

"Unnghh," Septimus mumbled.

"Ah."

"Yeah, I'm afraid he can't speak just yet," Dr. Ananth said, "He needs to keep his mouth still for it to heal. That was a job and a half – his mouth was cut up so badly I had to remove a few of his teeth just to sew it shut again. Not that it'll matter too much, he has plenty by the look of things."

"Yeah," Peter smirked. Septimus nodded in agreement. "So then," he added, turning back to the malkonar. He drummed his fingers against his knees, lowering his head just enough to hide his flushed cheeks. "I don't have much to say, really," he said with a shy smile, "All I have is that I'm glad you're okay. I know you probably expected something a bit more...emotional, but I can't really think of any other words to use. I'm just really, really glad you're okay," he looked up again, and began to laugh, "That's pathetic, isn't it?"

Septimus slowly shook his head.

"No, it's not?"

A nod.

"Well that's good." Another laugh. "Sorry, I'm not very good at heart-to-hearts."

Septimus grunted approvingly and tilted his head across to Darshana.

"It's time?" she said, and Septimus blinked his answer. "Okay." She turned to look at Peter's confused face. "He wants me to give you something on his behalf," she explained, "A little thank you for going to Edgeley Park last night."

She reached into the folds of her sari and produced a necklace, made of delicate silver with a single, pointed tooth dangling from one of the links.

"It was his idea," she said, holding out the jewellery, "A tooth and an old necklace go a long way for another person, don't they?"

Peter took the necklace and pressed his thumb against the point of the tooth. He felt a prick as it tore his skin. He looked at Septimus and smiled.

"This is your tooth, isn't it?"

The malkonar nodded.

"Thought so."

He slipped the necklace over his head and felt the cool tooth prod the skin over his heart. It felt nice, and suddenly everything in the world felt nice. No death, Averton or Malkonar. Just him and Septimus with nothing in their path.

"Thanks, mate," he beamed, sliding the tooth under his shirt.

"Ungh," Septimus grunted happily.

He lay back and snuggled into the sheets, moaning as his burns were pulled and pressured by his movements, but the awkward yet obvious grin playing on his face didn't slacken for a second.

"Do you want to sleep?" Peter asked. Septimus nodded. "Okay, I'll leave you to it, mate. I'll be back soon, okay?"

"Ugh," Septimus said, but as Peter levered himself to his feet he uttered another mangled word. "Fuhla."

"Yeah?"

"Cuhmurdun."

"Cuhmurdun?" Peter said, scouring his brain for the few scraps of Carcratian he had memorised, and somehow he found a match. "Comarden."

"Comarden? What does that mean?" Don asked.

"Have a guess," he smiled at Don, then turned it on Septimus. "Comarden," he whispered, and Septimus stretched his face as far as his stitches would allow.

* * *

The cave was cold. Dark too, the only light at its entrance and quickly fading away, but he didn't notice. He couldn't notice much. He barely even registered the cave, his weakened brain simply wouldn't allow it. All he was aware of was his breathing.

The bullets had rendered his nose useless so he was forced to breathe through his mouth. They came out loud and raspy, snagging on his twisted mouth and stinging his bleeding lips, but the pain was irrelevant to his focus. Every last ounce of his dimmed mind was devoted to breathing pink fire.

It was an arduous task that took too long and produced too little, but he didn't care. He was free. He had plenty of time to fix this damage, and plenty more to wreak havoc upon dragonkind. And Peter Vaughan, especially Peter Vaughan. What he had done would never be forgotten, and he would cling to him like pincers until death succeeded life.

He felt a stirring in his throat; he was ready for another breath of fire. He spat and small wisps of pink fluttered into the air, which he quickly inhaled before they could evaporate into nothing. A sweet sensation ran down his spine, and a little more sense crept back into his brain. He smiled a lopsided grin. Not long now.

THE MALKONAR TRILOGY
CONTINUES WITH

CATACLYSM

ABOUT THE AUTHOR

Alex Jackson was born in Gateshead, and has lived there ever since. His love of fantasy began at just age 3, when he was given a copy of *Spyro the Dragon*, and he has been imagining new worlds and creatures since he first picked up a pen. *Malkonar* is his first novel, but he has also produced poetry, and award-winning content for Gateshead Football Club. When not writing, Alex enjoys travelling the world and watching Gateshead FC, though sadly he hasn't travelled the world to watch Gateshead FC yet.

Made in the USA
Charleston, SC
25 July 2016